The Executioner's Son

BOOK 3
THE LONG WAR SERIES
2nd Ed.

Robert E Townsend

LIAR'S PATH PUBLISHING

Madison, Wisconsin

Robert E. Townsend
Liar's Path Publishing
Madison, Wisconsin 53711
roberttownsendonline.com

Publisher's Note: This is a work of fiction. Names, characters, places, and incidents are a product of the author's imagination. Locales and public names are sometimes used for atmospheric purposes. Any resemblance to actual people, living or dead, or to businesses, companies, events, institutions, or locales is completely coincidental.

Book Layout © 2014 BookDesignTemplates.com

Library of Congress Cataloging-in-Publication Data

Names: Townsend, Robert Ernest., author.
Title: The Executioner's Son : third book in the long war series / Robert E. Townsend.
Series: The Long War
Description: Madison, WI: Liar's Path Publishing, 2019.

Identifiers: LCCN 2019905780 | ISBN 978-7338827-1-2 (pbk.) | 978-7338827-4-3 (ebook)

Subjects: LCSH Soviet Union--History--German occupation, 1941-1944--Fiction. | Concentration camps--Soviet Union--Fiction. | Suzdal' (Russia)--Fiction. | Moscow (Russia)--Fiction. | Russia (Federation)--Armed Forces--Fiction. | Coming of age--Fiction. | Bildungsroman. | FICTION / War & Military | BISAC FICTION / Historical / World War II | FICTION / Coming of Age

Classification: LCC PS3620.O968 E94 2019 | DDC 813.6--dc23

For the Bronx Dancer

CONTENTS

Article I. BOOK I

Uneasy feelings
Gnawed at his heart:
"Beware of the water!
Tighten your girth!"

"Fairy Tale"
Boris Pasternak.

Larionov, Danton Volkov, Captain, Soviet Army, Government Reconnaissance Directorate, sapper by specialty, felt exposed. For this, there was no justification. The Vietnamese border was 30 kilometers distant. The Laotian jungle canopy was thick, the monsoon clouds unbroken. Rain fell in sheets. There had been no recent reports of partisan activity. American reconnaissance aircraft would not fly blind into fog-shrouded passes. The road, if you could call it that, was barely passable on foot.

By command of an unseen signal, the North Vietnamese Army column halted. Danton leaned against a tree using his pack to hold himself upright. The tree shuddered, rain dropping onto his poncho, making sounds like bullets impacting. A raindrop seemed to be crawling up his forearm to the pulsing vein at his elbow, and he flicked the black leech with a forefinger. He missed, and it coiled, defensively. The second flick sent it in a bush.

An NVA officer wearing a Nagant Model 1895 seven-shot service revolver in a shoulder holster, the theodolite tripod strapped to his pack, approached, and smiled. Danton's identification papers indicated he was a major in the Polish People's Army, a member of the International Control Commission inspectorate, but suspected that were he in any danger of capture, the Vietnamese lieutenant had orders to execute him.

He needed to piss but didn't want the slant-eye to see his soaked and shriveled penis. He turned to the bushes and stopped. He had heard that leeches crawled into your urethra, attached themselves and engorged. The surgeon had to cut off your penis before you could piss again. Who had told him that? The Poles attached to the International Control Commission monitoring the Laotian cease-fire? Yes, it was a lie; they lied constantly. He pulled his foreskin back and let it go, watching the yellow stream turn pale and clear as it splattering off a large jungle leaf.

The rain was cold on his face, while beneath the poncho, he was drenched in sweat and shivering. One *portyanka*, foot wrap, poorly tied at the last river crossing, had bunched into the toe of his boot. The blister on his ankle burned; that on his heel was beyond pain.

It had been cloudless that long ago morning, the breeze fresh and clear off the Caribbean Sea. The camouflage team had conducted a surprise inspection visit to assess the missile site's measures. The report would have been short and easy to write; no measures had been taken.

Colonel Petrovsky, furious and red-faced, rained curses upon the site commander's head. Colonel Varrenikov, an artillery officer in the Great Fatherland War, took crap from no one, or at least, no one equal or inferior in rank. "You headquarters dick-heads want the site operational by the deadline, or you want it hidden? Which? Tell me!"

"Both, you miserable son of a bitch, you set up the launch site, and you hide the fucking thing at the same time. Can't you squat and shit at the same time?" Had one been armed, surely the other would have been shot.

A silver apparition cut short Colonel Varrenikov's repartee. Both paused, gazed up with open mouths as an American aircraft, vertical stabilizer blood red, blue pod beneath the centerline, appeared overhead.

The pilot looked down upon white faces uplifted to the sun, surely smiled beneath his sun visor, saluted, and kicked in his afterburner. The recce aircraft flashed silver and gold in the sunlight and was gone, thunder echoing within open mouths. He was like the Firebird, Danton had thought.

The ZSU-23 AAA crew had been, unlikely though it seemed, on the ball. They had been tracking the aircraft and could have shot the smart-ass out of the sky, but there had been no orders. One had to obtain permission from Moscow. Later, a Soviet surface-to-air missile shot down an American U-2, but only after the Americans had taken enough pictures to build a photographic peace bridge that would extend from Moscow to Washington, D.C.

Cuba was forest-covered, Soviet intelligence had reported. What they hadn't said was that the trees were palms, not fir and pine, and provided no cover at all. Still, had Strategic Rocket Forces troops taken a few hours, strung netting from palm to palm, American photo interpreters would have had only a steaming pile on white linen to poke through.

Now, Khrushchev was on pension. Kosygin and Brezhnev had decided to stick it to the Americans here in the jungle, where you could hide things. The GRU forward reconnaissance assessed the battlefield, the point of the Soviet Army spear.

A Soviet mission had been sent to assess the material and manpower required to upgrade road networks in southern Laos sufficient to support the passage of a ZIL-131 truck. It had turned out to be a typical Soviet Army operation. The team chief, a general, had remained in Chita, Russia; the colonel had a girlfriend in Vientiane; Major Lipitov, the political officer, the fat bastard, shaking and sweating, claimed to have malaria, and remained behind in Attepeu. In the Great Patriotic War, they knew how to prescribe medicine to brace the courage of the shaking and sweating; insert a .7 gram dose of lead into the base of the skull.

Danton snorted. He was by his sweet lonesome the point of the spear. The Americans were too smart to get sucked into this muck hole.

Now only GRU Captain Larionov remained to fulfill the plan, his assignment seemingly limited to protecting the East German Carl Zeiss theodolite in its metal case, which the fraternal NVA officer carried inside a backpack. A chill clenched Danton's chest, knotting muscles across his shoulder.

What had he done to deserve this assignment? Connections. He had none. In Tolstoy' *War and Peace*, the rich kid, Pierre Bezhukhov, and the lieutenant, Dolokhov, both drunk, lashed a Moscow policeman to a bear and threw him into the Moscow river. Bezhukhov had connections; Dolokhov did not. Bezhukov got off with hardly a how-do-you-do. Dolokhov was reduced to the ranks, transferred to a penalty battalion and fought as a front line musketeer at the battle of Borodino.

In January 1963, Danton, his friend, Captain Roman Baranov along with his GRU camouflage and concealment team returned from Cuba. At Sheremetovo, they boarded buses, were driven downtown and into the Lubyanka. Were they to be executed for the failure of the maskirovka operation in Cuba? A gray-faced group of officers standing within the gray courtyard of KGB headquarters were ushered into the basement to the furnace room. The man was strapped foot-first to a board at the maw of a crematorium furnace. They burned him slowly, His screams echoing in the ears of fifty-five GRU officers. He was a spy, the KGB colonel said, a GRU colonel.

Baranov got an assignment to Dresden, while Danton leaned fevered against a tree in a monsoon-flooded jungle, black leaches crawling towards his penis. The NVA officer separated the foliage, gestured to Danton to approach. "*Au dessous est la rivière Xe Xou,*" he said.

'Speak Russian, you dirty foreigner,' Danton thought. He had not thought it possible to be sicker.

He looked through the branches as a ray of sunlight pierced through tumbling clouds to illuminate the waterfall. The river was like the Kamenka River during its spring flood. On the opposite bank lay a small meadow, which resembled the one upon which he had encountered the storyteller.

From beneath his poncho, Larionov retrieved the plastic cigarette case that protected his Marlboro cigarettes, extracted the American lighter, its fuel tank clear plastic within which floated a plastic image of a pike striking a lure. The Polish officers of the International Control Commission purchased cigarettes and trifles at the American Embassy BX and resold them to the Soviet mission in Hanoi. Lenin would have had them shot as speculators.

The *chuchmek* eyed the Marlboros, but said nothing, and stretched his hand inviting Danton to step out upon the escarpment. The latter shook from fever; it felt as if a spider web had clung to his face and neck. 'In the seventh kingdom beyond the seventh sea,' the distant escarpment like an erect penis spewed a white waterfall.

The GRU was in the shits now, but things turn around. The Communist Party watched the KGB, which watched the Soviet Army, which watched the Party, in one great circle jerk. The KGB would soon enough be on the outs. The GRU had intelligence officers in embassies around the world. He grinned at his porter, or his executioner, as the occasion required. He was down the shit hole and foul smelling little rats toted his pack. He was 'beyond the seventh sea,' his journey soon to end. He'd do his work, turn back, write his report in Chita, which the general would either accept or reject it, then return to Moscow to fix things.

Even the wizard Colonel Soroka could not lure the enemy to battle in such terrain so disadvantageous to combat that even q storyteller's wondrous carpet could not transport sufficient men and supplies from distant America.

He scraped the earth with his boot. Limestone. Limestone for road fill. He looked where the descending trail dog-legged back to the river's edge. Engineers could widen the trail, string netting through trees, and of course, limit movement to night-time using hooded headlights. When the road dried, the trucks could manage it. One built bridges under as well as over flowing water. These were problems sappers solved.

Mists hung upon the peaks. Danton closed his eyes against rising nausea, saw lightening of the atmosphere through his closed eyelids. The sun's rays had followed the river course to the escarpment upon which he stood.

He flicked open his lighter to light his cigarette against the rising bile, brushed away the malarial web entangling his face, sickness and beauty alternating for his attention. Something was wrong. The soldiers erecting a rope bridge across the river crouched as one, like chickens sensing the shadow of a hawk overhead. The NVA officer yammered, pointed. Despite his fever, Danton was adamant. He would not give up his American lighter. Then, a wondrous thing happened. Baba Jaga hoisted the chuchmek from the ground and flung him at Danton's feet. Then came the single knock of a knout upon a tree, which every Russian child knew was the signal that the Baba Jaga had stripped clean the bones of the interloper. Danton looked down into the lieutenant's open eyes, body twitching as if the forest witch were just now stripping the meat from the bones.

Danton shook his head. The order of events was wrong. He tried to organize a sequence of events. First, retrieve the cigarette. No, open the package. He noted with some interest as Baba Jaga lifted his transit from the ground, saw the flash of light, then darkness descended.

CHAPTER ONE- SUZDAL 1941

"Baba!" A peremptory shout woke the five-year-old Danton Volkov Larionov. Gray morning light backlit a drunken NKVD junior lieutenant in the doorway, his tunic unbuttoned, cap pushed back over his head, a Mosin–Nagant 91/30 rifle with fixed bayonet slung over his shoulder. Beyond, the morning was fog-shrouded. Chickens clucked the yard. A pig grunted. Wood smoke hung in the hut's still air. From out of doors came the smell of burning leaves. The family cow, its flanks manure-caked, crossed the muddy yard toward the Church of the Disposition of the Robe, now a state farm granary. "Make me some kasha before I stick my boot up your ass."

The lieutenant leaned against the doorjamb and unslung his rifle. From the yard came sounds ominous to the twentieth-century Russian peasant household: heavy boots in sucking mud, the thud of leather on flesh, curses and the squeal of the pig. A chicken squawked, and wings flapped.

There came a strangled croak, silence, then a burst of drunken laughter.

"You green magpie!" Danton's grandmother, Marfa, heavy-boned and broad-shouldered in a shapeless flowered dress, a scarf tied under the chin, appeared out of the darkness, a wooden bowl under her muscular arm. She lifted the spoon as if to strike the lout. "I'll knock you into next week, you come in shouting so. Wipe your boots, you pig! It's a new floor."

To interfere with the state security in the 1930s Soviet Union was to court death. The soldier lifted his rifle to block the attack. Evgenii Belodubrovskii, a prisoner-scientist in the Suzdal Chemical Institute, awoke, looked out from under his blanket, squinted and felt for his glasses. The shot reverberated through the hut as if fired in a kettle. Danton jumped, and the gentle scientist moaned, scuttling backward atop the clay oven.

"You dumb-shit," mumbled Marfa, "Put the gun down before you kill yourself."

"Progress, Mama. I'm transferred home!" The lieutenant pointed his rifle, a wisp of smoke curling from its muzzle, into the yard. "Look there, old woman..."

"*Da!*" the child Danton shouted. The drunken lieutenant was Danton's father, Volk Gregorevich Larionov, of the People's Commissariat of Internal Affairs, the NKVD, returned from months in Lithuania rooting out wreckers and saboteurs that had opposed the brotherly unification with the Socialist union of workers and peasants.

Danton's grandmother looked along the rifle barrel into the fog, squealed and shoved her son aside. "Ach, my God." A drunken peasant with drooping mustache appeared in the doorway, pushed the grinning Volk aside, and spread his arms, vodka bottle in one hand, dead chicken in the other.

"Eh, Marfa, thought you'd never see this old bastard again, eh?" His clothing was the color of the *rasputitsa*, Russia's spring thaw—brown, gray, black. "Can't beat the suckers, join 'em."

A third man appeared at the doorstep. Markov, a giant of a man, Danton's uncle and one of Gregory's sixteen sons, twelve by Marfa, four by a forgotten earlier wife, blocked the grey morning light. A fleeting smile passed over his serious face as he looked into the hut's gloom and found Danton in his bedstead atop the clay oven. "Boy," he said quietly.

"Ach, for Christ's sake, watch your tongue, Gregory!" Marfa's spoon made the expansive Orthodox sign of the cross in the air against demons and spying eyes. "You see nothing, Danton, you hear nothing." She slit her Finnish eyes squinting into the darkness to the side of the boy.

Volk raised his rifle into the darkness beneath the eves. "You didn't hear shit, eh, our little intellectual. One through the ears, fix your hearing good, eh, Professor?"

"I sleep," the darkness replied, its voice pleading. "I sleep."

"Get your ass out of here!" Gregory shouted and snapped a finger. "You know how I fix the louse?" A little bearded man slid off the oven—he slept in his clothes—shoelaces untied, and scurried out the door into the mist. "I pop them!"

"Still take boarders, Marfa, eh?" Gregory said. Danton liked the intellectual despite him being a blood-sucking capitalist louse. The Professor, a chemical engineer, had rid the hut of those lice. Danton had not been bitten this whole winter. He quivered with excitement though he remained silent as expected.

"How much the Commissariat pay?" Danton's grandfather, the wily peasant, nodded after the Leningrad professor. "If they don't provide food, the Zek doesn't eat, understand, Marfa? We've got the connections."

"He's lucky he's still alive...*Esser*," Marfa spit. Suzdal had been a Russian prison town since Ekaterina II, a tradition the Bolsheviks continued. It was a special prison in the GULAG, a 'political isolation' prison. Mensheviks, 'Essers,' i.e., social revolutionaries and other political bacilli were 'isolated' that they do not infect 'clean' workers with wrong thoughts. However, by 1941, most 'politicos' had been sent elsewhere to construct the Socialist fatherland some place or another. Suzdal was a prisoner-manned scientific institute.

"We've finished Irkutsk ahead of plan." Gregory withdrew a pouch from his coat, slapped the leather against his palm then under Marfa's nose. "Bonus. We're home to wet our lines...eh, Marfa, get the vegetables planted, then onto Poltava...another rush project. Bricklayers, the world always needs bricklayers."

"Where's the rest of my boys," Marfa hefted the money, slipped the pouch beneath her apron, then pushed her husband aside to look into the fog.

"They are sleeping it off at Masha's...in Bogolyubov," Markov answered.

Marfa pinched Markov's cheek, then turned to her husband. "You'll plant for the kolkhoz? Have you taken leave of your senses, Gregory? How does that get food on our plate?"

Gregory spat out the door. He was a different kind of muzhik; he neither beat his wife nor spit in her face. "We're planting the food plot."

"Crazy as well as drunk? Had a load of bricks fallen on your head?" Marfa fisted her free hand before his face, looked up to the ceiling, then went to the door and bellowed. "Anna, get your whoring ass in here...feed the men, Boil water...clean the chicken!" A pretty and slight young woman hurried into the hut, eggs in her apron. Marfa raised her spoon, and the young woman shied, protecting the eggs and disappeared into the darkness. Head bowed, she reappeared to set the table, putting grouts in men's bowls and pouring vodka. Marfa patted the hidden cache. "The Bolsheviks will take it."

"Mama," Danton's father said, "if Anna needs beating, I do it." He rubbed his unshaven face. The trip had been long; the vodka wore on him.

"Masha, Vladimir's wife, not Pavel's," Gregory clarified. He had many sons who had wives named Marina. "...says they changed the rules...bad harvests...one-hectare food plots permitted. We can sell to the prison." Marina, wife of Vladimir, was secretary to Fomichev, President of the Vladimir City Council, and herself a candidate member of the Communist Party. Like Baba Jaga, the Russian fairytale witch, Masha' listened to the wind,' interpreted its whispers, and told Marfa what was foretold. Danton had often tried to listen to the wind but heard nothing, now and then perhaps a little moaning in the eaves. It was a skill reserved those few gifted with magical wisdom, who knew *skazki*, tales, like his mother.

"More prisons...more guards. More guards...more food." Gregory, the clan patriarch, counted out the incontestable peasant math, finger by finger. He indicated the sleepy NKVD lieutenant. "Volk's general has a specific construction job. The leftover cement and bricks...," Gregory made a sweeping gesture. Gregory's sons would snitch 'extra' materials to expand the house. The material belonged to all, right?

Markus turned to his brother, Volk. "Your boy up on the stove..."

Volk peered with unfocused eyes into the ceiling gloom, "If it's a boy, it's Danton."

"Danton," Markov said, "You think you might like to go fishing?"

Marfa liked the idea. "Go to Pavlov's Pond...catch a nice carp for dinner."

"Can we still fish there?"

Marfa looked away, calculating the foods required for a family feast, thinking that one, two or three carp would replace several chickens. "Not for long. They're building dachas in Woman's Wood for bigwigs."

"Come, little boy." Anna extended her arms, touching her finger to his lips, and caressing his hair. "Ah, Volk, he has a louse."

"He's Russian. He'll survive." Volk looked out into the mists. "Typhus killed Ukrainians by the thousands...but they're weaker than Russians...littlest discomfort and they croak. We Russians are the stronger people."

"The professor has something that kills bedbugs...from Switzerland, he says," Anna said.

Volk mumbled, leaned his rifle against the wall, and it slid to the ground with a crash. It did not discharge for the bullet was already lodged in a ceiling beam.

Markov smiled, "I'll throw him in the pond, Anna. The cold water will kill the bugs. Boy, you want to go fishing? Come. Let your Da take your bed."

"Woman's Wood will be off-limits by mid-summer," Volk repeated, sleepily. "Dachas for the big wheels."

"Where are we going to get firewood?" Marfa said. "There's never enough coal."

"From somewhere else," Volk said. "Pavlov's Pond will be off-limits also."

Trembling with excitement, Danton skittered off the oven. Uncle Markov was taking him fishing where Baba Jaga snared bad children and broke their bones to suck out the marrow. The witch would think a bit seeing big Markov and go for another bad kid.

"We'll fish there until it's off-limits. Pond's still open, eh, Volk?"

Markov emptied his vodka glass, refused a refill, pulled a small packet from his vest pocket and waved it in Danton's direction. "Well, Danton, get your line. We will get us a carp for the homecoming feast, eh?"

Danton, mouth open, stared at the prize in Markov's fist. Fishing hooks! There were none to be found in Suzdal. There would be carp and chicken on the table. Uncles, aunts, and cousins would come for the celebration dinner. 'Life was good, all the time getting better and better,' just like the poster said.

Two moments, separate and distinct, that spring and early summer 1941, blended in Danton's memory. In the first, the sky was overcast, the air still, yet the clouds raced overhead.

Danton had clambered off the earthen oven, jumped into his trousers, and ran out the door. Leaping from grass hummock to hummock to avoidj sinking into the waist-deep animal-churned muck, he retrieved elm-switch fishing poles, fishing line, carved wood floats, and his precious few hooks. His mother made him eat breakfast, appealing to Markov's authority and packed cold piroshky into his kit.

Markov and Danton stepped out onto muddy Shakovski Lane, dead-ended in the east by the village grazing commons, in the west by the walls of the monastery of St Euthymius. The morning mist had not burned off. The onion-shaped domes of the Cathedral of the Transfiguration were dull, visible over crenelated fortress walls. Were the bells ringing that morning? No, that was impossible. They rang later in June.

The uncle and his nephew turned left onto Lenin Prospect, the ancient road that led past the Suzdal Kremlin and onto Vladimir and Kiev, then right down an alley between the Kremlin and an abandoned monastery and descended the bluff.

The Poles and Lithuanians had occupied the Suzdal Kremlin during the Time of Troubles, dug burial pits and mixed new bones with old. They passed through the intersection of Engels with Gastev Street where they could see both the Alexandrovsky and the Rezopolozhensky Monasteries onto Settlement Street. It has once been a village, which the inhabitants torched to protest Petrine reforms; those who hadn't perished in the fire died in the harsh winter.

The two fishermen paused midway down the bluff and stood for a moment. Above them rose a forest of multi-colored Byzantine mushroom domes; Beneath, the massed graves of a thousand years. Russia's blood-drenched history entered the Russian soul tombstone-by-tombstone, grave-by - grave, story-by-story. "What you think, boy. Fish the Kamenka, or up on Pavlov's Pond."

"I can always fish in the river," Danton answered.

They had stood where the river exited the ravines, where, in 1932, the gentle Social Revolutionary Belodubrovskii advised Marshall Tukhachevsky how to use mustard gas to clear the forest of armed peasants fleeing collectivization.

"Then, Pavlov's it is," Markov said.

Markov and Danton passed through the gate into the cemetery of the Church of St. Boris, built of wood without nails, since the time of Catherine II the Larionov family cemetery. Tall Brown grasses lay over fallen tombstones. Simple forest stones inscribed with name and patronymic in Old Church Slavonic, Boris Borisovich, 'Boris, son of Boris." With the emancipation of serfs, last names began to appear. "Larionovsky," 'belonging to Larionov family,' or 'of the Larionov crowd.' With time, the 'ski' disappeared, becoming simply 'Larionov.' Danton was the grandson of Gregory, born a serf.

There was no underbrush to obscure line of sight amongst the oaks of Woman's Wood. They cast their line in Pavlov's Pond there where the Kamenka's waters flowed over the concrete and wooden dam. Danton remembered it had been silent through the falling waters must have made some noise.

Neither the tsar nor the commissar built a railroad to the city. Industrialization passed the town by. The Bolsheviks had began to dynamite the churches for bricks to construct Socialism, but mortar was in short supply. The Orthodox churches with their fairy tale onion domes would remain until cement was plentiful. Meanwhile, some Soviet commissar noted the thick walls and fortified fighting points constructed against Mongol or Tartar or Bulgar or Polish or German or Swedish invaders. The enemy without had become the enemy within. The religious structure was the military structure; churches were fortresses. Thick walls held the enemy within as well as without. Suzdal became a Bolshevik prison town; local men again manned its walls and fighting posts.

Gregory had first married Marina, who starved to death during the Civil War, then Lyudmila, who became tubercular, then Marfa. Together, they bore him sixteen sons, fourteen surviving. The vicissitudes of Stalin did not disorient this peasant. Serve the Kahn; serve the commissar. In America, he might have founded a mid-sized construction company and bought a Cadillac. In Russia, he had a two-room hut, clay oven stove and a cow. *Naplevat'*. Spit on them. He was a Kulak in all but name, for his sons were in the NKVD.

The cunning navigated nation and civil and revolutionary war as they had the steppe warfare. They shifted sides. Gregory, drafted into the Imperial Army and rising to NCO, switched to the Red Army. He requisitioned Cossack grain in the Don. Born a peasant, he knew where another peasant cached his food, uncovered it, and was promoted. He rose not so high as to incite envy; not so low as to sink into the mud. Lift your head above the trench line; Get one between the eyes: Desert; get one in the back of the head.

Three sons guarded Suzdal prison complex # 160, and the fourth, Volk, father of Danton—an NKVD lieutenant, mind you—was the general's right-hand man. Gregory and Marfa served the commissar. Others were Red Army men, of whom two were literate.   Three worked at the foundry. Vladimir, the hero of Soviet Labor, had joined the Communist Party, and his wife, Marina, read the Suzdal Pravda, worked in the Vladimir city hall and listened to the wind.   There was food in the forests and fields surrounding Suzdal Prison complex # 160.

Marfa sold mushrooms and berries to the NKVD officers' mess and welcomed her husband and sons from Irkutsk and sent them on to Ukraine.   The matriarch would ensure the wives would not fuck the men remaining home. With four NKVD sons in Suzdal, local dogs sniffing in-heat bitches would think once or twice.

The khan, the tsar and the commissar each prized the agile and obedient servant.   Gregory and his family had steady work.   The Bolsheviks shifted and changed positions, and Gregory and Marfa rafted the revolutionary waters. In spring 1941, garden plots were again permitted.   Cabbage and potatoes rose from the earth. Mushrooms and berries sprouted in Woman's Wood. Pavlov's pond held carp. More prisoners equaled more NKVD, and the officer wives liked their fresh vegetables.

The obsequious and cunning peasant had skinned the khan, the tsar and now would skin the commissar. The Danton clan guarded the spies, wreckers and saboteurs, fed the guards and built Socialism.   Fierce and unsmiling Marfa wiped her hands on her apron, shouting an order to Anna, and gazed around at her wealth. "ah, a pike would be good, but better a carp."

Russian-Byzantine architecture, the motifs within its monasteries and cloisters the embroidery to a thousand skazka, fairy tales, a magical town to or from which the hero quests beyond the seventh land and beyond the seventh sea to rescue the princess from dark forces. For the Larionov clan, life was good and getting better.

Gregory Larionov, the bricklayer, would take his team to Poltava. The Soviet Union hummed with construction projects. Skilled workers were in short supply. The bosses made deals with skilled workers. A project completed *do srochno*, ahead of plan, paid a bonus. Delays meant summary execution. Communist purity would await the coming of Communism. That Spring 1941, the spring thaw again brought to the surface the contents of mass graves. Suzdal is the entrance to the Gulag.

The second memory was later, in early summer, the sun hot, the sky clear, the earth firm, the sunlight inspiring dread. Molotov's voice droned through the squeal, echoes, and feedback of the town's public address system. Somehow, the Orthodox priests had returned to the Cathedral of the Transfiguration, and he stood with his grandmother, transfixed and enraptured, incense smoke hanging in the stillness of the church's air. The priest intoned the story of the unseen God speaking from the burning bush to the dread-filled Abraham, as the unseen Molotov intoning to dread-filled Russians standing in the Suzdal Kremlin square.

Danton recalled the carp he had caught that day in Pavlov's Pond. Markov had clubbed it, then held it against Danton for the measure. It extended toe-to-chin. The Germans came not that day, but later, when Molotov spoke, as Gregory and Sons rebuilt the Poltava Opera House.

CHAPTER TWO

A March ice and rainstorm pelted the narrow windows of the second-floor conference room. Natalia Germanova Shtemenko, Deputy First Secretary of the Communist Party of Ukraine, a slight and handsome woman with dark flashing eyes, grey-streaked black hair wound in a tight bun at the nape of her neck, stubbed out her cigarette. She glanced over the rich and varied hors d' oeuvres spread across the linen-draped table. A silver-filigreed samovar stood in the center as a point of focus around which were arranged the vodkas, brandies, meat, and sweet meat platters, a European west Ukraine order imposed upon an Asiatic and Russian eastern Ukraine chaos. She judged the arrangement perfect. "Tea, Marshal Chuikov?" she said.

The general's aide, Colonel Chernomyrdin, rose to serve, but Chuikov seemed not to hear. Hands clasped behind his back, he stared into the swirling flurries as if looking out over an urban battlefield through the slitted observation port of a forward command post. Marshal Chuikov, the hero of Stalingrad, had held the city at the cost of one-half million Russians dead, some few of whom he had personally and publicly executed, thus fortifying those who wavered.

"Colonel," she said, addressing Chernomyrdin, a wave of the hand inviting him to partake of the table. Despite Party seniority and Communist equality, the woman attended to the tea. She calmed the impulse to throw herself upon the biliny and piroshky, swill down clear and frosted vodka, tilt up a bottle of sweet Crimean wine. Starvation, once endured, was never forgotten.

"Well, yes," the colonel said, conflicted, glancing to the Marshal and back to Natalia, then the table, but not moving. Natalia followed Chuikov's gaze through rain-streaked windows into the gray opaqueness. Whole sections of Kiev remained yet in ruin this early March 1953, little changed from when she had passed through in early 1944, Party apparatchik and German linguist, a member of the Intelligence Directorate, 1st Ukrainian Front. Beyond sight lay Kiev's ravines and Babi Yar, where on a September day in 1941, Sonderkommando 4a, SS-Standartenführer Paul Blobel commanding, executed the Jews of Kiev, Jette and Germann Buchsbaum among them. Yiddish-speaking Jew of the Pale, Germann had become a publisher of German, Polish, and Yiddish literature in Kiev, Russified his surname to Shtemenko. Natalie Germanova was born and raised In Kiev.

Had that old and gentle couple known a day's peace? Certainly, not from their daughter. Jette had given birth to a wild child, a 'stiff-necked' teen, who ice-skated over the dark and frozen waters of the Dnieper, the ice cracking around her. Who would have thought this skating-the-edge adeptness would become a sought-after life skill in the 1930s Communist Party of the Soviet Union? A brilliant student, she had read Marx in the original in her fifteenth year and therein discovered the certainty she sought, the key to history. When you understood the past, the future was bright and inevitable, like the mechanism of a clock.

She extended her hand and smiled kindly. "Please, it can only go to waste." She thought to cuff the colonel's ear, 'Eat, dammit!' She had once ordered food thrown away so that Western intellectuals visiting the worker's paradise would think the Soviet Union was a land of plenty, unlike a corrupt West then in the throes of the depression.

She had never married; she was a Communist, a Bolshevik. She had time only for the revolution. She had risen up the Party ranks because she was an organizer; she saw patterns and read hearts, a strong manipulating Russian men. Russian grandmothers raised Russian children; the two-year-old tyrant remained subject to the old woman's blandishment unto death. Death. She had risen up the ranks, the bodies of executed supervisors her staircase.

When Irina was born, doubt appeared in the afterbirth. They—imperialists, Whites, Greens, Kulaks, wreckers, and Poles—were the enemy, but when Dmitri was executed, doubt enveloped her like night fog rolling over the Pripyat Marshes. On one day, each and every word she spoke was the truth, hard and clear; on the next, the same words became unadulterated lies, dirty, vague, vaporous. Yet, to live, Natalie lied fluently. She could do little to ameliorate her foulness, but she would do what she could to save their child.

"Well, if you insist, Natalie Borisovna." The colonel crossed the room to pour a glass of tea and to fill his plate with sweetmeats. In the silence, the colonel clinked his spoon against the glass. Natalia opened her stenographer's notebook. It had been some time since she had taken shorthand. Well, you never forget, she supposed. The meeting was secret. The staff had set the table, then was dismissed. Today's agenda was the Doctors' Plot in Moscow, Jews that had plotted to murder the Socialist leadership.

Stalin had been, still was for all she knew, an acknowledged poet in the Georgian language, and he had taught the Soviet people to read language for symbolic meaning. The doctors had Jewish names, had confessed to being tools of an American and Israeli plot. A Jewish intellectual wrote a letter to Pravda asking that the Jews be moved to safety. The editorial condemned the letter. 'It was not yet necessary.' The meaning was clear. An all-Soviet pogrom was in the works. Four giant prison camps were ordered constructed in Kazakhstan, Siberia, and the Arctic north. It was the Soviet Union. The camps wouldn't be finished, but what did that matter? The Kulaks were dumped from trains onto the bare and wind-swept steppe. Die or survive; their choice.

The Soviet peoples had suffered grievously, and like in the Middle Ages, plague-ravaged peoples sought reasons. Under torture, a Jew would confess to poisoning the water, or casting an Eastern spell. Then, all the Jews were burned.

Natalia went to the samovar. Khazani regarded her with a slight smile. The pogrom would be the in Russian style; vast, bloody and uncontained, rather than the German manner; scheduled, gas chambers and crematorium. It would be as the collectivization rather than the Holocaust.

She removed her gloves from atop the locked leather courier pouch and placed them in her handbag. The Communist Party had called the Army and Ministry of Internal Affairs together to receive instructions. She guessed its contents, and her surmise made her sick to the core of her being.

Natalia's mind drifted. Irina's identification card was Ukrainian. Would she be taken as a mixed-blood? Irina was fourteen when Jette brought Natalia to the opera house. Irina danced like a winged fairy and Natalia had watched mesmerized, simultaneously fearful and awe-struck, that the child might fall from the sky, or fly away. Whence came this art?

Natalie gazed hard into the hot tea. Why had her daughter married the ruthless Nikolai? Many the time she wished to strangle the concrete-headed Yid, but he was gentle with Irina and became even more so in anticipation of the birth.

Then, Nikolai too was arrested. It was for the best, Natalie had thought. She snorted into her tea, not noticing the eyes turn towards her. Her grand-daughter, Ekaterina, blond and blue-eyed, had 'Ukrainian' on her identification card. An elevator door opened and closed. Footsteps echoed on the marble floor.

MVD General A. S. Khazani, affecting the wire-rimmed glasses and the leather overcoat and gloves of his master, Beria, entered, scanned the room, and paused to stare at Chuikov, who continued to stare out the window. Chernomyrdin stood, set down his tea and plate, and turned to the newcomers, as if to protect the general's back. Khazani, Hero of the Soviet Union, Second Class, had commanded NKVD flying detachments in the war, which provided the Russian soldier his battlefield choice; a German bullet in the chest or a Russian bullet in the neck. He had organized the execution of prisoners in the Ukraine jails as the Germans advanced, Natalie's son-in-law, Nikolai, certainly among them.

"Sasha not here yet?" Khazani said, using the familiar form for the Party First Secretary. She lit another cigarette. "I'm speaking to you," he turned to stare at her, widening his eyes, emulating a Russian thug on the edge of violence or a bad Eisenstein actor awaiting the German Templar Knights on the ice.

She regarded him impassively, he whom she hated with a white-hot hatred. "I regret, Khazani," she said, dropping the term 'general' "I don't speak Georgian."

He set his face as if prepared to execute her. He had intellectual pretensions, had published a book, ghost-written probably by an imprisoned Soviet academic. She hardly comprehended the cur's Georgian-accented Russian. She pressed the button beneath the desk's lip. "First Secretary Aleksey Kirichenko will come when he is ready."

Khazani's aide stepped forward to defuse. "Tea, Comrade General?" he slavered. Khazani ignored him, but the aide, a colonel, and ethnic Russian, hurried forward to prepare the Georgian's tea—four sugars— and placed it before Khazani.

From the floor below, a heavy door closed, then the sound of heavy footsteps on the creaky floor then steps clicking up marble stairs.

Aleksey Kirichenko, leaning heavily on a cane, entered the room. General Chuikov turned, nodded to the first secretary, and sat.

"Vasily Ivanovich, I congratulate you on your assignment to command of the Kiev Military District," the Party First Secretary said. The general had recently assumed the duties of Commander, Kiev Military District; the previous week he had been the Commander, Group of Soviet Forces

Germany. Soviet generals, peasant-born and raised, crude, practical men, indoctrinated against Bonapartism, had been taught from the womb to doff the cap before the master of the estate. Drunken and crazed, the peasant might well split open the master's skull, but he would not take the master's place. Still, care was needed.

"I also, Comrade General," said Natalie. Chuikov softened slightly, as marble might soften. He had been orphaned at birth; his grandmother raised him.

"Thank you, Comrade," he said, then looked a second time at Natalia. "Do I know you?"

"Front Intelligence Directorate, 2nd Belorussian," Natalia replied. Chuikov had commanded the 2nd Guards Army, a formation once seconded to the Belorussian Front. "I was your translator when you accepted the surrender of Berlin from General Helmuth Weidling."

"Ah," said the general. Khazani looked from one to the other. Was this a counter-revolutionary plot to be cut off at the root by the sword and shield of the revolution? "It was an emotional moment."

"Yes, I'll have tea, Natalia. Two sugars, please." The First Secretary took his place at the head of the table, withdrew a key from his vest pocket, unlocked the courier pouch, and withdrew three typed pages. He scanned the text, then looked up. "May I read?"

Natalie had risen in the Party as her predecessors had been executed. The previous month, it was clear that she was next, the writing was on the wall had been printed in *Pravda*.

'Get on with it,' General Khazani motioned.

"Summarize," General Chuikov said. "My staff will analyze the text."

Natalia wondered that her legs still functioned as she crossed the room, delivered the document to the aides, who, in turn, laid them before their generals. She had read the minutes of the Wannsee Conference, the German plan for the final solution, a practical, clean, and technical document. Germany's Jews were to be exiled. If no other country accepted them, then another 'final' would solution be found.

Somewhere in Moscow, a similar meeting had taken place. New gulags were under construction in Kazakhstan; the Jewish Autonomous Oblast was in readiness. She was a Jew. Irina was *polykrovnaya*, half-Jew. Ekaterina, her grandchild, blond and green-eyed—where had that one come from? Might she pass as a gentile? Darkness overcame the skilled dialectician, and she fell to the floor.

CHAPTER THREE

It was International Woman's Day, 1953. The Vladimir State Technical School where he boarded, thirty kilometers distant, was on holiday. Danton Larionov, grown tall and lanky, took the blue 'Cyprinus' reel, split bamboo rod and a wicker creel, war booty from East Prussia, from the tall and narrow wooden cabinet, also war booty. He ran his fingers first over the hand-carved lures, then factory-produced wooden lures, choosing one from each case, after which he closed the cabinet door.

He sat on the bench before the Lenin Corner, the large Soviet flag framing a Lenin plaster bust, which stood between color-tinted photos of Stalin and NKVD chief Lavrenti Beria. Two unframed photographs were tacked to the wall aside the flag. One was a black and white photo of sixteen broad-shouldered and heavy-handed Russians, clean-shaven, hair slicked back, staring fixedly into the camera lens over a food-laden table. Among them was a blond-haired child, the young Danton, who sat grinning before a large carp. Danton touched the second photo, a glass-covered and color-tinted photo of a blond woman in a nurse's uniform. He stood and walked the few steps to the kitchen, took three piroshky from the pantry shelf, wrapped them with an inner page of the *Suzdalskaya Pravda*, placed them in his war-surplus Red Army rucksack and stepped into the yard.

It was the *rasputitsa,* the thaw, the time between the Russian winter and spring when neither warhorse nor armored vehicle moved. Dry spring grasses lay flat between dirty patches of snow and ice. The log pigsty and chicken coop were empty, used now for storage and refuse. He stepped out the gate into the muddy street, paused, then leapt over the mud and dirty puddles onto the grass-covered centerline of Peace Street, walked several meters before he cut right and passed through a yard onto the macadam Lenin Prospect. At the wall of the Monastery of Our Savior and St. Euthymius, he cut left, walking carefully on the slick ice that tall defensive fortifications had shaded from the meager early season sun.

At the alley entrance, he paused, slapped his jacket pocket and cursed. He had forgotten his cigarettes. He turned around, considered whether to return home to retrieve them, but a memory diverted him.

It had been a winter afternoon. Danton and his cousins had been building trench lines in deep snow, emulating the hero Moscow University students, who had rushed into the trenches before Moscow two years earlier in the winter 1941. The German Panzer divisions slaughtered them all over the course of a single week's battle but their sacrifice gave Zhukov time to prepare the December counterattack. They had saved Moscow and the Worker's State from Hitler's evil legions. A commotion. People shouting, filling the street. A line of staff cars approached, Red Stars prominent on door panels, drove past and into the monastery gates. Open-mouthed, the boys looked into the faces of the German officers, then turned to look down Lenin Prospect.

Along the Vladimir highway, columns of marching men approached. It was, they first thought, the same Russian men returning that had in similar ragged and disorderly columns marched off two years earlier. No, they were German prisoners of war, and the boys watched open-mouthed from their own line of trenches. A prisoner stumbled and fell out of line, struggled to rise, his exhausted body unresponsive. He raised his hand, pleading. The NKVD guard, a Mongol, cursed, waved his pistol and shot him in the forehead. '*Domoi*! 'Get home!' he shouted and again waved his gun. The boys scrambled, abandoning their fortifications.

German Field Marshall Paulus, his staff and soldiers of the defeated German 6th Army passed by. 107,000 German soldiers were captured at Stalingrad. 6,000 would survive captivity to return home in 1955.

Danton turned away from the Vladimir highway. The north-northwest wind was cold. Clouds marched in straight grey lines, the gaps playing shafts of cold sunlight like anti-aircraft searchlights seeking the enemy. One dark cloud trailed a drift of rain. The March blizzard had become rains melting the snows and overflowing the banks of Kamenka River onto Kremlin and Illian meadows. He approached a guard shack looking to bum a cigarette, slapping his breast pocket to indicate his need. "Viktor Porfirovich on duty?"

"Buy your own fucking cigarettes," the guard rasped. "Your old man makes the moola." The Sphagin machine pistol with 71-cartridge drum magazine hung steady from a leather shoulder strap. However, he retrieved a pack of cigarettes from his tunic pocket. Danton nodded, lit one, stuck it between the guard's lips, lit his own, then stuffed the packet back in the soldier's tunic pocket. "You missed Viktor. Gonna catch me a pike, boy, take it to Masha?"

"Won't promise. The waters are high."

"Rains ain't stopping, eh? Good news there. You little boy and girl students won't be 'volunteering' to work the collective farms anytime soon. Gives time to fish."

"If I get anything, drop it here?"

"Don't come by early. You'll get run over."

"My old man was gone when I got up." They stood for some moments in silence looking over the river valley where the Kamenka River had flooded its bank over Illian Meadow and lapping up to the Pokrovsky Cloister wall. "Still snow...this late there on Mongol Hills?"

"Them's sheep, shit for brains. They belong to the The Lavrenti Beria Ukrainian Women's Sheep and Goose Collective. No luck fishing, you can wet your line there."

Danton shrugged. "I'm short of rubles right now."

His cousin snorted smoke. "What do you need rubles for? Your old man's Volk Gregorevich, Senior Captain, MVD. You get your pick of the litter." Danton looked off. The MVD ruled Suzdal. Some of the officers' children were spoiled rats, little aristocrats, but Danton didn't abuse his position. What honors he gained, he would earn on his own. The guard turned to look down the wall, the barrel of the submachine gun passing across Danton's chest to indicate the river valley. "Well, kid, there's a pretty one down there. We're keeping an eye on her for the chief."

"For Beria?" How'd he spot her?"

"Dunno. He probably saw her along the highway." He aimed in a general way south along the Vladimir-Suzdal Highway, then looked over his shoulder.

"Why didn't he take her on the spot?" Danton said. General Beria was by-the-books save his weakness for young women. Local commanders had come to understand the advantage of procuring. Good-looking female prisoners were set aside, and the word was passed among the NKVD families—hooded eyes, a nod toward Moscow—keep your daughters off the streets when the 'boss' is in town.

Danton cousin shrugged. He didn't know the whys and wherefores of the big wheels. "Okay, boy, get your ass someplace else." Danton acknowledged the free cigarette and advice with a lift of his hand. Ukrainian were primitive people who ate their own children, collaborated the Germans and spoke bad Russian. Two MVD uncles were still fighting remnants of Ukrainian Uprising Army in the Pripyat Swamps.

The Ukrainian women would return home when the bandits were suppressed. They had arrived in 1941 driving the Kolkhoz livestock before them, carrying fertilized goose eggs, saving their sheep and cattle while shedding their men along the way to Red Army conscription. Somehow, they found themselves in Suzdal. 'Whores, all of them,' his grandmother had spit out. 'You'll stay away from them, or I'll give you the hiding you won't forget!' Some of the younger ones were pretty and fought with the Russian women over the few remaining Russian men. Danton chuckled. They stunk like their sheep. They'd have to be soaked in the Kamenka a couple days before he'd touch them.

He moved to Kremlin west wall on the bluff. From this vantage point, he'd choose where to fish today. He had avoided on purpose the Kremlin front gate, the road to Vladimir and the Farmer's Market. There, his grandmother with other crazed old village women gazed down the Vladimir

Highway where their sons and husbands had marched off after Molotov had spoken on the radio.

A sheet of rain drove Danton to the lea of the fortress tower where the forty-foot-tall painted portrait of Vladimir Lenin posed, forefinger thrust up and forward, steady gaze resting upon 'Mongol Rise.' In April the pike migrated upstream to spawn. In the old days, one could fish in the pools beneath Pavlov's Pond, where pike leapt the stairs pool-to-pool. The pond was nowadays in the MVD secure area. What fishing was to be had was downstream from where the river emerged from the lime escarpments and ravines of Woman's Wood, where Baba Jaga lived and devoured children that strayed.

Long ago, these wild ravines and dense woods provided the Slav refuge from the Mongol, Tartar, and Bulgar raider. It was there that the people sought shelter when slavers approached. The horsemen had to dismount to enter and dismounted, lost the horseman's advantage. But later, when the Kulaks revolted against collectivization, Tukachevski's Red Army used mustard gas to clear the forests of the counterrevolutionaries.

Under this Kremlin tower, Markov, rugged face scarred with worry, stopped, the stone walls echoing the ringing bells of the Church of the Resurrection, and lay aside the sack heavy with carp.

The tinny drone of Molotov's voice echoed out over public speakers. The enemy had invaded Mother Russia. Its fields and cities were aflame. Mounted enemy formations advancing at a trot before billowing smoke when they broke into a gallop giving out unearthly whoops, like the whine of racing engines. In 1941, the whine of the diving Stuka had replaced the howls of Asiatic horsemen, the tank-mounted enemy firing machine guns into packed ranks of dazed Russian foot soldiers as had shit-smeared Mongols fired arrows. They—Mongols, Tartars, Bulgars, Poles, Germans— came in springtime after the rasputitsa and when the grass had greened.

Always came enemies to fall upon the Russians without warning. One day the sun would be shining, the men working in the fields, the women tending the gardens before from the south or north or east a feeling in the earth beneath their feet– –horse hooves, or marching feet, or caissons, and at the horizon smoke spreading along the horizon like an unnatural storm. Kamenka floods and mass graves fertilized the meadows and clearings.

Once the fortified convents, monasteries, and Kremlin had kept the enemies without. Now, the enemy, internal and eternal—the Rumanians, Poles, Czechs, Latvians, Ukrainians, Russians; spies, turn-coats and wreckers—was within the walls. Danton shook his head. Had that been Markov besides him when Molotov spoke? He glanced up at the clouds, which marched south like echelons of enemy aircraft; the Americans would attack over the Arctic.

He looked down where the river cascaded from the Woman's Wood. Recent rains had mostly melted the heavy snows, so though the channel flowed fast, the waters covering the meadows could be fished. He could float the lure into the eddies to see what might be lurking there. There might be pike resting. If not, there were carp on the flooded meadow rooting for worms and grubs. Often, when the waters receded, fish became stranded.

He considered whether to go back to bum another cigarette from his cousin.   A fall of rain swept across meadows and obscured the Pokrovsky Convent; the sheepherder and the sheep formed a single field of slowly moving dirty snow.   He wondered whether that was the shepherdess, which was to be served on General Beria's table?

The gusting Arctic winds that had swept over ice and taiga and boreal forests moaned and whistled amidst the ancient towers and belfries.   The flock of sheep disappeared over Mongol Rise where, it was told, Mongol general Ugedei observed the drafted Jewish Khazar tribesmen attacking the city. Small whitecaps formed on the waters flowing over the wide expanse of Illian Meadow. Danton made out where the log church of St. Nicholas Church stood upon a slight rise behind a screen of bare oak and birch branches.   There, by the church, he would cast his line.

He leaned forward, allowing gravity to carry him down the bluff, his feet pounding, dimly aware of the centuries of bones layered beneath his boots. The bones of women blind with terror, caught between field and gate, steppe tribesmen drafted to deplete the arrows of defenders, the defenders buried in mass graves. He clambered over a memory of the great defensive trench, its wooden palisades becoming brick, then stone walls—behind which the farmer stored his grain, his cattle, his gold, his women, which tempted the irruptions of the herder, stinking Mongol horsemen leaping their steppe ponies over earthen breastworks.

From the bluff's bottom, he turned to view Suzdal's medieval skyline, the rushing clouds seeming to scrape their undersides against ornately fashioned lightning rods atop gold-starred blue domes. Such was the roofline of this ancient Russian medieval town, the towers of the fighting positions interspersed with the onion-shaped towers of Russian Orthodox churches. The tsar, the church, and the army, priest, and soldier, joined shoulder-to-shoulder against the approaching horde. Spiritual progress was military progress; the monastery was the fortress; the convent was the redoubt. On these slopes and meadows, battles were fought between farmer and herder until the farmer's wall, military organization, and gunpowder exterminated the herder.

Steppe warfare was extermination. The fortunate were killed, the survivors beaten, raped and marched across burning plains to the slave markets on the Black Sea. Thus had the Europeans named the Slav. For a thousand years they were the Europe's slaves.

He crossed the shallows to the footbridge, walked to the middle, turned and lifted his fishing pole to salute unseen cousins manning turrets. The past became present in Danton's youthful certainty. The Communist Party, the Soviet Army, and the NKVD defended against that which lurked beyond the horizon. Danton would wet his line where the Kamenka River flowed from the Woman's Wood.

He stepped off the opposite side of the bridge onto Illian Meadow, noting with disapproval the muddy waters—a collective farm manager upstream was abusing Socialist property. He splashed to the abandoned Church of St. Alexander Nevsky. Within lay the detritus of young Russian men and women—empty vodka bottles, cigarette butts and a dirty pair of woman's bloomers. Someday, it would burn and within they would find the charred bones of the fornicators who sought rapture in sex and found oblivion in the bottle.

He passed through the church to the vestry door that looked out over the cemetery onto its leaning and fallen gravestones, tangled brambles, birch and aspen sprouting from grave sites, the encroaching forest. This had been the Larionov church until the 1930s, where they had been buried from times when peasants had no last name; only the baptized Christian name 'Boris,' and patronymic, Borisovich, 'Son of Boris.' Whence came the name 'Larionov' was uncertain. A Suzdal peasant in the time of Catherine II given to the Army to fight under Suvorov had returned from the dead with a name.

Here at his foot, the Kamenka emerged from Woman's Wood's limestone ravines and spilled onto Illian meadow to form still waters where carp rooted in the meadow grasses for grubs and worms, sheep and goose droppings and cattle manure.

Neither Danton nor the ungulates nor the fish could enter Woman's Wood, the pike restrained by the force of the water, the young man and sheep by triple-strand barbed wire topped with concertina wire. Cattle and sheep grazed to this line, the meadow behind, dense and tangled brambles before them. On occasion, a child with beating heart could scurry across to retrieve an errant goose. Several yards further on, was a second fence line, the wires fastened to concrete posts. If the sheep or pig strayed across, he was summarily executed— 'These saboteurs, at least, you can eat!'—and served in the officer's mess. Danton pursed his lip. Flood waters had damaged the fence and snapped wires. It must be reported.

The teacher had treaded with care about Danton, but he took no pleasure in terrorizing them. His cousin, Timofei, was a different story. When Sofia Vladimirova once corrected a grammar mistake, he looked upon her with cold practiced eyes, and she fainted. Danton was not unimpressed, but it had caused story hour to be cancelled, which he looked forward to. When she returned to her duty post, shaken and white, she read with a broken voice, a poor performance. Marx, Lenin, and Stalin stared from the poster "Glory to Soviet Education." She had deserted her post, an offense punishable by a prison sentence of up to five years. Danton after school beat up his cousin. A young communist did not misuse his power.

He cast into the rushing stream and allowed the current to pull the line and cork into a backwater, but fished without luck, the waters too fast, flood detritus interfering with his casts. The winds swayed the trees. Dark, rushing clouds darkened the forest. Winds moaned down the ravines. There was a better place to fish. He crouched and looked into the wood. Wild pigs had worn a muddy path through the underbrush. Danton stared long and hard into the forest, looked back to the Kamenka and its unsatisfactory currents, then again into the woods. For within Woman's Wood was Pavlov's Pond, where once he had fished with Uncle Markov. The old people told how long, long ago the manor lord had the ravine dammed, the fish pond constructed, then when the carp and pike were judged of sufficient size, allowed his serfs to fish, the catch divided by the medieval rule of apportionment: *Pol' nam, Pol' vam;* 'half to me, half to you.' The dam had spillways, four stone pools stepped down. The landlord's son—he had studied in Germany—had designed it according to most advanced engineering principles, wherein waters flowed from pool to pool, allowing the pike to continue their migration upstream to spawn. It turned out that the smaller had the easier time of it while the larger and heavier swam beneath the dam, surfacing, submerging, evil-tempered, disinterested in bait and hooked with the gaff. But still, pike swam upstream and spawned.

Danton looked toward the town. The wooden church blocked the view. There might be pike waiting in a pool near the mouth of the dells. Thick brambles and thorns marked the transition between forest and meadow. Floodwaters had submerged the path that ran within the ravine and along the river. There, where it was forbidden to enter were prize pike. How extensive was the damage? He had a responsibility to inspect, to report. He was a Komsomol. He dropped to his knees and entered the tunnel, pushing his fishing pole before him.

Danton now moved along the top of the ravine using the sound of cascading waters to orient himself the half-kilometer to the edge of Pavlov's Pond. It was not as he remembered. Flood waters reached into the forest; shoreline trees stood in water. Logs floated in the pond and had blocked the sluice gate, backing the waters, which flowed over the top of the dam. On the far bank, where he remembered a meadow gently ascending a hillside, were trenches gouged with backhoe from which muddy rivulets flowed.

He looked around. As children during the spring thaw, they had built stick and snow dams in series along the muddy streets. When the top dam had filled, they broke it, and the water cascaded washing out the successive dams one after another. If he could clear the spillway, the lake level would lower safely. He'd save the town. He smiled at the memory of some half-recalled childhood tale. Suzdal was eighty meters above the river course. The town was in no danger. Anyway, he'd clear the blockage.

Danton lifted a fallen sapling to thrust against the floating log. It sank slowly under the surface of the muddy waters. As Danton pushed the log away, music penetrated the wood and knifed through the shush of falling water. Dirge music like a miasma filtered through leafless oak and birch trees, as it had the day Molotov spoke on the radio.

The log resurfaced and rolled. It had become a woman, black hair streaming with the current, staring up at him with one eye. A second eyeball, optic nerve still attached, winked at him from behind her flowing tresses. The logs were the bodies of the executed that had been stacked along the shoreline to await the thaw.

The dirge ceased, replaced by speaker hiss, squeal, and echo. A man's voice—Molotov announcing the German invasion—droned through the woods. Danton recoiled, slipped and fell amongst the dead into the waters of Pavlov's Pond.

CHAPTER FOUR

A magpie, its wings black, its sides white, flew along, not hurrying, looking here, there, all around. She saw a wolf— tail down, head hanging, walking on the path. The magpie landed on a branch and asked, "why so sad, brother wolf?"
Bulgarian Folk Tale

Her sandals ravished his eyes, her beauty made his soul captive, with a sword she cut off his head. Judith 16:11

The Soviet Union stood silent, stunned, dumb. Stalin had died; the crazed father had croaked, and the household sat fearful and lost.

A troika—Malenkov, the Russian, Beria, the Georgian and a third, some fat little Ukrainian—had taken his place. A troika, yes, three horses in tandem harness pulling a sleigh; it was a good thing, but only one could hold the reins. Beria controlled the Ministry of Internal Affairs, the police and secret police and the MVD divisions; none dare oppose him. His friend, Malenkov, commanded the government and the Army. The Ukrainian? Ach, an ignorant peasant and party apparatchik; Beria would make short work of him.

It could not come too soon. The Soviet Union was in crisis. The state required firm hands on the reins in spring 1953; wolves lurked in the forest.

Work discipline declined. Workers in groups of three hung near the gates of the Dolgoruky Tractor Factory in Vladimir to leave work at shift-change. The tear-tab sealed .7 liter Soviet vodka bottle required a three-some to drink; the bottle, once opened, could not be resealed. The vodka rule of thumb was; if one drinks alone, death is inevitable; If two, death is courted; If three, blissful oblivion.

The Gulag prisoners in Suzdal moved from building to building more slowly, their eyes lifting from the ground. The prisoner amnesty released the malleable; the hardcore and troublesome remained.

The Soviet soldier performed heroic feats, stood against the German tanks, advanced in unbroken ranks against the entrenched enemy to die by the hundreds of thousands...millions. For those cowards who broke, NKVD flying squads awaited. Bullet in the chest; bullet in the back. Your choice. Always there were Russians who went over to the enemy, spies to be uncovered, wreckers to be neutralized. The names—Cheka, NKVD, MVD—changed, but the secret police remained.

The Larionov family was the secret police in Suzdal. Silence followed Danton. The boy was powerful. He was the son of Volk Gregorevich Larionov, the secret police major, Vladimir Province.

Danton looked up, a shadow blocking the sunlight, the fine nuts and screws of a dismantled German fishing reel falling into darkness, the elegant Tiffany lamp as inadequate as the pre-war kerosene lantern it had replaced.

Stalin, who understood the Russian soldier, had permitted war booty proportional to rank to be shipped from conquered countries. Then Lieutenant Larionov had been practical in his plunder. He sent good German steel; kitchen knives, honing stones and awls and, for his young son, a creel, German reel and rod. The single bauble was the lamp, which had arrived too late. Danton's mother died of the same typhus that had devastated the German prisoners of war. Danton for a moment saw his father as he had seen him on the eve of war, save now he wore a holstered Makarov 7.62 pistol with the shoulder belt, the symbol of his authority, rather than Nagant Model 1891/30 rifle.

Gerda, his mother's sister, whose husband had disappeared in the 1941 battle for Moscow, had taken his mother's place and maintained a German orderliness in the Russian house—a polished wood floor, lace curtains over clean windows, white bed linen. Thus it was and had always been: when the invaders left with their booty; women, slaves, and plunder, the survivors emerged from forest and ravine, found one another, dug through ashes for unburnt timbers and smoke-stained pots, and rebuilt. The Soviet Union had won a great victory. And the survivors found one another, paired, rebuilt, planted, and from time to time cast a worried glance to the horizon.

"How's luck?" Volk said. Danton returned to his fishing reel. His father, short of stature, Slavic stocky with large hands and long arms, rummaged through his pocket as he surveyed Danton's project. Eyes sunk deep on a ravaged face, he was clearly sick. Danton towered over his father, his height an inheritance from his mother's side, Volga Germans. "Got any smokes?"

Danton touched his shirt. "Two," he said.

"Give me a pack."

"Two cigarettes."

"We'll share." Danton handed over the pack, which his father eyed with skepticism. "Czech?"

"Beggars can't be choosy."

"Foreign cigarettes are unmanly, not a real Russian smoke. A Russian smokes the papirosa, harsh black makhorka, long cardboard tube so we can smoke wearing heavy mittens. What was the new generation coming to?"

"Since the Czech cigarette is so unmanly, I won't charge you for it."

"In that case," his father said, grinned and took the cigarette. Yes, life had improved. The dirt floor now wood, a house with all the conveniences; running water, an iron stove, and electricity; two electric light bulbs, one in the kitchen, the other over the table, hung from the low ceiling, and an imported lamp. The clay stove on which the Russian peasant family slept warm through the bitter cold of a Russian winter night remained. The pigs and cow were absent from the courtyard, the front yard no longer a mire, though a dozen chickens and three geese still wandered upon bare dirt. The outhouse and the chamber pot remained.

Gerda called from the sink where she chopped cabbage. "Vanya called."

Volk was assigned a telephone, which connected him to the MVD command post in the Vasilevsky Monastery and through the exchange to the district Party headquarters in Vladimir. Whereas the war had treated Danton's father harshly, it had treated his Uncle Vanya well. "He's coming with Tamara tonight. We need a bottle of vodka."

"Ehh," Volk groaned. "Danton, you go to the commissary...the new one. Pick up cigarettes and two bottles of vodka. What does Vanya want?" he asked Gerda.

"Don't know where the comissary is," Danton said. The reel mechanism needed to be re-engineered and rebuilt. He could use the lathe at the technikum but needed good quality steel.

"Rumors are flying," Gerda said. "Vanya says it's important."

"Ah, fuck it," Volk said. "Come, Danton, you can fix that later. We'll show your face to the guard and clerks. Then you can run the errands while you're home."

The spring shower had cleared the air. The setting sun cast long filtered light through tall greening elms that edged the field. Danton measured his pace to his father's limping gait along Garden Street, which marked Suzdal's town edge to the west, beyond which spread collective farm fields. "Modern Soviet youth, eh? But you shouldn't smoke."

"By your bad example, shall I learn this lesson?" Volk gently struck his son on the back. Danton continued, "Why did they build a commissary there? The one at Vasilevsky Monastery seems good enough."

"Security," his father replied. "They built some dachas in the wood...for the big wheels. The Georgian likes his privacy when he comes on an inspection trip...once in a blue moon. He doesn't come often."

They crossed the bridge over the Kamenka River where Lenin Street became the Vladimir Highway. To their right stood the Church of the Resurrection and the old Trading Arcade. Built in 1806 with open-ended arched stalls, the vagaries of Soviet politics sometimes permitted peasants to sell vegetables there. The wives of Party officials did not buy there, but the grandmothers did. "Beria is a Communist, but not an idiot. People need more discipline, of course, but they need cabbage." Boris stopped to gaze across Efrimov's meadow to the Church of the Holy Redeemer. The setting sun passed a frieze of shadows into the cemetery through the greening branches of the five great Russian elms. Danton inhaled from the cigarette, the softness of contemporary Soviet youth no longer an issue, while his father spoke, voice soft and hoarse, Danton holding his breath to hear the words. "You'd come to a kolkhoz. Silence. Go into an *izba*, they are all sleeping on the stove. There is the butchered carcass of a calf on the table, but it wasn't a calf. It was a child's." Volk inhaled a lungful of smoke and fell into a paroxysm of coughing as if he wished to eject his burned lungs from his body. Danton waited for the coughing to pass, his father's face to fade from red to its accustomed gray pallor. "We'd shoot the murderers. It was a hard business, picking the nits from the body of our new Soviet State."

Danton nodded. He had studied Soviet history. The English and Germans had collaborated with Poles to orchestrate the famine, withheld grain from the Soviet Union, and before the Soviet State could requisition grain already in short supply, famine struck.

Beyond the Kamenka on the eastern hills, flocks of sheep grazed. The Poltava Goose and Sheep Cooperative had been moved here from the Ukraine when the Nazis attacked. Despite enormous Russian sacrifice, the Ukrainians had flocked like children to the Germans. Ungrateful savages. It was a hard business constructing Communism.

The old man looked west, shading his eyes, over Illian Meadow on the far side of the Kamenka. "What's that there, boy?"

"Nothing wrong with the old eyes, eh, *starik*?" Danton said.

" I can still see as far as when I was your age."

"No doubt you could read the fine print of Suzdalskaya Pravda were I to prop it on the far hill. Those are sheep."

"I know that you...I'd call you 'son of a bitch,' but that won't do, will it? That sheep herder...what the hell she's doing."

"One of the Ukrainian girls, I suspect." Danton shaded his eyes against the setting sun and made out the figure in a green cape, blond hair spilling down her shoulders. She stood on one leg, her hands above her head, then with a slow movement bent forward from the waist, sweeping her arms to touch her fingers to the grass before returning to an upright pose. "She's exercising, I guess. At the Komsomol meeting awhile ago someone noted it was popular in America."

"America, now." Volk lifted a bushy eyebrow, a 'what next' expression on his face and motioned to his son for another 'foreign' cigarette. Danton spread his hands. No more. "Before the war, it was the Germans we were supposed to copy. Must mean we're going to fight the fuckers." They heard the tinkling of girlish laughter. The dancing shepherdess had stumbled over a sheep, which she now chased on hands and knees. The sheep bolted several steps before turning to face its pursuer.

"So many," Volk murmured, "so many."

'Just fifty or so,' Danton ready to correct his father's estimate of the size of the flock, then understood and spoke no more.

They had crossed over the Kamenka River Bridge and turned into Woman's Wood where the MVD barracks, special dachas, and firing range were located. A thick border of wild brambles, thorns and vegetation grew along the fence. Few passed this line. At the sentry post, Volk snapped a finger. The guard smiled and gave him a cigarette.

"You run into Baba Jaga in here?"

"What brings old woman stories to mind all of a sudden?"

"Mother warned that if I wandered off, the witch would snatch me, strip the meat from my body and cook my bones."

Volk gazed distantly, but what brought Baba Jaga to Danton's mind was the odor of decomposing meat, strongest during the spring thaw. He bent to change his angle of observation, discerning amidst the brambles, saplings and young trees straight lines and geometric form. It was a tractor of some sort. Danton touched his father.

"Ah, That. It's a D-5, Caterpillar, from the American lend-lease." The elder Larionov paused to catch his breath. "Their tanks were horseshit...lit up like roman candles when a German 88 hit them...gas engines, not diesel like Russian tanks. But their trucks and bulldozers were good."

"Ah," said Danton. "Can we take a look at it."

"It doesn't work...salvage," his father said.

"We could probably repair it at the school foundry."

His father shrugged. "That right? How long will it take?"

"Not long. I suspect the comrade students would like to study American technology. A few graduates will get jobs at the Vladimir Tractor Factory." For a moment, Danton visualized weeds undulating in flowing water but forced his eyes to the hard line of the bulldozer blade. In Suzdal, Russia, mass graves were layered one upon the other over the centuries. Socialism would bring such horrors to an end.

CHAPTER FIVE

Her feet were bare. A hooded green cape fell to her calves. In her left hand, she held the goose herder's long hooked staff. In her right, she whirled a sling. Boys in white shirts and red scarves circled hefting stones, prepared to scatter her geese. It was good fun.

Danton laid aside his fishing pole, "What the fuck..." and loosed a string of curses. "Are we to damage Socialist property? Aren't you marching in the May Day parade?" Face hard, eyes cold, he regarded the boys as his father regarded Gulag prisoners. Eyes fell to the ground and stones to the grass. Danton jerked his head in the direction of the town square. 'Get out.' They retreated before the tall youth, the light too bright for their eyes, the shadow of the secret police too dark for their thoughts.

Sentries upon the Kremlin towers, rifles upright, gazed down, Russian watchman scanning the horizon, as they had since the time of ancient Rus', spears upright, for the Mongol's mounted archers.

"Good way to get yourself hurt," Danton said as the boys disappeared into an alleyway.

"I would have handled them," she said.

"You are a fool," he said and turned to examine the impertinent snip. She removed her hood, shook her long hair loose, which fell to her waist. Her complexion was clear, her teeth white and straight, and her blue-green eyes looked straight into Danton's grey. She retied her kerchief at the nape of her neck, careful to not catch her large hoop earrings. She wore the Ukrainian woman's blouse, blue-trimmed with puffed sleeves, cinched at the waist and falling over a black ankle-length skirt. Danton mumbled, then cursed to provide a pause for his thoughts. "Your dialect isn't ignorant Ukrainian," he said. "You speak Russian well."

"Do I now? And tell me, hero-*bogatir*, what an ignorant Ukrainian sounds like?" He guessed she was at least fourteen years old, judging by her sauciness. "What's behind there?" she said, pointing to the fortress. "We are expecting Genghis Khan, soon, perhaps?"

"Mind your tongue, girl," Danton rebuked. "Enemies of the people. Stay away from those walls with your silly ducks."

"Geese," she corrected.

"Stay away from here with geese, ducks or magpies...," the warning begun harshly ended softly. Which tone to use? Of which class was she—proletarian or intelligentsia? She was a goose herder, which could not be more proletarian, but her vocabulary indicated education. She retrieved a pair of sandals from her musette bag and bent to wind leather thongs around her calves, like a Roman lady. There was a rise of new breasts beneath the light peasant shirt, her calves white and strong, like a runner. "And stay away from there...those woods...those fences...Woman's Wood."

She emanated the young woman's impatience at the stupidity of young men and posed the eternal dumbfounding question. "Why?" then, "Dark spirits?" She was a stranger who didn't understand unseen borders. "Baba Jaga?"

"Worse," he replied.

"Ah." Her eyes widened, but the rise of an eyebrow hinted at a tease.

"Firing range. Stray rounds may hit your geese." Her laughter like the lark's song, spilled into the sky. Her teeth were perfect; her eyes bright, her lips full. She wasn't from around there. She wasn't from Russia. She wasn't from this planet. "How old art thee?" Danton said gruffly.

The girl looked aside as if asking an unseen presence had she given this uncouth boy permission to address her with the familiar form. Danton felt his face heat despite the cool spring breeze. She was young, a stranger, who didn't know rules. "I am sorry, countess, how old are you?" he said, now using the formal form.

"I am no countess."

"Then tell me your name, if I am not to continue calling you 'countess.'"

"Soroka."

"Sorokin?" Again, Danton was confused.

"Soroka," she corrected. "Ekaterina Nikolayeva," she said. "What? Are you a policeman? Or do you just ask questions to hear yourself talk?"

"You seem to be doing well enough with the questions." He now understood. 'Sorokin' was the Russian name; Soroka the Ukrainian form, and which meant 'magpie.' She certainly yakked like a magpie. She was of the Ukrainian women from Poltava who had been resettled here with their sheep and geese. Their animals and fowl grazed in the uncultivated lanes and fallowed slopes. They spoke with heavy accents, and fought Russian women for the right to screw the Russian men. Danton glanced around. There was neither copse nor ravine into which to lead this Ukrainian to a private place. Cousins along the Kremlin wall surely watched him, then aunts would note his malfeasance, and he felt the restrictions on youth that came from living in a small town the world over. And, as a boy in small towns the world over, he now sought some way to keep the conversation going. "And you can read too?" There was a book in her musette bag. "Fairy tales, is it? I read them too."

"I am glad you can read, really, I am." This saucy, jumped-up goose girl with a bit of schooling and who stood on ceremony clearly did not know who his father was. Did this silly thing suspect nothing when 400 kilos of muscled and drunk peasant boys slunk away like meek kittens? Danton changed his voice to that of an uneducated peasant.

"You, Katya, you tell me good skazka?" She looked at him, expression severe. "Ekaterina Nikolayeva," he corrected himself.

"The fishing was bad today?" she smiled, and he felt gratitude. She was young, new, full, like the blossoming apple and pear and plum trees upon the slopes of the bluff. Danton acknowledged that the fishing had been bad. "Then, come with me before the geese wander off. In the time the geese take to cross the meadow between the Church of St. John the Baptist to the Church of Tikhvin, I'll tell a tale of fishing for pike in the Kamenka River." She stepped off, guiding the flock with her staff. "On the night before St. John's.."

"Are you a believer?" Danton interrupted, raising one finger, like the great Lenin surveying with Mongol eyes the valley of the Kamenka River. "We don't treat believers well here. We are Communist."

"Do you want to know where the fish have gone or not?"

"But of course. What fisherman would not want to?"

"Then, come."

The geese led the storyteller and her devotee from the Kremlin meadow onto the Illian Meadow. "There was born in the Kamenka a pike with teeth so long that God preserve us from any such," the girl began.

A shaft of sun broke through the overcast brightening the gold stars upon the sky-blue domes upon the Cathedral of the Nativity. How had he not noticed the gold upon the blue? Had the sun not shone before?

There in the meadows that bordered the Kamenka, the Ukrainian goose girl told the Russian youth tales of ancient kingdoms in the incantatory euphony of a Slavic tale as told to the open-mouthed child.

I was at their wedding and drank mead; it ran down my mustache but did not go into my mouth. I asked for a cap, and received a slap; I was given a robe, and on my way home, a titmouse flew over me cackling; "Flowing robe?" I thought she was saying, "Throw away the robe," and threw it away. This is not the tale, but a flourish, for fun. The tale itself has not begun!

The girl touched an errant goose with her staff to tell him to cease his wandering. It hissed. Danton flared with protective anger and stepped forward. But Ekaterina the Wondrous scolded Andrushka the Gander for his bad manners before an honored guest and that Andrushka would feel the price for bad behavior were he was alone with wolves, river trolls and bad boys. Chastised, the foul-tempered gander returned grumbling to the flock. Thus, they crossed Illian Meadow in the valley of Kamenka River to the walls of Pokrovsky Convent at the speed of grazing geese.

On May Day, 1953 the son of the NKVD walked with the Ukrainian girl and thought that surely in her presence even Vasilisa the Fair might hide her face in the gloom of Woman's Wood.

CHAPTER SIX

By June, the kolkhoz fields had been planted in potatoes and rye, though the Maxim Gorky Technikum of Vladimir student work brigade had not been mobilized. So, Danton fished either the Kamenka upstream of Woman's Wood or on the Nerl River before it merged with the polluted Kamenka. The Kamenka downstream from Woman's Wood had suffered a fish kill. The fishing overall had not been good, but any day on the river was better than killing time at a kolkhoz. The student work brigade had been assigned to the Heroic Leningrad Collective farm, where the planting—potatoes and cabbage, rye and cauliflower—had been completed. The farmers did not trust the students to provide more than labor, so if transportation from Suzdal to the Heroic Leningrad did appear on Suzdal's Trade Square, and often it did not, Danton would fish. He would pack his rucksack with piroshky, bread and cheese, break down his fly rod, and watch through his German-made Zeiss binoculars the Ukrainian shepherdess exercise or read or chat with her Mongol girl.

Danton descended the stairs of the MVD commissary, displayed his internal passport to the guard, passed through the heavy door, and stopped, his way blocked. Colonel Vargonov, commander, Suzdal Prison Complex 160, was standing before a bespectacled MVD general in the black leather coat, who was speaking. "Don't pick her up now. Fear takes the shine off." The general was short and gaunt with misshapen teeth, the incisors prominent. "The boss likes 'em fresh."

"Of course, of course, Comrade General Khazani." Vargonov was a toady and survivor. "We'll keep her under surveillance. We don't have to feed her, then, eh?"

"What's the condition of the dacha?"

"It's a castle...spotless...silk sheets."

"And the hillside?"

Colonel Vargonov inhaled. There was sweat on his brow. "The damnable frost...can't keep anything buried. Yes, yes, The Estonians reburied them, then we split up the troublemakers...half to Perm...half to Tashkent." Colonel Vargonov had larger issues. "If I don't get those two detachments back, there'll be trouble. We're stretched. There's too many prisoners."

The Georgian waved dismissively. "We've cut the prison population," he said.

"Those remaining are the most troublesome."

Khazani, patience at end, snarled, "You can't handle it, others can..." Colonel Vargonov blanched. The Suzdal detachment had been reduced in manpower. There had been an incident in the East. The staff of a Magadan gulag had gone over to the Americans, who had communicated with them using a balloon tethered over Alaska. The Americans, magicians of technology and duplicity, had rearmed the Japanese to the East, the Germans to the West, Iran to the South while deploying technically advanced bombers to attack from the North. The Soviet Union was surrounded by enemies. The capitalists were wealthy and could buy wondrous things to tempt the slacker Soviet citizen. The ever-vigilant MVD had uncovered the GULAG plot and executed the blackguards save for the few that had provided evidence. Suzdal Complex # 160 had to send a replacement company to the Far East, while the firing range detachment had to be moved to St Euthymius Monastery, thus to show Beria full manning if and when he showed up.

The general waved his hand. "Solve the problem. Shoot the leaders. Transfer the activists. Keep them moving." Vargonov seemed to quickly calculate how many troublemakers that might be. The general broke out a pack of Benson & Hedges from a brown carton, opened it slowly, put a cigarette between his thin lips, and relented some little bit. "Patience. The boss is aware and will solve all problems in due time."

Vargonov had pulled his lighter from his pocket, unsuccessfully tried to get a flame, smacked his lighter against his palm to move lighter fluid to the wick, all to no avail. Danton struck a match and held up the flame to the general's cigarette. Through exhaled smoke, General Khazani looked him over. "Larionov, son of Volk," Danton said.

"Ah, Larionov...one of our best...chosen to escort the American vice-president on his tour of the Far East." Colonel Vargonov, ever the opportunist, used Danton to divert a superior's attention from his successive failures. Even his cigarette lighter failed to fulfill the norms. "Stalin himself noted the success. Then Lieutenant Volk Larionov...wounded at the front...manages the 'business.'" The word 'business' was emphasized.

General Khazani lifted an eyebrow. "One of our best. Please," he said, extending his arm, elaborately inviting Danton to pass, but changed his mind, holding up his hand, looking Danton over as if examining a horse for purchase. "You're a good-looking young man. Your plans?"

"Plans...?" Danton watched Vargonov's expression tighten, but Danton knew the catechism. "Yes, sir, currently in technical school and Komsomol...I wish to be selected to the Soviet Army engineering academy."

"And to follow in your hero father's footsteps?" The general was short, and Danton flexed his knees so as not to tower over him, but the general remonstrated. "No, the new Soviet man bends his knee to none. Stand!" Danton stiffened, rising two heads taller than the Georgian. "Give this boy a copy of my book," he said, not taking his eyes off Danton. Vargonov snapped to, about-faced, and was gone. "You have a girlfriend?" Danton demurred. "Yes, I understand," Khazani said. "The new Soviet man takes little time for his own needs...but that is wrong." The general lifted a didactic finger as Vargonov reappeared and held a book out so that the Georgian could take it without looking, as if out of the air. "We must not neglect our responsibility to teach as well as to learn. Now, young man, fulfill your tasks. Look me up when you wish to further your education." He turned back to Colonel Vargonov, cold replacing warmth. "We've got shit on our plates...plenty," the Georgian said. "I'll tell you when to pick her up."

The MVD officers ascended the stairs, leaving Danton to wonder for the fleetest moment who 'she' might be. He read the book title, *The Moral Outlook for the Soviet Man*. General Khazani was General Lavrenti Beria's man. Beria's itinerary was a state secret, but news passed quickly enough—the hooded eyes, a nod toward Moscow and a whispered "the wheel." The news was good. Beria was like cheese swimming in butter. Stalin had purged the Party, scattered the generals to hell and back, then died. Beria had only to push aside a few Stalin cronies, and the Ministry of Internal Affairs was in charge of the Soviet Union.

"Cigarettes, Anna Markovna," Danton said, opening Khazani's present to the autographed first page. What had his father to do with the Vice President of the United States? Over vodka NKVD agent had joked about American spies who had come to the Soviet Union, allegedly to build Communism, whom they had unmasked, and shot. "Anna, what the hell you staring at?" Danton said. The shopkeeper was standing rigid, her face white. Another unknown 'she' lifted into his mind, and he pushed her down, like a log floating in a pond.

CHAPTER SEVEN

Danton paused beneath the wall of the Aleksandrovsk Monastery, set aside his fishing gear, and faced west. The view gave him pause. The earth lay in subdued dusk colors under an exuberant sky. The sun rested split in half by the horizon, high western clouds turned blood red, the arch of the heavens a color spectrum, red at the earth-sky boundary becoming azure blue overhead becoming black in the East. The evening star rested about the onion dome of Cathedral of the Nativity dividing the sky into equal halves.

He spied two distant figures in the dusk light of Slobodan Road, one cloaked in red, as if that person had stolen red from the sky. The pair disappeared among the log houses of the settlement to reappear where Slobodan Street intersected the Pokrovsky Convent Road. Their direction was for the Kamenka footbridge where old women washed clothes and which gave onto a path ascending the bluff.

He lifted his binoculars. One was a squat Asiatic female in Russian dress—brown skirt, grey sweater, black hair under a scarf. The second wore a hooded red cape that fell to her knees and over an ankle-length embroidered skirt and valenki, Slavic felt boots. The pair talked animatedly, the laughter reaching his ears. He lit a cigarette to slow his heart. The pair paused at the middle of the bridge to watch the water, then moved on. It was the Ukrainian girl. Why were they coming into town?

He watched them from within the shadows of the beech trees that edged Stalingrad Square. The pair stood in the ticket line, Ekaterina towering above her squat companion, above the majority of people in line, mostly old people. The sky's light seemed to remain within her cape, and she spoke with animation in a grey and silent line, though when she spoke with someone, they seemed to illuminate, as if reflecting the girl's internal light before returning to grey as she turned away.

"Eh, Danton," Danton smelled his cousin's approach—vodka, cabbage and sweat—before he heard him. The cousin elbowed him, "Sneak in a bottle in for me. Verochka won't check you."

Danton thought to give some excuse, but when Ekaterina laughed, he said, "Fuck you, Sasha. Aunt Vera won't check me because I don't sneak shit in. Figure it out yourself."

Sasha pressed the theme of socialist unity, "Nail that stands out, asshole, gets hammered down," then noticed Danton looking elsewhere and followed his line of sight. "Eh, my friend, you're following the split tail. Mother fuck, that's a cute one! Tall one, well fed, eh. Big girl, big twat." Ekaterina and her companion entered the movie house. "But you're going after the slant-eye, I'd say. What they say...wider you spread'm, tighter they get."

"How about I break your jaw?" He crossed the square to the ticket booth.

"Good evening, Verochka." Vera, a war widow, was an aunt by marriage.

"Danton, my dear, what ever's getting into you. Fishing must be awful. Not yet assigned to farm work? What's the world coming too?" She paused, lifted her glasses, and looked closely at her nephew. "Is our Danton learning culture at the technical institute...now become a member of the intelligentsia?"

"Some," he said not understanding, took his ticket, and entered the theater. Aunt Vera was a dear woman, but her questions rarely made sense. As the ticket taker, a veteran missing an arm and eye, closed the loggia door, Danton spotted Ekaterina unwinding her scarf and removing her cape. She had taken a seat on the main floor. He slipped into the balcony, where he could watch her, taking his seat as the crashing chords of Tchaikovsky rolled through the theater. He grimaced. Tchaikovsky meant a heroic war or harvest movie.

He saw Ekaterina clasp her hands, touch her companion, and squeal, crashing chords drowning her exclamation, and turn an enraptured face to the screen. There, the black-inked outline of a ballerina balanced en pointe upon a blue background, Stars of the Russian Ballet in white letters spread across the screen. A woman's name, 'Maya Plesetskaya', in italic script and a title, Swan Lake, in block letters appeared in black on red background. He was for a moment confused— the music called for tanks crossing snow-covered fields and artillery exploding or the open maws of combines devouring grain fields. What the hell, Danton thought? Mosfilm was sending culture to the uncultured. It would be a long hour and one-half.

And he silently cursed. Sasha had found his team-of-three and they were seating themselves beneath the projection booth. For a moment, he thought to join them. Vodka-oblivion seemed a more appealing way to kill time. He looked down. The Tatar women, Her smile benevolent, had shushed Ekaterina who, eyes wide and mouth open, now sat transfixed before the rolling screen credits.

A young man's plan formed in a young man's mind. This Ekaterina loved ballet, of which Danton knew nothing. Soviet education was memorization; in this he excelled. Thus, would he find common ground with this Vasilisa the Fair. She would teach him. He would watch her and the dance. What she loved, so would he; what she didn't, he wouldn't. To deflect suspicion that he was a mere flatterer, he would reject one dance that she favored, then she would educate him. Girls were like that.

He was a young man of principal, but to gain a young beauty's smile, he would toady enough to make Colonel Vargonov seem a paragon of honor. The movie was one and one-half hours long. He could hold his breath that long. If six hours fishing could pass like six minutes, one hour of fruity men dancing with gaunt women wouldn't kill him.

His gaze returned to Ekaterina, upon whom the Tatar woman smiled as a mother. What was that about? That mystery was for later. If Ekaterina Nikolayeva Soroka judged this gaunt woman named Maya Plesetskaya as incandescent, so too would Danton Volkov Larionov. He looked again upon this Ekaterina's face, her expression changing in the screen's changing light like clouds passing over a village pond. Had he ever seen a face—in picture, film or dream—so beautiful?

A music crescendo widened his focus. Dark and slitted eyes regarded him from afar. He leaned back into the dark and the Tatar woman turned back to the screen. He too turned to the screen to see there what so affected one so beautiful. There, childhood tales of knights, princesses and distant lands began to spool into the eyes of he who would be an engineer.

In a theater in Suzdal, Russia's magical city of walled monasteries, white marble churches bedecked of onion-shaped and star-sprinkled blue, red and ochre domes, its kremlin with turreted towers, churches, a bejeweled princess who told wondrous tales of faraway lands had appeared as if by incantation. Dancers crossed the screen. Strong men and faraway music lifted weightless young women dressed in diaphanous cloth into the air, the screen's reflecting off spectacles in the audience as if off sapphires.

Outside the theater was the Gulag. Long column of grey prisoners moved through the night, head downcast, as if descending into the earth. Screams rose from behind stone walls. Shots rang out in the wood. Spring brought dead from the earth with the spring flowers. Danton drove from his mind the wisp of smoke, shadowy forms rising from the earth, at the edge of the endless steppe.

A princess had appeared, as if by spell; she could disappear, as if by spell broken.

The film credits ran. Danton stood, and fell to his knees. One leg was dead to the touch, the other tingling. Mosfilm had distributed the film in two segments, one and one-half hours each, to be played on successive evenings. The projectionist had run them both. He stood, tested his weight, limped around Sasha and his team, passed out and sprawled as if shot in their seats. He cursed them under his breath, but thankful for small favors. The vodka had not been home-brew, and they had not thrown up over the balcony. He made his way to the street, lit a cigarette, shook out the tingling in his leg, wondering if the film might have been meant to be played on three nights. With Stalin gone, the Soviet Union was going to hell. Shooting was too good for the projectionist-saboteur.

Ekaterina and the Tatar were among the last to leave, she looking into the night sky, chattering and excited as if a third film canister would have been a pleasant surprise. The Tatar limped, sharing with Danton cramped muscles and aching bones. He inhaled, tossed his cigarette butt to the ground, and stepped out of the darkness. "Good evening, Ekaterina. Did you enjoy the movie."

"Ah, Danton, you startled me," she said. "Were you there to see Stars of the Russian Ballet? I would not have suspected you to be a fan. You...a boy...sat two hours? I mean, you are no longer a boy..." She inhaled, paused—the dreamscape ended, reality begun. She smiled at him, and he thought the street lights brightened slightly—were the power station crew also drunk, become inattentive, allowed the power to surge? "The movie was beautifully filmed, don't you think? I only regret they filmed segments...not a complete ballet."

He had lifted his hands as if to forbid the thought "It was hardly any time at all." Danton lied so baldly that it was not a lie at all. Her sympathetic smile, understanding of mere mortals, reassured him. "I like parts of it; other parts bored me."

"Really," she said, one eyebrow lifted. "Which?"

"Plesetskaya can do no wrong," he said, watching her eyes. "I liked especially her dancing Rasa's Death." He looked up. The dim and interspersed streetlights little interfered with the star-filled night sky. "but I did not like the Giselle."

His audacity was rewarded. "Danton Volkov!" she reacted as if he had spoken unkindly to the bad-tempered gander, and deserved to be battered about the shoulders with small fists. "You are wrong, a thousand times wrong..." Ekaterina spoke rapidly to the *chuckmek*—Amenya was her name—in the ignorant language, fluttering her fingers toward Danton, faux-exasperated. The young man loved ballet, certainly, but took this odd position—not objective, mind you—that Lyudmila Semeryaka and Mikhail Lavrov—stars of the Kirov, mind you!—had interpreted Giselle badly.

Silent and unsmiling, Amenya watched Danton. She followed Ekaterina's words while looking him up and down, then paused her eyes at his midriff, which was her level gaze. She uttered a few words, and Ekaterina gasped, hand to mouth, then lightly touched a finger to Amenya's forehead, a remonstrance. The tatar was not his friend.

In the cool evening air, Danton's face felt heated. Lavrov danced in see-through black tights, his dance belt a bulbous protrusion, the crack of his ass clear for all to see. The slant-eyed witch had compared Danton with Mikhail Lavrov, the latter doubtless queer as a lead kopek. Ekaterina now spoke that language in scolding voice, and the Tatar's suspicious mien softened ever so slightly—Danton had protected Ekaterina from the Russian hooligans—then hardened; he was still a Russian.

"Amenya raised me almost since birth. She is from the Crimea." The last street light illuminated a wisp of sadness on her face, then a smile. "I wouldn't think you'd like ballet, Danton?"

"I like it well enough," he prevaricated. "I'll walk you to your compound. You shouldn't be alone."

"No, no, Danton, that's unnecessary. Amenya is with me."

"Amenya appears capable of destroying one, even two assailants, but not a gang," he replied.

Ekaterina giggled and translated. Amenya spread her fingers. She could destroy five. "Amenya has been my companion since forever. We've slept in the same bed since I've been a child."

Danton held up his hand like a Soviet film hero facing down the Basmachi, the bad Central Asian bandits in the movie, Red Guard. There would be no further argument about ballet—his position on Giselle was unshakable.

"Thank you, Danton, as you wish..." She has used the familiar form, and it felt to Danton as if she had kissed his cheek. They now stood on the bluff path at the corner of the Aleksandrovsk Monastery. "It's a half-hour walk, though. Now tell me a story that takes place in the Vladimir district."

"I'm not a good story-teller," Danton demurred.

"Tell me the history of Suzdal. It's an ancient city. Tell me about this convent...Pokrovsky, is it?"

"The history of Suzdal is the history of Russia," Danton said. "Peter the Great exiled his first wife here after he divorced her."

"I bet she wasn't happy about that."

"She plotted with the kulaks and nobles to overthrow Peter and undermine his reforms."

"Kulaks? Were the kulaks plotting against Peter also?"

"Well, not the kulaks. They plotted against Lenin and my father and uncles routed them to secure the fruits of Socialism for the Russian people."

Ekaterina paused, "His wife plotting against him must have displeased Peter."

"Indeed, it did. He executed their son, Aleksey, because he sided with his mother."

"Don't you hate it when families fight?"

"Are you teasing?" He sensed a smile in the darkness and he was pleased. "Imagine where you stand," he said, "and what do you see?"

"I see a Russian sky with uncountable stars. I see the outline of Orthodox churches against those numberless stars. I imagine their faded gold stars as the full-bearded architect in his Byzantine robe saw the sky, domes emulating our star-strewn Russian sky."

"What else?"

"I don't understand."

"You must also see walled monasteries and fortresses. The convents are fighting points, the churches defensive fortifications, domed observation towers for there is always the enemy lurking to fall upon the Russian people. Here, where we walked, the enemy camped and besieged our peaceful people and it was the Soviet security forces that protected our homeland from the foreign armies." Danton scraped the earth with his shoe. "Here...stinking Mongols, their bodies covered with dung..." He sensed the slant-eyed Amenya watching him in the dark. "Here stood the tent of the

Mongol Khan amidst his cavalry; before the cavalry and here, at the base of the bluff, shuffled the *strafbats*, captured Russian peoples, given the choice...attack the walls on order or be killed now. Most chose a few hours more life...."

"Strafbats?" Ekaterina looked up at him, the teasing gone, seeming to have stepped back, but not; Amenya stepping closer, but not; both poised, one to flee, one to attack.

"Suicide battalions," he said. He pulled a cigarette pack from his pocket, shook one out, and looked up through a gap in the tree canopy at the star-strewn Russian sky. Here, in the silence of a grove of great Russian trees, there would be no scream, no curse, no thud of a rifle butt on flesh and bone. "Savages used slaves on the front line. The Soviet Army fought with honor...No such thing with us. The Soviet Union had wanted only peace. Hitler had attacked without warning. The Soviet soldier fought heroically. "

"Danton," Ekaterina's voice murmured somewhere in the darkness. "Are you all right?" The shock hit him like a rifle butt to the forehead. A fragment of ballet music, dirge-like, sounded in his memory, as the swan-ballerina's white costume became black. Could Ekaterina be she whom Colonel Vargonov had reserved for General Beria?

CHAPTER EIGHT

The military-surplus American Studebaker sped along the rutted roadbed spewing mud up through the floorboards and upon the battered   Bakhtiar Komsomol Student Shock Brigade. It had been a crisis. Potato bugs infested the shoots. Students were mobilized to save the new plantings, to save the Soviet Union. The brigade had picked well enough, and the beetles had multiplied well enough.

The collective farm driver twice buried the vehicle to the axle. Danton browbeat the Komsomol to free the truck from the sucking mud, the driver content to finish his bottle, pass out, sleep, and perhaps die on the road. Only Lyuba refused to descend into the mud. "My nails," she said.

The rain had been cold and steady for the two weeks; none, neither boy nor girl, had gotten warm nor dry. Using the shadow power he held as his father's son, Danton organized the stringing of wires between bunks to dry jackets and foot cloths, scheduled shifts that stoked the night fire, ran down malingerers. At night, he met Lyuba in the mow above the horse stable for warmth, to ward away images.

Water. Water and logs. They floated to the surface of his consciousness, and he willed them beneath the pond debris, yet they rose again. Beria had come and gone. Of this, he was sure. The Russian summer of 1953 had been late arriving; the wheat fields blanched, mildew threatened the potato; ergot the rye. Would these gray and grim clouds not part to allow but a single shaft of sunlight?

The Studebaker struck a rut slamming his head against the sideboards. He cursed for a long minute until the pain subsided into a low throbbing. The shaft of sunlight illuminated the crossroads where the dirt track to the Bogolyubov State Farm at Petroskoye intersected the macadam Pereslav-Suzdal highway.

"Stella, they're suffering," protested Ekaterina. The shed end doors stood open, the air within still and redolent of lanolin and the eye-watering methane stench of decomposing goose manure. The collective farm women, hair tied in scarves, aprons to their necks, sat five to a side along the long table, plucking goose down.

"Better we cut off their heads?" Stella, stocky and short, heavy forearms and fat hands, her face wrinkled like a Slavic baba, reached with a wire hook into the wooden pen to catch a goose at the leg. As she lifted the bird, the prisoner shot a beak into the attacker's face, but the old woman knew the trick well enough, turned the bird sideways, and the well-aimed shot struck empty air. She set the irritated bird upside down onto Ekaterina's lap. "Practice plucking on this black fucker. Dark down ain't worth shit. The Russian bitches want only the white down warming their lard arses."

"Doesn't it hurt the geese?" Ekaterina pouted.

"They're in molt, silly. The down comes out easily."

The black goose, not to be plucked without a fight, struck Ekaterina on the chin and, squawking like a goose, she buried her face in the gander's breast to avoid the flapping wings, thus exposing the back of her neck, which the gander bit. "Hold him between your legs and stroke his neck, darling." The black goose had won round one. The women gossiped, watched the show, providing Ekaterina lewd advice on handling 'the gander' as they stripped feathers and down.

Amidst fowl and feminine cackling, Stella snagged another, which she set upon Amenya's lap, who flipped the bird and began plucking. Ekaterina's companion clamped the bird between her legs, then grasped Ekaterina's opponent at the neck. "It calms them down," she advised.

"There you go, honey. Learn from your nana," a single-toothed crone chipped in. "Pretend you got your man tight there." Raucous laughter and lewd commentary smoked the air.

"The girl has got strong legs. When she mounts'm, he'll not throw her."

"Ach, look how she blushes. Hold those legs tight together, girly. You're too young to breed."

"Men are easy to manage. Keep their stomachs full and dicks empty." The women acknowledged each astute truth with high-pitched cackles and side glances at the Ekaterina.

"I haven't seen that Russian boy...the one who carries a stiff pole when he's hanging around you. He's a good-looking boy, but keep him out of your bush."

"What are they saying?" Amenya asked, but Ekaterina waved her away. Even had the young girl wanted, she simply did not have the Tatar words to translate the ribald advice.

"I'm not looking for a husband," Ekaterina replied.

"Are they talking about the Russian bastard at the movie?" Amenya said, her slitted eyes slitting further. Ekaterina half-nodded while warily watching the angry gander, her arm positioned to block the hard beak.

"What'd your Tatar say?" Stella carried another goose to the table, her finger flicking a deposit of goose shit from the bench. "She looks pissed. Tell her to cheer up."

"She was helping my mother on tour when the Germans occupied the Crimea." Amenya had been hired to help a Russian dance troupe passing through Balaklava. The prima ballerina had a blond and blue-eyed child, a handful. Amenya, who spoke only the most basic of broken Russian, was hired to watch the child the few weeks the troupe toured the Crimea. "Her family disappeared."

Ekaterina had learned, as children do, the languages which surrounded her—Russian and Ukrainian and Amenya's Tatar language, stories, and tales, fact blended with fancy. Ekaterina was an adept student. She held the goose firmly between her legs, her left arm ready to block the beak, right hand coming away with small bits of down. She lifted a handful to show the women she was learning, and stopped.

The women had become silent, eyes focused on the indefinite distance, Stella looking into the west. Even the geese seemed to become quiet.

"You are quite the storyteller, they say." The woman who spoke sat some distance from Ekaterina, younger than the Ukrainian women, though at least twice Ekaterina's age and watched her with dark smoldering eyes. Clearly, she has once been a striking beauty, her complexion dark, though lighter than Amenya's, her eyes shining beneath epicanthic folds, two long black braids falling across large breasts, clear genetic evidence of Asian and Slavic tribes crisscrossing the Central Asian steppe. She spit on the floor. "I was a sniper in the Great Patriotic War. I have a medal. I shot seven Fascist officers, one a general. Enlisted Fascists didn't count unless they were snipers and I've shot a bunch. Let me tell you another story."

Ekaterina listened, open-mouthed. The woman's Russian was correct, spoken without Ukrainian lilt. "God descended to the earth. He looks around. He sees a German sorting through heaps of iron bolts picking all sorts of nuts. God stops and asks the German, 'Tell me, what is your heart's desire?' The German immediately responds, 'I want a factory!' God gave the German his factory and went on. After a while, he sees an Englishman sitting with needle and thread, sewing something onto a ragged coat and asks, 'Tell me, what is your heart's desire?' The Englishman immediately responds, 'I would like weaving factory!' God gave him the factory and went on." The woman at the sniper's side, eyes dark, gentle and sad, Jewish perhaps, began to sing softly.

"God goes on. He sees a Russian guy with a shovel digging in the earth. So, God asks him, 'Tell me, what is your heart's desire?' The Russian thought and thought, and replied, 'I want my neighbor's cow dead.'

The women nodded, fingers plucking down under their own guidance, at a fundamental truth. The dark beauty, silent for some moments, now continued. "The Russian is tainted. He smiles, shares his vodka, swears eternal friendship, then..." She inhaled. It seemed she was finished, but after a long pause, Ekaterina heard her say..." the spawn of corruption." The warrior beauty's eyes had misted over as she joined softly singing the women's song.

> If I only had wings
> I would lift myself to the sky
> To the clouds

Where there is no pain and no punishment

'Spawn of corruption,' had been the curse the poet Lermontov hurled into the face of Russia's Tsar upon hearing of Pushkin's death by duel. Every Russian school child learned his 'The Death of a Poet.' Ekaterina's eyes moistened for these lost women of the Poltava District, Ukraine Soviet Socialist Republic.

CHAPTER NINE

Gerda looked up from slicing cabbage, distracted, as if she had been transported back from elsewhere. "Ach, Danton, look at you! Have you been wrestling with pigs? You look cold. Some hot tea?"

"Yes, thank you, Gerda Fillipova. Tea would be much appreciated. No, I have not been wrestling pigs, but the roads are pigsties. Where's Volk Gregorevich?"

"He was not here when I awoke. Start the samovar, then change your clothes. A towel and dry clothes are in the drawer. There are rumors, he..." Her Gerda paused. Beria's name, even among his trusted, was not spoken aloud. "Has not been here."

"The general hadn't come yet?" Danton asked.

"You look feverish," Gerda replied. "Take your tea, then go straight to the banya before you get pneumonia. The heat will do you a world of good."

"Only a headache, Gerda." He felt as if he were suffocating in dark narrow closet. Ekaterina in whom all magic resided had not yet been despoiled. "I need to see a friend." He dare not oppose his father.

"The pretty one? And you go looking like that? Now, wash and take your tea and to the bath house with you. It's the poor suitor who meets an educated young lady not wearing a clean white shirt."

Gerda's image blurred before him, the room's light rippling, as if looking into a clear pool of still water, into which a stone had dropped. "I have too much to do...to have to do with girls." His words were ungrammatical, their sense changing in mid-sentence.

"Yes, yes," Gerda said. "You have many tasks, young Hero-Communist, but put on a white shirt."

There were no secrets in a Russian village; there were no secrets in a Stalin's Soviet Union. Gerda's kind words belied the strain in her face. He glanced out the sink window. Had the sun broken through those dour Russian clouds? Danton inhaled. He was the son and grandson and great-grandson of Russian peasants of the northern forests. The ravines and woods hid them from voracious horsemen. He would hide the storyteller; the MVD would pick among those women slow to hide.

"His body lay in the graveyard behind that wooden church." MVD General Blokhin sat on the sofa, erect, bleared eyes set in a vodka-ravaged face, Russian-confident in his certitude, and waved his hand vaguely to the west.

"Would you like a vodka, General Blokhin?" Gerda touched this and that; the concrete sink, the cross beneath her apron jacket, the electric samovar's frayed cord.

"No, no vodka, Gerda Fillipova, 'he' is supposed to come today or tomorrow, this week for certain."

"Tea then?"

"Yes, tea would be just what the doctor ordered. It's been a damp spring."

"I'll do that, Gerda Fillipova," Danton said. She had yet to learn how not to shock herself when she connected the plug to the electrical extension.

"Volk Gregorevich was stalwart in the defense of socialism." Blokhin shifted on the Volk's chair, regretting the refusal of vodka. "He has revenged your loss ten-fold," Danton was uncertain what 'loss' might have meant. "Are you all right materially...food...supplies?"

"Fine, I am fine, General. I have the children." Blokhin was confused. Children? Her husband had died in the battle for Moscow. She had no children. "The children, Simon...the school." Gerda taught in the kindergarten on the west edge of town.

Blokhin nodded, satisfied. He had no further responsibility. Danton looked around. The house had been refurbished using profit from "black" labor and decorated with the knick-knack plunder of the Great Patriotic War. Socialism had profited the Larionov clan, those few left living. Once, the house had been full of uncles, aunts, cousins and bustle, doing those tasks Marfa commanded. Danton's grandfather and sons would depart to construct Socialism and return like Tsarist merchants bringing riches from distant lands.

In the strained silence, the house echoed with memory of din of an extended pre-war family excitement when the men returned. Then as now, the town public address system exhorted and condemned like an Old Believer's God, speakers hung on electric poles along Lenin Avenue echoing and squealing in otherworldly voices, against vices—public drunkenness, under-fulfillment of plan, hooliganism. By the Trade Arcade at the edge of town, his grandmother and aunts waited for the ghosts to return, as they had once waited for the men to return, before Molotov spoke.

He looked out the sink window into the neighbor's ramshackle yard, a pile of burning leaves, the earth turned over for onions, potatoes, and cabbage. The original occupant had been a 'middle peasant', but when the rich peasants, the kulaks, were repressed, he became a 'rich peasant.' A 'poor peasant' took over his house, minus cows and chickens, and remained so. He grasped the frayed samovar cord and connected it to the hanging plug. The woman's long hair drifting in the river's current appeared in neighbor's slow-swinging willow branches. He gasped and squinted the image from his vision.

"Well, must get going. Much to be done, no rest for the wicked..." General Blokhin slapped his thighs with both hand and stood.

"You sure you won't have something stronger..." Gerda held the vodka bottle "for the road?"

"Well, yes, now that you offer, Gerda Fillipova. Odds are the shit will hit the fan sooner rather than later. A little fortifying never hurt..." Both Gerda and Danton read the signal. "He" was coming soon. "None for you?' Gerda demurred. She did not drink. "Then the boy. He had impressed Khazani."

Danton and Blokhin clicked glasses. "To the victory of Socialism"

"To victory," Danton replied, and drank.

CHAPTER TEN

The Kamenka River flowed clear across Illian Meadow that early June afternoon 1953. White tufts of cloud moved sedately across the sky, save two which billowed into the stratosphere. The sunlight rendered the black and white geese and red poppies upon the blossom-dotted meadow as dollops of paint upon the canvas of a Russian impressionist while random clumps of purple iris softened the artist's taste for primary colors.

The ill-tempered gander squawked and chased a gosling. Ekaterina caught him with the crook of the shepherd's staff. "Ah, Petya, what should I do with you? You are the commissar. You must be a good Communist goose. Am I going to have to make you confess your thought crimes to the collective?" She giggled as the bird muttered and goose-marched away.

Her blouse was brilliant white with red and blue threads tracing her neckline. Where did the Ukrainian women find such colors with which to decorate their clothes or clean water and bleach to whiten blouses? Russian clothing was dull gray or ash-flecked black. Danton propped the vodka bottle in the crook of the Linden and stepped out. "Do you have a story for me, goose girl?"

Ekaterina squeaked, hand to mouth, then seeing who had appeared, lit him with a smile. "Danton, you startled me so. Where have you been? I haven't seen you for days." She lowered her eyes. "I thought perhaps you no longer liked to hear stories?"

"The Komsomol was mobilized. We were sent to combat insect infestation."

"Ah, the best sons of the motherland marching forward, bravely I'm sure, to do battle with...potato beetles?" She smiled to soften the sally. Had she the only white teeth in the whole of the Soviet Union? "Danton, You stare at me so." With her hand, she shaded her eyes to survey his face. "Are you ill?"

"I need you to come with me." He motioned from whence he appeared, the wooden Church of St. George standing in the noonday shade of massive Russian elms.

"Danton, you know I can't leave the geese."

"The geese will take care of themselves." He glanced toward the Vladimir-Suzdal highway bridge where the old women held vigil. He hardened his gaze. "" Did you not understand me?"

Ekaterina looked towards the Pokrovsky Cloister as if searching for something not there, gripped her staff, then looked back to Danton "Danton, let me tell you a story, a new-to-me but old-to-the-world tale."

"There is no time." Beria was coming. He would hide this innocent for a mere moment until corruption passed her by, before she became the apple blossom torn from stem to decorate the tip of Beria's dick. Danton would lie to Blokhin. Someone should have told him, he would say. 'The Ukrainian girl was no virgin, let me tell you, then Danton would leer. He would play the good-looking boy, the spoiled son of the nomenklatura, who got all the pussy he wanted. Khazani had even given him a signed copy of his book.

"There is always time." Ekaterina looked to the straying flock, lifting a finger, a tale ready to be told. "Long, long ago a poor peasant went to the Bogoliubov market. He had very little money, and his wife told him that he was to buy only potatoes for the feast of St. George."

"I've heard this story," he said, glancing to the Kremlin towers.

"He trudged from Rykov to Bogoliubov holding his few coins tied in his handkerchief. He was dizzy with hunger, and the thought of a good potato soup rumbled his stomach."

Could the infernal girl not smell the danger? "There are spies among the Ukrainian women," Danton said. "One of them asks too many questions about security."

"The peasant met a woman on the road, and she asked, 'Batioshka, what are you holding so tight.'" With her shepherd's crook, she touched a fowl, which waddled back to the flock. "I suspect you have a great deal of gold coin gripped in that fist, eh?" Her staff guided the flock into the meadow in the direction of Pokrovsky Cloister. "No, nothing, grandmother, I have nothing. But she made short work of his deceptions. She could read a poor peasant like our dear leader, Vladimir Lenin, could read a capitalist."

"So, what did she have to trade with him," Danton said. Perhaps, he had not heard this story. The conflict ripped his innards; he longed to earn her love as a gentle protector, the dissonance twisting his features. They stood in the midst of a Gulag camp, the forests mass graveyards, the inhabitants slaves. Did this innocent need to know corruption and danger?

"So, old man..." The gander lowered his head and spread his wings, hissing. "I have here a wondrous goose, which I will trade for that gold coin in your purse."

"Did the stupid peasant get fleeced for his gold coin?" Time was passing. Ekaterina had grown distrustful. Through ruse and deception, he sought to hide Ekaterina until they found some other girl for the voracious Beria. To admit to the truth was too awful.

"No, the old peasant was not so easy to fool as that. For a gold coin, you should sell me twenty geese!" Danton could not make out who guarded the Kremlin gate, some cousin or the other no doubt. His family was the state in Suzdal gulag. "But this is a special goose, the old woman said, for it lays golden eggs."

"That's crazy," said Danton. He moved between the dark goose, which turned, and flock followed, beginning to understand how this might be done. "There is better grass there among the gravestones," he said.

"Ah, Danton, you clever goose. That's what the old peasant said. 'ah, nonsense,' he said, but the old woman assured him that indeed the goose laid golden eggs, and the peasant rubbed his chin and scratched his head. The old peasant was a hard bargainer, not to be fooled. 'Every day he lays a golden egg; not just on holy days?' 'Of course, Batioshka, every day one golden egg." So finally, after much hemming and hawing, they finally agreed to the trade, spit on the ground and over the right shoulder to close the negotiation, and the old woman walked away with the gold coin, and the old man put the goose in his sack."

"Ekaterina, you'll do what I tell you."

"Now, Danton, where was the peasant and the goose which laid the golden eggs?"

"He had the goose under his arm and going home to his wife, probably very nervous."

"Well, yes, Danton, he was on his way home, but not nervous at all for he truly believed that the goose indeed lay golden eggs and that their money problems were gone for all times. Foolish man, don't you think?"

"Yes, foolish man. But what happened next, then?" Danton sensed the distant hum of motors. He scanned the Suzdal streets that opened onto the bluff. Was some guard now searching the fields seeking his Ekaterina? "Now, I shall tell you. When he got home and told his wife about the wondrous goose he had purchased, she began to rail and curse him...aii, it was a terrible thunder, and the neighbors stood nervously in the commune and wondered if they should rush in to rescue him..."

"I would never allow my wife to abuse me," Danton said.

"And no woman would abuse you for you are a new Soviet man, kind, strong, respectful of women."

The engines of the approaching convoy grew distinct. Danton did what he knew. He commanded by terror, a bully who wanted love. The conflict shook him, and he did what he knew. Ekaterina pulled a book from her musette. "Are those foreign codes?"

She looked at him. "Foreign codes? Whatever are you talking about? They're German fairy tales." She scanned pages, glanced up as if recalling a passage, then looked at Danton. "Why do you watch the fortress walls so?"

"We need to be eternally vigilant for spies." The girl searched his face questioning. Her innocence touched sparks to the wisps of vodka vapors swirling in his soul. Did she not understand the danger he courted for her? A gust of wind whipped her skirt against her thigh, baring her ankles. She was barefoot. "Komsomol Pravda reports that German spies in the employ of the American have infiltrated deep within the Soviet Union," Danton said. "Ukrainians are working for the CIA." Danton hardened his gaze like the Soviet hero, Baktunin, from the movie, "Road to the Sea," who had discovered the Imperialist agent infiltrating the switching yard.

Ekaterina's face drained of color. "What are you saying, Danton? The Germans murdered their husbands, their fathers, their families. They have no one. They want only to return to bury the dead. You would denounce them?" The roar of engines, the rumble of tires across bridge planks, the drums of doom.

"There is a possibility of a spy among them, and it is important for Soviet citizens to be vigilant and report suspicions. We can discuss my suspicions there. Now!" He pointed imperiously to the abandoned church. "Perhaps I am foolish, and you can convince me that they are indeed loyal Soviet citizens. We just can't be too careful."

"I don't understand you," pleaded she who had faced downed the toughs with a pebble and sling.

"Nothing will happen to you. I assure you. What I am saying is that I can say the right thing, that your Tatar is too curious about the operational detachment in Camp 121, subsection 14. "

"You are saying what? Are you going to denounce the cooperative or denounce Amenya? Which?" Finally, there was fear in her voice, and her bare feet stepped one way, then the other, uncertain.

"I can only speak the truth."

"Truth, truth? What is that? The truth is in Woman's Wood?" Ekaterina said, and flinched.

"What happens in Woman's Wood?" Danton saw his cold expression reflect in Ekaterina's fear, and he attempted to gentle his voice. "We protect the people, Katya...We are the sword and shield of the revolution." He caught her collar, and she recoiled, her blouse tearing, exposing her breast."

The convoy rolled over Vladimir-Suzdal highway bridge, a black limousine in the center of the column. Ekaterina, wild-eyed and confused, covered her nakedness with her staff and arm. The geese, confused, moved as a single thing, gabbling as if they were a thousand strong and flowed between and around them.

Danton resolved to brave execution to spoil her before Beria could touch her. He lunged for her waist to carry her from view, but a grey devil and beating wings struck his face, chest, and waist. He lashed out, caught the gander at the base of the neck, somersaulting it, and it flopped about the ground, bleeding at the mouth.

Automatic gunfire rolled down the slope and over Illian Meadow. Two guards sprawled on the cobblestones before the Kremlin Gate. Those on the towers stood, hands raised. A Red Army truck gunned its engine and crashed through the Kremlin gate.

Ekaterina, eyes wild and wailing like a baba, pressed the dying goose against her chest, blood smearing her skin, the torn remains on the once white blouse. Danton looked uncomprehending as soldiers leaped from MVD trucks, gunfire echoing down the ancient Suzdal streets and out onto the Kamenka River and Illian Meadow.

CHAPTER ELEVEN

In a troubled time in a troubled land, a Tsar died without an heir. Within the Moscow Kremlin, his captains struggled for ascendency. From outside its crenelated walls, the people might discern the rise and fall of the pretenders to the throne by a close reading of the pages of Pravda as in another land and in another time by the close reading ;of sheep entrails. The Moscow doctors had been wrongly accused, their tormentors arrested. Kaganovich had been sent to Tashkent to celebrate the fulfillment of the wool production five-year plan production 'ahead of plan."

There were strange doings in the countryside. A woman arrested in the middle of the night is released in the gray of the day following. The gulag barracks gate swings in the breeze. Enemies of the people walk In broad daylight to the train junction in Vladimir. The citizens lift their heads to the horizon. Invaders? There is no smoke, but a murder of crows flies cross the wind.. Who can interpret these strange signs and strange happenings?

The Soviet Army general replaced Colonel Vargonov, driven away shaken and ashen-faced, as Commandant of the Suzdal Prison Complex # 121. With him arrived the bulldozers. Pravda reported the General Lavrenti Beria was a pervert and that he had been arrested.

On a certain day in a certain land, she had appeared on the meadow at the first loop of the meandering river. She reappeared beneath the south portcullis of the Nunnery of Saint Catherine where the Kamenka flowed into the Sergei's Dell when the setting sun outlined the Monastery of St. George. On the fields where once the smoking campfires of the Tatar prince who held the captured Russian queen, Vladimir launched his magic arrow from the fortress wall to pierce the rapacious slant-eyed warrior. Simultaneously, Alyosha the Fool broke the dam flooding the river, cutting off the Tartar reinforcements, the rushing waters extinguishing the flames of the faggots as Russian forces sallied out of the fortress and slaughtered the isolated attackers beneath the fortress walls. Strange happenings, I tell you.

Gone. The storyteller who danced had gone. The Lavrenti Beria Sheep and Goose Collective had dispersed, God knows where. She touched him and disappeared, as in the Skazka.

Stalin had died. Beria had disappeared. Khazani had been shot, Vargonov arrested, the NKVD abolished. In summer 1953 columns of Gulag, prisoners marched south from Suzdal to the rail station at Vladimir as in 1943 columns of German prisoners had marched north.

He saw the shepherdess in flowing green cape on Illian Meadow, leaning on the hooked staff watching over sheep. He approached from behind and spoke her name.

She turned a broad, flat, and stupid face to him, her expression becoming saucy. Slow-witted, she knew enough what a Russian man sniffing around wanted.

"Where's the goose girl?"

"Heads chopped off," she croaked and waved in a general direction of the town.

"Ekaterina?"

"Eh? Ah, that one. They're gone," waving her dirty hand westward. "Can't help you now, but come back...we can work something out." She cackled like an old baba.

Danton turned away. The green meadows, red flowers, white walls, and blue star-spangled Byzantine domes had turned to black and white, Suzdal once and again the gray Soviet Gulag.

How was it that the sun shone every day that remained that summer, the birch bark chalk-white, its leaves deep green? The moon rested full within the forest of cupolas of the Pokrov Convent. How was it that year the waters of the Kamenka were clear, the pike and the carp lying in still water, and upon his tread swimming lazily into deeper waters?

Pravda announced Beria's fall on July 10th, crediting it to the initiative of Comrade Malenkov and referring to Beria's criminal activities against the Party and the State'.

Fall came, then winter. Low-hanging grey clouds raced south off the White Sea, the winds rustling the few oak leaves clinging like sailors to a shipwreck. Neither fish nor vodka relieved Russia's bleak countryside.

The apple doesn't fall far from the tree. But on a Russian spring day between the bluff on which stood the Rozhdenstvennij Monastery and the Kamenka River, Danton resolved that this apple would roll downhill from the Suzdal Kremlin to the waters of the Kamenka River onto the Oka River and into the Volga.

Danton completed technical school and joined the army as a combat engineer in fulfillment of his three-year obligatory service. He had ambition. He used a phenomenal memory to learn by heart whole tracts of engineering technical details and Marxism-Leninism. He would join not the new Committee for State Security, the KGB, but the Government Reconnaissance Directorate, the GRU, as an engineer and with time, perhaps transfer to the Kiev Military District, in Ukraine.

BOOK II

In the England of 1500 children were singing a rhyme and playing a game called "Ring Around the Rosies." When I grew up in Canada in the 1940s children holding hands in a circle still moved around and sang:

Ring around the rosies
A pocketful of posies
Ashes, ashes
We all fall down.

The origin of the rhyme is the flulike symptoms, skin discoloring, and mortality caused by bubonic plague. The children were reflecting society's efforts to repress memory of the Black Death of 1348-49 and its lesser aftershocks. Children's games were—or used to be—a reflection of adult anxieties and efforts to pacify feelings of fright and concern at some devastating event. So say the folklorists and psychiatrists.

Norman F. Cantor, In the Wake of the Plague

It is a family portrait in black and white of a father and mother with child kneeling before them. But where the husband should be, his face is scratched out so that it appears as if it is an apparition's arm that lies protectively on the woman's shoulder. And so it is.

Photograph, 1991, Kiev, Memorial Museum, Victims of Stalinist repression.

CHAPTER TWELVE

Ekaterina Soroka looked at the man who had knocked at the door to the artists' communal apartment on Alexander Square, Poltava, USSR. Beyond, actors and stagehands, all members of the Tchaikovsky Poltava State Artists Commune, stood in the dim light, passive, uncertain, eyes to the floor, awaiting their turn to the bathroom.

"Can I help you, comrade," she said. He stood not speaking but rolled a cigarette in newsprint from Red Star. The flaring match illuminated his burned and scarred face, skin grown over one eye like an eye patch as if he would in a moment remove a carnival mask, and the disfigurement would disappear. A veteran, she guessed, a *tankist*. Where the leather helmet had protected his hairline and the chinstrap the jaw, the skin was healthy. He had probably served in one of the gasoline-powered American tanks, which burned like roman candles when the German Panzerfaust or 88 ignited the vulnerable gas tank. The Soviet tanks were better, safer, and faster with diesel engines. She looked closer. His teeth were broken and chipped, save the incisors, which were filed to points. Ragged hand-drawn tattoos interlaced with burn scars crossed his face while a long white scar circled his neck. He wore the awful Soviet brown suit, short at the wrist, shiny at the sleeve, baggy trousers reaching above the ankle, shoes laced with twine. He exhaled, and smoke wreathed his face. He was as Beelzebub come to their door for his own reasons. "Can I help you," she repeated.

Katya," he murmured, then rasped, "Get your mother."

"Comrade," Ekaterina said firmly. She controlled an involuntary shudder and only later wondered how he knew her name. As a Pioneer and Communist Youth candidate, she must treat veterans with respect for their sacrifice. But rudeness should not be countenanced. Beyond, in the hallway, the communal apartment dwellers stood in a line before the single bathroom, eyes to the floor, the light from a dirt-streaked skylight rendering them black and white. "Can I tell Irina Sergeevna who is calling?"

"Nicolay Isaakovich."

"And your family name?" He did not answer but looked beyond her into a room no larger than a broom closet. Housing was in short supply. The Germans had occupied Poltava; that which they had not destroyed when they advanced, they burned to the ground when they retreated. She squinted as if she might look through the theater mask, a little shock vibrating her chest as if she had leaned against the poorly wired light switch. "Comrade," she repeated, to give herself pause, "your family name?" It became clear. He was a *frontovik* that had seen Irina Germanova perform at the front or perhaps in a hospital ward. Occasionally a veteran passed by to thank her and sometimes her mother would give the veteran a little money, a ticket to a performance at the Poltava Opera House.

"You are more beautiful than it was possible to imagine," the monster said.

"Comrade, Lenin teaches us that it is our contribution to the social good that determines our worth and not externals like beauty."

"Screw Lenin," he said.

"Comrade!"

"Who is it?" her mother's voice came from inside the communal bathroom. The door opened, and the ballerina emerged. "For the love of God, Alexei Alexeevich, I have my allotted five minutes. Why were you pounding so?" She stopped in mid-sentence, the communal dwellers silent, neither grumbling, muttering nor cursing. Irina looked into the gloom, focused her eyes, fussed with her musette bag as if searching for her glasses, and suddenly recoiled, as if the impatient Alexei Alexeevich had struck her face. He had not, his head hung as before, his eyes averted. A sadness sagged the body of the prima ballerina of the Poltava Ballet, Odette's body pierced not by Prince Siegfried's arrow but crushed under the weight of 1941.

"We cannot know you," Irina said, tears coursing down her face.

The Gulag gates had opened. The survivors stepped out, tentative and blinking, to make their way back to where long ago, a knock in the night wrenched them into an inferno beyond the pitiful imagining of Dante Alighieri. Released, not free. Released. The dead had arisen to wander without blessing, strangers among the living.

'I am not guilty.' Pharisees with names foreign or familiar-Wallace, Sartre, Marcuse, Chomsky—sung choruses in praise to Socialism while in the Soviet Union, one did not discern the sound of the false witnesses from the wail of Arctic winds.

A tear slid down the grotesque face. The ballerina's hand touched her own face as if searching for feeling. Ekaterina's heart felt as if it might burst in a silence rancid with the smell of burnt sunflower seed oil, boiled cabbage, and the effluvium smell of the communal toilet.

Batu Kahn's horse-mounted bowmen or Guderian's tank-mounted grenadiers slew the Russian soldiers by the millions. On the approaches to Kiev, a single witness—a Genoan merchant, a German army cameraman—recorded the bones of Russian soldiers' littering the landscape to the horizon.'

"Go to school, Katya, now!" commanded the ballerina's disembodied voice.

"Mama?"

"Go!" she commanded.

The frightened girl slipped past the beggar. Only later did she puzzle why the dwellers waiting in line didn't curse the beggar, or drive him off, had not lifted their eyes from the floor. Only later did she remember the tattoo on his neck—a dagger thrust into a man, a splatter of red ink on clear skin—a prison tattoo, worn by gangsters, not political prisoners.

We will have wars of national liberation as long as imperialism exists, as long as colonialism exists. These are revolutionary wars. Such wars are not only permitted, they are inevitable because the colonialists will not voluntarily set the people free. Thus the people have to struggle, and that includes armed struggle, to gain their independence and freedom.

N.S. Khrushchev before representatives of the world's Communist parties, 19 January 1961

Let every nation know, whether it wishes us well or ill, that we shall pay any price, bear any burden, meet any hardship, support any friend, oppose any foe, to assure the survival and the success of liberty.

John F. Kennedy, Inaugural Address, 21 January 1961

CHAPTER THIRTEEN

The long and dreary Moscow winter endured. The rear echelons of the night's storm retreated to the southwest, a few laggard clouds obscuring the distant St. Basil's Cathedral and Kremlin. Standing alone before the window atop the Ostankino Radio Tower, Alexander Soroka gazed through the steam rising from his tea.

"Now perhaps the mother-fucker sun will put in a full day's Socialist Labor," he muttered. 'Ach, Wash your mouth out with soap, Sasha,' he thought. Fifteen years since the war and still you curse like a front-line soldier.

He mumbled on. "You pretend to pay me, I pretend to work, saith the Socialist worker and so saith also the socialist sun." What can one pay the sun? Sacrifice a bullock, a virgin, millions of the best sons and daughters of the motherland? "Were that so, the lazy son of a bitch should be burning twenty-four hours a day and incinerate this god-forsaken land." He paused a moment, then said, "One lucky yid, you...Sasha." Many the time Soroka had heard the proverbial, often enough real, bullet whistle past his ear. Somehow, he remained among the living to drink good Indian black tea. Few in Russia drank Indian tea, available only, so far as he knew, in the Gostelradio commissary. Reason enough to work for the USSR State Commission for Television and Radio Broadcasting. The theater had served him well.

The screening clouds dissipated, and the Kremlin appeared. He held in his hand a worn US newspaper clipping from the American journal, *This Week*, dated September 7, 1952. Henry B. Wallace, who had almost become President of the United States of America, had written the article. It was a confession, at which, God knows, Communists were past masters. A mealy-mouthed piece. Wallace was shocked that the Soviet Union spied upon the United States. Shocked!

A Soviet self-criticism collective would have insisted Wallace make a full confession of his false thoughts. It would be recorded and entered into evidence upon which the NKVD would have prescribed 'ten years,' or perhaps that beyond cynical euphemism, 'ten years without the right of correspondence.'

"Was it my fault he was a moron?" Alexander supposed Wallace might have written the article. He was probably on a pension now without a speechwriter. Aloud, he said, "Well, God be with the holy fool."

Soroka had begun his professional life in the theater; had been no mean impresario and had been tasked to organize the 1944 US Vice President Wallace tour of the Soviet Far East. The American had been like a peasant with mouth agape at his first magical show, eyes fixed the red ball. "It is the Socialist future," the American vice-president wrote. He wasn't too far wrong there. What would be the English translation of the Russian proverb, fools are neither planted nor produced, but born?' Well, of course. 'There's a sucker born every minute.'

He withdrew a teletype flimsy from the folder. Soviet Intelligence reported the former Vice-president had died, incorrectly, it turned out. Soroka snorted. Russian intelligence. It could kill you, and often did. General Goglidze had the sick and injured at Kolyma executed—Three thousand, he'd heard—that Wallace need not see them. Soroka was the Soviet Union's foremost expert on Wallace, an academic discipline whose time had passed. Wallace had missed becoming US president in 1944 by what...89 days?

Soroka sipped. It was essential to use a small samovar. One mustn't make too much tea liquor. The secret was to bring the water to boil, and then let it settle a moment before pouring it over the tea leaves. A mystery wrapped in an enigma, eh? He had to admit that the electric samovar was not an unmitigated catastrophe. The old-style charcoal samovar was better, but not by much.

A 'President' Wallace would have been Soroka's winning lottery ticket. The Jewish magician would have become a Special Consultant to the Ministry of Foreign Affairs and eligible for overseas travel.

"Good morning, Comrade Soroka." Three secretaries--they hired pretty ones at Gostelradio—walking along the ring corridor inclined slightly away from the powerful mumbler. He nodded without turning.

Alexander had kept a small suitcase packed, sending Rachel, his son, and daughter, to Kiev to her parents, and awaited the NKVD. Irina danced and also waited for the nighttime knock. On June 22, 1941, Hitler saved them. In the confusion of the invasion, Alexander and his brother's wife fell through the NKVD cracks.

He fingered an article torn from the Odessa Pravda. There was a local radio program, which was devoted to family reunification. The correspondent had written in crayon in block letters encouraging Alexander to create such an All-Soviet Union radio program.

There was evidence his brother had survived Stalin, Hitler, and the Gulag...somehow. Stranger things had happened in this crazed land.

"Olga, come with me to the bathroom while I splash water on my face. That Comrade Soroka frightens me terribly."

"Ah, Masha, hard eyes. Those Jewish Bolsheviks..."

"He had been a Menshevik, they say."

"How'd he survive?"

"I don't know," Olga whispered. "Pity Comrade Stalin missed him." They ducked into a door. "Cigarette?"

The Soviet Army senior lieutenant stood on Moscow's Red Square at a point equidistant from the portal of St. Basil's Cathedral, the main entrance to the GUM department store and the gate to Lenin's tomb. By his collar tabs, his military specialty was sapper, combat engineer. Geometric relationships occupied his mind. The shadow of a cloud crossed the square darkening the long line of Soviet citizens standing in stoic patience before the reliquary of the saint, Lenin's Tomb.

Danton Volkov Larionov exhaled moist breath into the frigid air. His grandmother had told him stories how pious Russians, ignorant peasants as well as educated nobles, had stood in similar lines to view the reliquaries of the holy relics of the Saint Euthymius of Suzdal. A gust of wind lifted crystallized snow off the cobblestones, strafed his great coat and carried away his thought and moist breath. He pulled the fur cap down over the top of his ears, but left the ear flaps up; uniform dress regulation permitted earflaps down while in the field, but not in garrison or on leave.

The Revolution had enriched the Larionov family; the war destroyed it. Danton, two uncles, and widowed aunts remained. Without goal but with inchoate yearning, he had joined the Soviet Army. The storyteller who danced in the meadow overwhelmed his dreams. She had mentioned Poltava, in Ukraine, where on the war's eve his grandfather and uncles had gone to reconstruct a theater or opera house or philharmonic hall; he couldn't remember exactly. They had disappeared without a trace.

Chance had found Lieutenant Larionov assigned to Dnepropetrovsk, Kiev Military District, a few hours by army truck south of Poltava. Even in the late-1950s, the devastation the war visited upon Ukraine was visible and utter. The German army had advanced rapidly into and retreated quickly from the territory of the Russian Soviet Socialist Republic; it was in Ukraine that the Great Patriotic War was fought. The Soviet Army and the Wehrmacht each destroyed what they could in retreat. As expected, the Germans were more thorough. Danton would wonder how even one Ukrainian had survived the invasion, occupation, and withdrawal.

An opportunity presented itself. He volunteered accrued leave to help rebuild the destroyed Poltava Gogol Theater. He inquired among survivors for family news. Family reunification was a permissible discussion topic. Survivors spoke volubly. There had been no information concerning a 'black' pre-war construction team accepting under the table money to do special projects, nor of a ballerina named Soroka.

Soldiers talk, and veterans tell war stories. A veteran combat engineer spoke of a Soviet Army colonel-magician who made whole armies disappear to reappear hundreds of miles distant and fall upon surprised and stunned Nazis formations with tanks, artillery, and fire.

His name was Soroka, and this Soroka taught an advanced combat engineering course on maskirovka at the Valerian Kuybyshev School of Combat Engineers in Moscow. A 'first' in this advanced course would advance his career. He had little else to do.

"Ah, Katya, must we walk so far out of our way." Vera Vishnevskaya whimpered through mittened hands over her face. A metallic cold Moscow wind gusted a flurry of snow crystals off bare tree branches to envelop the girls. They paused until the wind and snow settled.

"Verochka, it's only 150 meters extra. It won't kill you."

"Yes, it will," Vera said but followed her friend. The young women had become friends that fall day the fourteen-year-old Ekaterina had appeared at the Kirov Gymnasium of the Language Arts on Moscow's Old Arbat. She was tall with a long blond braid circling her head like a laurel wreath, wore an embroidered white blouse, and spoke with a hint of Ukrainian accent, a yokel country girl dressed for the cattle fair. 'Now here is a white crow,' murmured the boys, sons of the nomenklatura and circled to have a little sport. Vera, already a renowned verbal swordsman, stepped forward, cutting and stabbing with words and knitting needles to rout the horde.

"We'll get their blessings," Ekaterina replied. Even bundled against the 1960 Moscow cold, Ekaterina was a beauty. Green eyes peered out beneath knitted cap, over the wool scarf and through strands of long wind-whipped blond hair. In the winter's iron-grey dawn, she stood out, appeared disembodied, a red knitted cap with matching muffler, grey coat and wool skirt and embroidered *valenki,* ankle-high felt boots—peasant– or child-wear—with multi-colored knitted stockings, as if head and boots were advancing without a body. It was an odd costume in socialist-grey Moscow, but such that the older women would glance upon her kindly, remembering when they too wore *valenki.* If the stray Moscow drunk might be tempted to accost this beauty, her straight white teeth and healthy skin warned him off. Her parents were nomenklatura, whose children during wars and famine had enough to eat, privations apparent among Russian youth in the pallor of the skin, bad teeth and curvature of the spine.

"Don't get your hopes up, dearest Katya. The competition is fierce, and we don't know how many openings there might be." Vera thought to pluck a single dark hair which had appeared on Ekaterina's brow. In the genetic stew that was the Soviet Union, Ekaterina's mother was light and lithe; her father dark and, well, Jewish, while this daughter, tall and statuesque, had a tendency towards an unfortunate unibrow. and on which Vera used a light bleach solution.

"No, Vera, I forbid you to be negative. Moscow State University will accept us in the language arts department. We will speak perfect German and English. We shall study together in Berlin. Then we shall become translators in the foreign service..." She stepped over a fallen tree branch. "...To serve the working man and the Soviet Union. And we shall dance in Paris. Things turn out well when they turn upside down, don't you think? Hasn't everything turned out well so far?"

Ever the optimist, Ekaterina had grown too large for ballet, and sought alternatives. Things fell her way. By some magical Soviet incantation, Alexander Soroka had obtained one of the larger 'Khrushchyevki' on Argunovskaya Street in Moscow's Ostankino district, throwing the sixteen-year-old friends into despair. How could they bear being parted, leave the Arbat, live without Vera? Ostankino was in the boondocks at the end of nowhere! Then, General Vishensky received quarters in the Soviet Army housing complex near Timoryevskoye Metro station, mollifying the girls. Things weren't so bad. The Soroka's new apartment was private with kitchen, bedroom, living room, and balcony—the living room became Ekaterina's bedroom where Vera often slept over.

Vera was dubious. "If I survive till the streetcar arrives, then maybe. These mittens—bless your sainted grandmother for knitting them—will stave off death until after classes today only if I am lucky."

"I promise you," Ekaterina said, "the heater on Streetcar Number 11 will be a blast furnace this morning. So, if we don't visit the spirit people, they will punish us by causing Lydia Borisovna to make us compose sentences using English modal verbs to form conditional sentences only, and for every mistake, she will beat us with a pencil."

"Katya, the Bashkirs have made a pagan of you."

"No, not a pagan, but a fabulist," Ekaterina said, pursing her lips at the unjust accusation.

"No," Vera contradicted, "...a pagan. 'Fabulist' is the word you use to deceive us, to mask your trail. My dearest Ekaterina, I'd kiss you, but my lips might freeze to your cheeks." Vera raised the mitten to her face. "Even in this cold, they still smell like lamb."

They had entered a small clearing in which some unknown artist had carved wooden statues from oak tree trunks, human and elfin figures—gnomes and fairies and men and women and children—frozen in a frolic-some moment by a Baba Jaga spell. Ekaterina paused a man, woman, and child hewn from a single tree. The years had given their faces a tragic, even horror-stricken mien, one man's face disintegrated as if erased from memory. After some moments, she spoke. "Boris Leonidovich first took me here." Vera looked at Ekaterina and thought for a moment that her heart would burst with love. Often she awoke upon their narrow bed, their limbs intertwined, to gaze upon Ekaterina's sleeping face and to kiss her on the cheek. She seemed a slash of steppe sunlight fallen upon the Moscow's morose cityscape. "I haven't seen him for such a long time." Ekaterina stopped before a man's figure, its face weathered and haggard, but warmed beneath a cape of snow. "He's ill and doesn't leave Perdelkino in the winter." She caressed the wooden figure's head, looked up, and memory became visible among bare branches.

The morning had been fog-shrouded. Rain fell in a light mist. Long lines of ragged and starved men marched south down Vladimir Road.

"Fascist murderers," the Kolkhoz deputy had said, "Criminals."

"But they're Russian," Ekaterina protested.

The woman struck Ekaterina across the shoulders, knocking her to the ground, then burst into tears, knelt and took Ekaterina into her arms. "Life's getting better. Life's growing sweeter," she said

Vera's voice interrupted the vision. "Come, Katya, we'd better run, or we'll have to stand on the streetcar."

"His friends were so horrible to him," Ekaterina murmured.

"Who?" Vera said, hand on Ekaterina's back, guiding her from the grove.

"The poet..."

"Pasternak?"

"Yes."

Streams of Moscovites emerging from the pre-war "Staliniki" high-rises fronting on the All-Russian Agriculture and Industry Exhibition Center grounds. The intersection of Academic Korolev and Argunovskaya was the end stop of the #11 streetcar line, which would take them to the Foreign Language Institute on the grounds of the Ismailovskii Monastery.

An Asiatic man appeared out of the commuter crowd and thrust a carnation into Ekaterina's hand. Though the militia arrested beggars and homeless where they might encounter foreigners, they congregated at suburban metro and bus stops to sell this and that. Vera stepped forward to shoo him away, but he said in heavily accented Russian, "Soroka?" Ekaterina, seeking a few kopeks in her handbag, thinking him a beggar, paused. "Ekaterina Nickolaeva?"

Ekaterina tilted her head questioningly but spoke kindly. "Yes and no...I am Ekaterina, but Alexandrova, not Nickolaeva."

"Dancer?" She looked into his face, again confused at his accent and his use of the masculine form of the word 'dancer,' and smiled. "A dancer only in my dreams."

Vera watched Ekaterina's expression turn quizzical, and her friend spoke a few incomprehensible words. A slight smile creasing his face, and responded in kind. Ekaterina spoke rapidly, and the slant-eyed man understood.

Vera pulled the two from the pedestrian flow, understanding nothing, following the conversation through expression, gesture, and the occasional Russian word. Clarification came slowly, he shaking his head either in the negative, followed by rapid words, then, the affirmative nodding. Ekaterina alternately perplexed, then questioning, not understanding, then understanding.

Ekaterina spoke rapidly in the the stranger's language, pointed to the Gostelradio complex, but he held up a finger, pausing her contradiction, and gave a cascade of instructions in which Vera heard only the Russian word 'Baumanskaya Metro.' Ekaterina repeated what seemed to be instructions and the Asian man, satisfied, retrieved a knitted cap from his bag, gave it to Ekaterina, and disappeared into the metro station crush.

"Whatever was that about?" Vera asked of the thoughtful Ekaterina, but before she could form an answer, the streetcar arrived, the Russian crowd, yet to learn the art of the queue, swept the young women to its door.

Aboard the streetcar, they stood in crushed silence for the half-hour ride. Vera could not question Ekaterina for if they spoke in Russian, a bothersome babushka would listen and if they spoke English or German, then said bothersome babushka would report them as spies. Vera would make Ekaterina join her for a cigarette at lunch in the Ismailovskij Forest.

CHAPTER FOURTEEN

Ekaterina fumbled In the vestibule darkness for the keyhole to the inner door while simultaneously waving her hand above her head seeking the hanging light switch. Vera reached the chain first, and a dim bulb lit the room to expose rubber overshoes and boots, coats, and fur hats. On the opposite wall hung framed black and white photos of ballerinas in various poses plus two posters, one the schedule of the 1934 Kirov Ballet tour to Odessa, Sochi, and Crimea, the other the Bolshoi Ballet 1955 season. Ekaterina mumbled 'thank you' and opened the door.

"Katya, is that you?" The vestibule door opened onto the living room, which at night became Ekaterina's bedroom, the bed a convertible sofa. The apartment was Soviet palatial: three rooms; bedroom, kitchen and living room plus bath, all the conveniences.

"Yes, Mama. Verochka, also. Where are you?"

"I am entertaining in the distant reaches of the palace...the Red Room."

"Mama, don't tease."

"And don't ask silly questions. I'm in the kitchen." Vera following Ekaterina down the short hallway past the bedroom door, and at the bathroom door, turned left into the kitchen. Irina wearing her dressing gown sat at a Formica table, cigarette in one hand and tea glass in the other, a portrait in quiet elegance. She was a handsome woman, tiny with her hair piled atop her head and held in place with two knitting needles. Her unlined face was, however, ballerina gaunt, her eyes shining. The door to the balcony was cracked open through which vapor slithered along the floor while smoke drifted out over the transom. "Come, darlings, tea?" Irina kissed her fingertips and fluttered it across the kitchen at Vera. "Vera, darling, you don't need my cold. Be a dear and make the tea, would you, angel?"

"Still a touch of the flu, mama?" Ekaterina kissed her mother's cheek.

"I can't seem to shake it," Irina Soroka looked into her daughter's eyes." What's wrong, my dearest?"

"You should see a doctor."

"What, you want me dead already? "

"Momma," the daughter's tone disapproving of her mother's flippancy.

You know I don't trust doctors." Irina Soroka, her family and stage name Shtememko, caressed her daughter's face, then grasped her chin to examine her eyes. "What going on in that little creative mind of yours?" she said, smoothing her daughter's forehead. "Don't frown, darling, your face will wrinkle."

"The oddest thing happened today."

"In your imagination or...?" Irina looked to Vera for confirmation, who had long ago been judged to have the firmer grasp of reality.

"Don't ask me, they...Ekaterina and the *chuchmek* spoke gibberish."

"We don't use that word in this house, Verochka," Irina said.

Vera was, however, opening the cabinet above the sink--she chose three teacups with floral designs and rejected the tea glasses--finding a match, igniting the burner and speaking over her shoulder. "Where's the sugar, Irinochka? Ah, never mind, I found it."

Ekaterina had knelt and laid her head on Irina's lap. "His Russian was awful. I thought, at first, he was one of Amenya's relatives with a message. It was the oddest coincidence. He was Bashkir...quite stunned when I spoke Bashkiri, but he had nothing to do with Amenya. Can you imagine the coincidence?"

Vera lit cigarettes for herself and Irina. Irina blew the smoke towards the door, holding the cigarette aloft that she had not lit her daughter's hair afire. "Irina, you are not well. Your eyes look like you're a raccoon. I don't like the color of your skin."

"Why thank you, dearest Verochka, you know how to make an old ballerina feel young again. Katya, did you understand the man?"

"I understood the words, but he made no sense, momma."

Vera set the tea tray on the table, laying out napkins and dessert plates. "I called the policeman to send the chuchmek...Asian man...on his way...I know the cop saw him, but he turned away. Such lack of discipline contravenes socialist norms," Vera sniffed.

"Bashkir, Verochka," Ekaterina corrected. Vera let the correction pass for a bit of unresolved gossip was in the air.

Irina stubbed out her cigarette, and with a graceful flick of the ballerina's wrist, she tossed the butt through the narrowly cracked door and over the balcony. "So, darling," she said, running her fingers through Ekaterina's long blond hair. then lifting Ekaterina's face from her lap, "what happened?" They exchanged smiles, the memory of mother encouraging an excited child to hew closer to the main plot line.

"It was the oddest thing, Mama. He said that my father wanted to see me. I told him I had had tea with my father that very morning. I thought I had misunderstood as he could have meant 'uncle' or 'grandfather' on the maternal side. Mountain people remain tribal...progress still hasn't reached them...and family relationships can be confusing to us."

"And he gave Katya a white carnation and knitted cap. Now wasn't that odd?" Vera poured hot water into the teapot, but paused, looking into Irina's face." Are you all right? If possible, you are even paler than when we came in."

"I'm fine," Irina touched her daughter's cheek. "I'm fine. Girls, Alexander will be home soon; wouldn't you two like to see a movie. Tarkovskij is screening a new moving at the Writer's Club on Myasnitsa Street. Would you see it first and tell me if I should go."

"Ach, Irina Alexeeva," Vera smirked. "Hero Wife of the Soviet Union, sick and you send the children to the movies so you can fulfill your wifely duty? Might I send you out for a movie one of these nights?"

"Verochka, you can be the little slut, can't you? Bring your face closer, so I can twist your ear. Just because one wishes to speak in private with one's husband..." here Irina paused a beat "...does not mean we are going to do 'that.'"

Ekaterina, blushing, buried her face in her mother's lap, but Vera merely raised an eyebrow above the lip of her cup and sashayed her hips.

Danton dismounted the Moscow Metro at the Chistiye Prudy station, rode the escalator and stepped off into the narrow alleyways of the seventeenth century Pokrovka neighborhood; it was scheduled for urban renewal; until then the ancient houses and apartments housed soldiers and workers. The winter's snow had caved in the roof of the open bay barracks to which Danton has been assigned. Now, Danton shared with seven other junior officers two rooms, a hot plate, a single toilet and cold water shower at the Vasili Pushkin House, the poet's uncle, on Staraya Basmannaya Street.

Senior Lieutenant Herzen, the barracks chief, a 6'4" 270 lb. Estonian, whose father was an entomologist, and whose family had been exiled to Central Asia in 1940, ordered a three-front attack against bedbugs, lice, and cockroaches. 'Fuck if I have to listen to some fucking Herm,' snarled Naval Lieutenant Vasilevsky, whom Herzen promptly kicked in the crotch. The lieutenant, the scion of a Vladivostok naval family, had zero influence in Moscow.

The attack on the cockroach infestation was a holding action. The quarters were scrubbed first with bleach, then washed down with a boric acid solution. Cockroaches, Danton learned, navigated by odor; remove the scent, and the cockroach was lost.

Bedbugs came next. Danton accompanied Lieutenant Herzen to the Chistiye Prudy post office to make a long-distance phone call. There was much shouting in Estonian, many "ah ha, ah ha...," and notes taken before he finally hung up. In their quarters, Herzen ordered the door and window jambs sealed with rags, turned up the heat, then marched the 'unit' to the bathhouse. There, he had their bodies steamed and soaked, doused with DDT and rewashed. Civilian clothes and military uniforms burned, the eleven Soviet Army officers were issued new uniforms, but left to their own devices to restore rank and insignia. The Navy officer wanted his unformed merely doused in DDT and rewashed. Herzen leveled a KGB stare at Vasilevsky, then loosed a string of Russian and Estonian curses upon the others. "You fuck-heads wear uniforms. Inspection every Saturday morning, bathhouse every Saturday night..." Soviet Army brutality defeated the Germans; Soviet Army brutality would defeated the louse. "Save your Red Star newspaper to wipe your ass. No using fingers, dirt bags!"

CHAPTER FIFTEEN

Alexander hung his hat and coat in the vestibule, removed his overshoes and judged by the absence of coats, hats, boots, and gloves that Ekaterina and Vera were out. He entered the apartment and stopped. Beyond the window, new housing construction was underway twenty-four hours a day, floodlights illuminating the apartment interior. He closed the curtains, and the apartment immediately quieted. He sensed movement on Ekaterina's bed, a sofa in the day time. "Irina?"

"Katya and Vera went to a movie."

"Long movie?"

"Not so long." She switched on the table lamp and smiled up at him, and he felt again as if he were seventeen, the awkward stagehand before a prima ballerina of unfathomable grace and beauty. She coughed.

"My love, you need to stop smoking. The Americans say it is bad for your lungs."

"And you, Sasha, are you going to stop?'

"I only half-believe the Americans; thus, you should stop, not me." He smiled for a moment at his advantageous reasoning.

"We Russians used to believe everything the Germans told us. Now we believe the Americans."

"We are impressionable folk."

"It is hot, don't you think?" She fluttered her fingers, as if to move the air, then stood to open the window. "I wish we could somehow adjust the heat in the apartment. The Germans and Americans install those things—what are they called?—where you can turn the radiator on and off."

"Valve," Alexander said, "it's called a valve. We once had no heat, you remember?"

"True," she mused. "We Russians don't do half-measures, do we? I don't understand why I feel so peevish."

Alexander waved his hand; his Irina by definition could not be peevish. "It would be better in the long run if the government installed these valves. Moscow apartment buildings are centrally heated. Each radiator is connected directly to a district boiler. Thus, each Soviet citizen is equal, his portion of heat equal, and one opens and closes windows to adjust the temperature. We once froze, now we boil."

In the blood-drenched Soviet Union, Alexander had been gifted a thing of grace. On the streets of Moscow, crude and blustering drunks paused, seemed to doff their hats before Irina, as if inherited memory told them they beheld an aristocrat. But within, her spine was as a stainless steel rod. "But I have good news, Irina. The apartment next door is ours; we can expand, provide Ekaterina her own room, and create your practice studio. I'll have the radiators disconnected. The windows will give good cross ventilation in the spring, summer, and fall; In winter, the vestibule radiator will heat the studio sufficiently."

Her gaze had moved to the room's far corner, her eyes pausing on the single white carnation aside the lamp. "We need to talk, Sasha."

She went to the window to retrieve a bottle of vodka from the sill, the outside air so cold, the vodka had the consistency of oil. She retrieved two aperitif glasses and poured each a drink. "Let's toast."

He touched her nose with his glass. "To what, may I ask?"

"A Tatar gave Ekaterina that flower."

"Kolya is in Moscow," Alexander said.

Alexander and his brother, Nickolai, had begun their professional lives in 1920 in the Poltava National Folk Theater, first as stagehands, then actors, directors, producers. Cold, hunger, twelve to a three-room communal apartment, it didn't matter. They were building Socialism. The energy was intoxicating. Even more intoxicating was seventeen-year-old Irina Alexandrova Shtemenko—blond, green-eyed and a statuesque 5'4"—already the prima ballerina of the Poltava National Ballet. Nickolai was a brilliant director and producer; all knew it, as did he. He was good-looking, and Irina chose him. Alexander married the plain, steady, and observant Rachel. In late 1940, Stalin moved to eradicate the 'last deadly cells of the Bukharin cancer.' Nickolai was arrested.

Alexander, thus tainted, awaited his own extirpation. He packed a small suitcase, sent Rachel, his son, and daughter, to Kiev to her parents, and waited. He received the summons by mail. The words remained imprinted in his memory. 'You are invited to appear at the Poltava City municipality Building, room 23, on Monday, June 23, 1941, between the hours of nine and eleven in connection with your application.'

Irina was dancing Giselle. After a performance, she appeared at Alexander's apartment, her face white, stunned, as if struck with an iron bar. Alexander read the article in the

Poltava bi-weekly *Iskusstvo*. The critic had brutally reviewed her 'wooden' performance.

The message was clear. Irina too was to be arrested. Stalin's terror, like a fever, raged, abated, raged anew, never-ending, had resumed. He wept, and she comforted him. They woke to the howl of sirens the morning, June 22, 1941. Hitler had saved them.

"Nickolai wants to meet Ekaterina," Irina said.

Alexander Soroka ascended the Baumanskaya Metro Station escalator, and at the top, paused. Mistake. Impassive faces—students, professors or workers in rabbit fur hats and dull overcoats--jostled him aside and swirled through the station exit. He sought shelter within one of the wall alcoves housing bronze hero-workers and -soldiers, hammers or machine guns at ready, ready to deliver prompt and severe Socialist justice upon the deviationist. He placed the white carnation and Bashkir woven hat at the soldier's foot, lit a cigarette, and closed his eyes, as an enervating sadness sagged his shoulders.

The order of events that summer and fall of 1941 confused him. Rachel would not abandon her parents. The Soviet peoples fled east like the Israelites in the Sinai, but fleeing rather than following a dark cloud by day, fires by night. In July 1941, these Moscow State Technical School, "The Baumanka," students volunteered as a group in September and died en masse in October before Moscow. The student division suffered 90% casualties, so wrecked the Red Army disbanded it. The Eighth Volunteer Division of the Krasnaya Presnya district was wiped out in its entirety. NKVD special detachments executed the disoriented and fleeing, German *Sondereinheiten* and NKVD *Osobiye Otryady* differing only in the alphabet on their insignia. Neither took prisoners.

In August, the government evacuated Moscow's artist community, but the NKVD intercepted the set designers, directors, and producers. They brought them here to the Baumanka where Alexander was assigned to Mikhail Kalatozov, the Georgian, to film patriotic films. In early 1942, Colonel Brezhnev, the 40th Army Director of Deception, drafted the Kalatozov's studio to work on army-level, then front-level *maskirovka* plans. Kalatozov went to tour the United States, and Alexander became Colonel Brezhnev's deputy, the eternal Soviet deputy, the Jew.

And this Jew did the best set designs of his life. The German soldier listened with thudding heart to the recorded tank engines revving in an empty forest while in the next sector T-34s by the hundreds attacked, appearing as if out of the earth.

Alexander had returned to Kiev in 1946. His father- and mother-in-law, Rachel, Isaac, and Judith, that sweet and gentle child, Judith—had disappeared utterly, machine-gunned into the ravines of Baba Yar. In Kiev, he saw the hand-written sign posted on a kiosk. SEEKING SOROKA, then the penned details. That's how it was after the war. Russians sought after one another--parents for children, wives for husbands, children for parents—like fireflies on a summer night, signaling in the dark, seeking. The NKVD also posted notes, seeking, like the voracious firefly, *Photurus*, that mimicked the signal of the seeking *Photinus,* and devouring him.

It had been Irina, and she had found her Soroka, Alexander, the brother, and he was enough. And they throve, in the Soviet sense of the word.

Ekaterina too, blond and blue-eyed, thirsting for stories, lighting the Moscow gloom with the sunshine of the Caucasus Mountains, was found. Khrushchev was the first secretary, the killers grown weary of killing.

'We didn't know,' wailed the Weimar homemaker and Alexander had wanted to crush her face. How could she not know? The ovens of Buchenwald overlooked the city of German enlightenment, of Goethe and Schiller. The evidence of mass murder was clear, plentiful, and brutal beyond all telling.

Alexander and Nickolai, once they had been exuberant Jewish teens freed from the shackles of family, tribe, doctrine. As had the evidence of Soviet mass murder. And each had hands drenched in the blood of the innocent. Like the old Bolshevik he had been, he would sacrifice himself for the 'future.'

Nickolai had arisen from the grave. Alexander was not astounded at the seeming miracle. Socialism had murdered tens of millions of Soviet citizens, yet so many he had known—twenty, perhaps thirty—had returned from the front, or the gulag, or the past, alive.

The station had filled and emptied several times; The Bashkir stood in an opposite alcove, watching him. He extracted two cigarettes and matches from his cigarette holder and lit both. They both inhaled deeply, then the Bashkir inclined his head, and Alexander followed. Nikolai's messenger crushed his cigarette beneath his foot. Alexander retrieved the knitted cap and faded carnation and exited the station.

Ice crystals swirled at his feet on a cold and bright Moscow March morning. The Moscow winter teetered on the edge of spring, a high thin cirrus ameliorated the sun as if not to injure Muscovites ascending from the depths of the Metro into Moscow's northern winter. Alexander followed the Bashkir gangster into twisted alleys of medieval Moscow.

"Did he come alone?" The harsh, hoarse voice echoed in the cavernous darkness, the reek of damp, mold and hashish assaulting Alexander's nose.

"Girl no there," the Bashkir said in Russian but continued, presumably, in Bashkiri.

The voice replied in kind, but haltingly, the language not native, before finishing with the command, "Check him" in Russian. The Bashkir motioned Alexander to lift his arms, removing everything--cigarettes, matches, cash, coins, knife, and pens—and dropping them into a woven basket. "Khorosho," the Bashkir said.

"Go to the street," rasped the voice. The Bashkir disappeared. "So, Sasha, much blood flowed under the bridge."

"Kolya?"

"None other."

"Your voice has changed."

"Time does that."

"You're a gangster."

"For which I thank Comrade Josef Vassarionovich. Gulag...prison...army. The worst of us, heroes of the fatherland. Glory to the defenders of socialism."

"You survived? How?"

"As one survives these things. Time's really the motherfucker, isn't it, Sasha? You, however, are much the same. Always asking questions, never answering."

"What happened, Kolya?" His hands searched his pockets. Where had he put his cigarettes? He needed water. He needed vodka. "What has happened?"

"What hasn't?" Alexander, despite all, smiled. Nikolai retained the youthful habit of answering a his brother's question with a question. And the smile vanished. Nikolai stepped into the light of the hanging lamp. Burn and blast, the ravagers of the battlefield, the German 88, mortar, grenade, flame thrower, had rendered him faceless, as if the Yiddish demon Ra'Ah had materialized from the gloom. Alexander felt burning the length of his esophagus, pressure building within his skull.

"Shocked, Sasha?"

"Irina had told me...Poltava," Alexander croaked.

"I gifted her a small bag of groats."

"Black market?" Nickolai snorted, Both had been righteous youth; Each, members of the thirty-five-thousanders, Komsomol recruited to collectivize agriculture, and after whom Hitler patterned his 'Hitler Youth,' had campaigned against hoarders. There was no mercy given to lice sucking the blood of the working man. No mercy, indeed. The lice and the Ukrainians perished by the hundreds of thousands. "You survived. How?"

"Sasha, you repeat yourself. But, as one survives these things. The Germans tended not to shoot the *strafbats*, it was said. In my attack, it was true, anyway. The counterattack annihilated the main force. We survivors continued forward to either join up with partisans, become bandits, or both. Such freedom, there between the lines, I had never before known."

They became silent. Nickolai's unblinking eye shone through drifting dust motes. The suicide battalion and the regular battalion, the latter's reward but a few extra minutes of life. In the darkness, a match was struck illuminating the face of another bodyguard. Cigarette smoke drifted through the lamplight. Nickolai broke the silence. "I will see Ekaterina when?" rasped the Ra'Ah.

"It can not be," Alexander said.

"I have evidence you informed on me, Sasha."

"I don't understand, Momma." It was 5 PM, already dark in January Moscow. Ekaterina stood between Irina and Vera at the window of the new and empty apartment overlooking the abandoned three-domed Church of the Holy Trinity, the ice-covered Ostankino Pond, the darkened oak forests. The nine-story concrete apartment buildings, the Khrushchevki, had yet to cross Academician Korolev Street into the Moscow forest and, fingers crossed, never would.

"What is there to understand? I teach ballet; I require a practice studio. Alexander knows how to do these things."

"Might I have a key, dearest Irina?" Vera said, arched eyebrows reflected in the window, innocence feigned. The coyness faded, and youthful ignorance blossomed. "You were lucky to be young then. You had privacy. The Germans messed up our lives, destroying so much housing. There is no place to be alone with a boy."

Irina paused, inhaled slowly, and turned as if taking advantage of the opportunity to view innocence born anew. "Trysts have implications, dearest Verochka," Irina said brushing hair from her face. Privacy? One did find privacy to be with a lover when opportunity presented; Acquaintances traveled, were imprisoned, executed. Intimacy happened.

"Alexander is late, Momma." Ekaterina stepped away as if to explore the new apartment, but changed her mind, returning to the window. The Construction floodlights had been turned on and illuminated falling snow, enclosing the world as if the three women watched the empty stage from the second balcony of a grand opera house. "It has something to do with the Bashkir, doesn't it? Did I do something wrong that I can't remember? I know the Bashkir wasn't KGB." She grasped her mother's hand and released it. "I shouldn't have told you."

Irina retrieved her daughter's errant hand, pulling her close, her face to her own, breathing her daughter's sweet breath. "Remember the Poltava veteran?"

"Which one?" Ekaterina shook her head, maybe yes, maybe no. "The soldiers loved you, Momma. It made me so proud, those heroes coming to our door. You were gentle with them."

"The one that was burnt." Ekaterina squinted, uncertain. Many were so. "The one that frightened the neighbors," Irina added.

"Ah, that one," Ekaterina smiled. "He scared them, alright. He was a gangster, I think."

"That's probably true, and he was probably your father."

Ekaterina tilted her head, not understanding, but Vera leaned in. A titillating tale was soon to be told, and she would encourage the narrative. "You had two lovers at the same time? How exciting it was to live during the revolution. It's so boring now." She was not one to step lightly upon emotionally quaking earth.

"Momma..." Ekaterina gasped, but Vera interrupted.

"Katya has two fathers? How exciting! When I want a private moment with a boyfriend," Vera raised her eyebrows. "... I have to wait until father is at work, mother is visiting relatives, and browbeat grandmother into standing in line for women's pads, which are always in deficit, mind you, but it gets her out of the apartment for a while. In the good old days, you could have time with a lover without the whole family watching?"

"But Momma, my patronymic is Alexeeva?" Irina touched her daughter's face to comfort and put her extended forefinger to Vera's lips.

"After your great-grandfather." Both young women paused at the deception implicit in Russian naming customs. The patronymic was the father's name. If ten children are born, then ten have 'child of Boris' as their middle name; Borisovich for the males; Borisova, the females. If the child was fatherless, then one sought continuity in earlier generations.

Ekaterina was speechless; not so Vera. "Ach, Irina Alexeeva, your mother had no husband, and you had...have two. It does even out, doesn't it? Everything in balance."

"Vera, can you possibly be quiet for one moment?" Ekaterina snapped. "The veteran...who was the veteran?"

"How interesting," Vera said. "Bulgakov's Master and Margarita was a fantasy...Margarita and the artist had a private apartment."

"The gangster is Alexander's brother, Nickolai."

"Was he my father?" Irina motioned helplessly. "Which was my father?" Ekaterina demanded. "Can't you tell me? Can't you tell me now?"

"Each cares deeply for you," Irina said. The ambient city light reflecting off low hanging clouds lit half Ekaterina's face, her expression vexed, her patrimony a vexing problem, like the use of the English modal verb to create the conditional sense of the sentence. The ballerina considered her own aching heart, observed the tear sliding down her daughter's cheek. Were these children so unaware as to how one chose in a lawless land fallen into chaos? The horsemen came, pillaged, murdered, and passed on. The survivors emerged, found the living, paired up, rebuilt the hut, planted turnips and survived, perhaps, to the next harvest. One lived for another day. It was what Russian women did. It was then as it was now, and would be forever. Siegfried drowns, and the swan flies on.

Irina caressed the child's face. Alexander sought, and Nikolai was sought. She took as husband he who could provide shelter and food for her and her child. It was what a Russian woman, elegant ballerina or squat peasant, did.

The spring blizzard struck Moscow mid-morning. Wind strafed snow against the windows, the storm out of doors giving within the lecture hall a sense of silence. Reserve Soviet Army Colonel Alexander Soroka grasped the lectern, pausing to gaze up to the ascending tiers of student officers, varied in build, age, health, and ethnicity. Revolution and war had ravaged them. Bolshevism had boiled the Imperial Russian ethnic cauldron to create the New Soviet Man. With the cooling of revolutionary fervor, an odd stew had congealed. In the lawless Soviet Union, the Communist Party district secretary was like the Mongol *Baskak*—spy, enforcer, and collector of taxes. The revolution had not created factory line-like millions of muscular, tall, and strong Communist *Koloboks*—gingerbread men. Rather, the survivors had formed clots of odd loyalties—family, yes and mostly, but also bands, clans, and tribes; the Army, KGB and Communist Party, for mutual protection.

"Comrades," he whispered. The students leaned forward. It was a theater trick, his actor's murmur projecting to the theater's most distant corner. "Good morning," he said aloud. Here and there a lift of the eyebrow, a hint of recognition. Some were on to him. He nodded to the grizzled infantry Captain Kulikov in the second tier. A Leningrad *frontovik*, he had fought in the trenches, charged across long stubbled fields with pre-sighted artillery and interlaced machine guns fire, had fallen prisoner to both the Germans and to NKVD special units. Few Russian soldiers had survived either encounter, much less both. He was, as in a typhoon or massive earthquake, which killed tens of thousands, the babe found atop the rubble in his crib, asleep. He was as Maxim Maximych of Lermentov's *Hero of our Times*, good-hearted, cunning, a survivor.

"You are honest and honorable Communists soldiers, firm in defense of our worker's paradise." He paused as if he were Henry V addressing his men on the eve of Agincourt, at least as Shakespeare imagined it. "...whom I will teach to lie like rugs. Our objective, however, is to deceive the enemy; not our comrades. My assistants and I will teach you deception, and we will warn you against self-deception."

The veterans of the Great Fatherland War had witnessed massacres aplenty. Soroka himself had watched the 6th Siberian Volunteer Rifle Corps enter battle across a vast and snow-covered rye field. 22,500 of its 30,000 men died in two days, half lost in those first few hours. Senseless death was a Soviet strength, such as it was. Stalin chose not to relieve the siege of Leningrad. Hitler wanted Leningrad. Fine. Twenty-five German and Finnish divisions parked in the sucking, mosquito-infested swamps and frozen lakes surrounding Leningrad as 900,000 Russians in service to the principal of misdirection starved to death. Coincidence did not surprise. Born and raised a peasant on Leningrad's Lake Illmensee, Kulikov fought for three years the German 502 Jager Division, farm boys recruited from the shores of Germany's Lake Illmensee.

"Comrade officers," he began. "Deception is a deceptive business." He raised an eyebrow. Alexander's humor was subtle; Nickolai was a past master of shtick, slapstick, and peasant crudity. On tour in the provinces, he made the Russian peasant guffaw. His brother had timing, self-confidence, and bluff, quick to read an audience as he walked onto the stage. He had that certain something, but his act panned before the NKVD audience. He disappeared into the maw of the Soviet Union's vast gulag. Now, decades later, Nickolai, the Magician, reappeared. What a performance!

"Deception is in the end storytelling. Storytellers and liars; the first we revere; the latter we curse. You are artists that move your audience into an alternative world using suggestive description, 'realistic' scenery, convincing dialog, and character motivation. 'Yes, that make's sense,' your audience decides, and they will go where you take them." An illiterate orphan had given him a piece of paper fluttering on the street in Dnepropetrovsk. He raised his voice. "The director manipulates props, light, sound, and movement to guide the audience eye here away from here..." He ostentatiously pointed to himself." To there," pointing to center stage, "... as I did in the introductory lecture." He raised his fist, lowered his voice, pausing a beat, "you will learn four concepts, one no less important than the other." He held up his clenched fist, opened it one finger at a time. "Truth. If deception is to succeed at all, there must be a truth that can be manipulated. All deception works within the context of honesty."

'The dancer, Irina, in Poltava, seeks...' written on a scrap of paper.

"Misdirection is the fundamental principle of magic. In magic, misdirection directs your attention elsewhere. The keyword is attention. At your first lecture, a rabbi turned into a Soviet Army colonel. I could have nicked your foreskins...made Jews of the lot of you while you followed with open mouths smoke, mirrors, and movie screens. "

Soroka watched Roman Baranov—surly and handsome, slippery and charming, with the morals of a street rat, light a cigarette. He was like a Guards officer from 'War and Peace,' whose place in Soroka's class Colonel General Baranov purchased for a chit to be cashed at Soroka's convenience. The slime ball would do well in this man's army.

"Denial. Denying the target access to the truth is the prerequisite to all deception. Denial makes deception possible. Lacking access to all the facts, the target must make do with what few real signals he can obtain from the mass of data available and must subsequently rely on previous experience, preconceptions and, as is often the case, wishful thinking to analyze the situation and develop a course of actions. Denial creates the opportunity to manipulate the target's perceptions by offering the target something highly desirable. Information that the target considers to be true."

Soroka passed onto the face next to Baranov, Larionov, Danton Volkov. His face was familiar, but he could not place it. So many faces.

"Deceit. All deception requires deceit. As your ten-year daughter might retort, 'Well, no kidding, Einstein.' Deceit is not synonymous with deception. Lying looks to one side of the interaction between liar and audience. "Someone whose fairy tale is not believed is still a liar but has not been deceived. One does not fail at lying because the audience is not convinced, but one does fail at deception if the audience does not believe the lie."

Crazy, he thought. Revolution and war had passed thousands of faces before Soroka's eyes; who remembered them all? But why does he see Larionov, and think 'German'?

"Imagine, you are traversing a large and dark room. Light bulbs glow and grow dim, here and there, without illumination. There is sound; now loud, now low, its source and direction uncertain, then silence. Smells; oil or burning rubber. Memory; you had been in the room, possibly, once before, long ago. Touch; your shin strikes an iron bar, a white light of pain. Your enemy is in the room. Perhaps. Disoriented."

Afternoon darkness settled in the auditorium; students were having difficulty taking notes. He signaled to his sergeant to turn on the lights. Men looked up, grateful. The darkness had crept up upon them.

"This you will do for the enemies of the Soviet Union. Yet, there is another among us who is the world's great deceiver, who has convinced you of any nonsense, yet who leaves you with all your heart believing the truth has been spoken." He would choose twelve or so for advanced deception training and assignment to the General Staff. Soroka had created his own band and a network of interlocking alliances. "Who might that be?" he whispered.

The officers looked around. Here and there came flickers of uncertain understanding. Could it be...? Baranov fiddled with his cigarette lighter, bored. Larionov watched Soroka intently, a good student, or at least faking the appearance of a dilligent student.

"Your grandmother!" Alexander roared. Nods and smiles rolled across faces as Soroka's tone became conversational, homey. "The Russian grandmother is our greatest storyteller and yet our greatest deceiver. Pay attention to your grandmother, and you will graduate well in my class. Your end-of-course assignment will depend upon the quality of deception plan you write. You may write conceive an operation to deceive America or your wife, but it must be complete, artful, creative."

Soroka pounded his chest, like a wealthy American automobile salesman. "I make your follow-on assignments. There are assignments in Moscow..." He paused. "....and on the Arctic Circle." Knowing looks appeared in the auditorium. These were soldiers, after all. "The best will be rewarded not only for their diligence but also for their artistry, discipline and creativity. These words seem contradictory, They are not." Soroka stepped from behind the podium, his battle ribbons telling veterans he knew what war was.

"Only by studying carefully the guidance Vladimir Ilyich Lenin provides us in his collective works can we hope to have the clarity of vision required to bring about Communism in the lifetime of you young men yourself and the certain eventual victory of the proletariat of all countries." The student searched for hats and coats, touched pockets for matches and cigarettes, and capped fountain pens. Communist doctrine was the benediction which ended each lecture. One needn't pay attention. "The main enemy, The United States of America, is in its final stages of disintegration, but remains as dangerous as a wounded wolf in a thicket."

CHAPTER SIXTEEN

Spring comes barging loutishly
Into Moscow's private houses.
Moths flutter behind the wardrobe
And crawl over the summer hats,
And fur coats are put away in trunks.
Boris Pasternak

On Monday, the sun shone hot upon ice-covered Chistiye Prudy Pond, casting laced shadows through the bare branches of Russian elms upon patches of snow. There was, if one looked with hope, a hint of green in the tree's buds and branches. The young held their greatcoats in their arms and wished they had left the heavy burdens behind. The old remembered. The Sunday night previous the snowstorm blanketed the city, temperatures falling to -45C, public transportation halted, water pipes bursting, drunks seated upright and dead on park benches. But today Muscovites sat on these same benches, watching with stony gaze grim-faced passers-by. Now and then, a child in the arms of a passing young mother melted sour miens into smiles, like an unnatural ray of light brightened the weak northern sun.

"Eh, Grandmother, summer's arrived," Ekaterina said, buying roasted chestnuts wrapped in newspaper. Summer, like victory in the Great Fatherland War, was inevitable.

"Maybe, girl, maybe not." The old woman loosened the top button of her coat and untied the string beneath her chin, the ear flaps still dangling over her ears. She squeezed Ekaterina's hand as she passed the purchase over the charcoal brazier. She, too, had once been hopeful.

The metro ride between the VDNKh station and Chistiye Prudy lasted but ten minutes, a Moscow millenium. Ekaterina missed old Moscow's Kitai Gorod and the Basman Districts and often found excuses to return to walk the convoluted streets and sit in the hidden, ancient courtyards. She paused before the park bench where two massive Moscow policemen played chess. "May I?"

The larger awoke from his concentration. "Yes, yes, of course, young lady. Is there room enough for you?" She picked up his black and white police baton, and he smiled. "And if there is any disturbance, junior comrade auxiliary militia girl, take care of it, will you?" he said before returning his attention to the board.

Ekaterina sat beside the giant, and for a moment, enjoyed the illusion of being 'petite.' Irina had resigned herself to her daughter's teenage growth spurt. 'The Russian boys can lift you, but foreign dancers, surely not.' Ekaterina soon grew beyond the Russian boys. It was a shame this policeman-*bogatyr,* who could lift her easily didn't dance ballet. Ah, to dance the foxtrot in London. In fables, a woman could voyage beyond the seventh sea to dance in great golden salons under diamond chandeliers. In the Soviet Union, only the special and the reliable traveled beyond the border. Would she be judged reliable to study even in the German Democratic Republic? She tapped the policeman's billy club lightly to her forehead. For a moment, prickly anxiety skittering within her throat.

She looked up and spotted Vera in a bright red summer dress, sweater over her shoulder, standing on the metro station stairs, searching. Ekaterina waved the black and white baton to catch her attention. "Hey, young lady..." the other policeman looked up. "You aren't supposed..." Vera waved and smiled.

"So, what's the excitement?" Vera said, taking the baton from Ekaterina's fingers, and kissing her.

"Vera, you just won't believe it!"

"I don't believe it," one chess player mumbled. His opponent looked up, grinning, noticing for the first time the two beauties.

"Okay, I don't believe it. What?" Vera said.

"I'll tell you over tea."

He preferred, he decided, the heavier-busted red-head, but wouldn't chuck the tall blond out of bed, if it came to that.

'Ekaterina the Third," Vera said, "You have a lover, who has a private apartment, but you won't let me use it."

"Don't be foul, Verochka."

"You prefer I call you Ekaterina the Great?" Vera raised an eyebrow, current or ancient gossip; it didn't matter. "She did have her predilections, didn't she?"

"I don't share good news with pigs," pouted Ekaterina.

"I am going to arrest you both for disturbing my peace," said the larger policeman, his board position untenable and seeking diversion.

"And I, my dears, will testify in your defense," his opponent said. "Sergey is distractible." They all stood, by chance arranged in descending size, like Russian matryoshka dolls, but missing the figurine that should set between Ekaterina and Vera, who was 'petite.' "Could we treat you two to a touch of vodka?" he said.

Ekaterina touched the baton to the cop's nose, severe, like a teacher.

Chattering and arm in arm, Ekaterina and Vera wove in and out of chaotic pedestrian traffic, the Russians having yet to learn to hold to the right as Napoleon had taught. They entered the Tea House on Myasnitskaya, ornately decorated with Chinese porcelain figures, golden dragons and ceramic tile dormers over copper-trimmed windows. The three-story building recalled a time when wealthy Russians indulged their taste in tea. In the late 19th century, a whimsical tea merchant had decorated the façade to celebrate the presence in Moscow of the Chinese Emperor's plenipotentiary, an advertising gimmick. Less whimsically, Tsarist Russia and Imperial China had signed a secret agreement--the Russian Empire received transit rights to build the Trans-Siberian railroad across Manchuria in return for China receiving Russian protection against foreign predations. In 1905, the Imperial Japanese Navy sunk the Russian squadron, thus ending Russian Imperial pretensions.

"Katya, why here? Are you deranged? Why here?"

"We were happy when we lived here, weren't we?"

"Tell me the news now," demanded Vera.

"I am unsure whether it is good or bad."

"Tell me, for the love of Jesus, in whom we don't believe, and I will judge. This is what I do well, pass judgements." Ekaterina acknowledged her girlfriend's skill set. They passed beneath a haphazardly constructed arch of boards installed to protect customers from falling porcelain figurines. Ekaterina grasped the heavy and unyielding oaken door, Vera joining her and, crouching slightly to use leg power, opened it sufficient to slip in. "Hinges haven't been oiled since we had last done it," Vera complained.

"We oiled it with sunflower oil. It never lasts, does it?"

"So, what's the news?" said Vera, not to be put off.

"Patience. I said we'd discuss it over tea. Ach, Yefima Borisova," A stocky lady blocked their path, and whom Ekaterina grasped with both hands. "It has been so long!"

"Ah, Ekaterina, I hadn't recognized you, you've grown so," Ekaterina becoming not a customer, which in the Soviet Union was the exploiting class and enemy of the worker, but a friend. "Aren't you still a polite young lady. Children nowadays are such hooligans. If we are not vigilant, we will have American gangs." She offered her cheek to Ekaterina, waved them to seat themselves, but turned on Vera. "What's with you, Verochka, standing aside like a young aristocrat? You don't greet your elders? Kids, no manners nowadays." Vera glanced at the ceiling—it wouldn't collapse anytime soon—relented, made appropriate noises, and entered the empty tea house.

They took seats near a dusty window looking out onto the street. They spoke of this and that until a waitress might arrive to take their order. As had become customary in the Soviet Union, none did. The counter girl standing before empty shelves that once held ten thousand tins of tea stared distantly. Three waitresses stood in a far corner chattering. Vera slapped the table, rose, went to the counter and thrust her face between empty eyes and infinity.

"Thou! Tea. Now!" The young woman focused slowly on Vera as if she were gazing upon an aristocrat thinking 'Stalin knew how to give it to your kind.' "And biscuits, fresh or otherwise, or are you hoarding them for atomic war?"

"When you get free," Ekaterina placated.

"But before hell freezes over if you can at all manage it," Vera said. The three waitresses, equal by state dictate, gazed at one another. One of them would soon have to move.

Yefima shooed the two young women the table aside the dusty window looking out onto the street and the recalcitrant counter-girl into the room behind the counter. The three distant waitresses laughed raucously, their backs turned to the cafe. Ekaterina looked out onto the street, then about in the teahouse's ornate rococo interior, as if it were this day exactly one-half century earlier. Vera too looked about, but saw it as it would be next week or next year in a Berlin or London as seen in the American Life Magazine or the English Picture Post, which the privileged students could read at the foreign language institute. The waitresses' again retrieved their vacant states, their world the grim 1961 Soviet reality with neither past nor future.

She clattered the tea tray onto the table. "Thank you so much," Ekaterina said to the retreating back.

"Fuck you," murmured Vera. Seated at their table, tepid tea before them, Vera's mood was black, and she shook her thick red hair as if to cast it off. "Your Alexander has influence, but not so much in here. So, Katya, I've almost forgotten what we've come to talk about? Is it that you are pregnant?"

"If I were, Verochka, it would be the second immaculate conception in history, after which we'd have to disavow Communism because a miracle had taken place. Remember when we worked as guides at the American Exhibition in Sokolniki."

"I shall forgive you again because I love you. Yes, I remember. It was only the most important time in our lives with all those cute American boys. We have nothing more to live for."

"They were exotic, weren't they?" Ekaterina put her hand to her chest as if to still a racing heart. "But..."

Vera reached across the table to grasp Ekaterina's hand.

"You did make love to that Chicago boy, didn't you? I knew it," she said, slapping the table in triumph.

Ekaterina raised her hand in a 'slow down' gesture. "He wasn't from Chicago, Verochka," Ekaterina raised her eyebrows significantly, then stopped the tease. "And if I had, it would have had to have been with Ludmilla Borisova observing. The 'aunts' were supervising us constantly. I don't think they ever even went to the toilet. But listen, Vera dearest, and stop talking for a second. I have a problem." Vera looked her up and down and found no problem. "I might be getting a car."

"This is a problem?" Vera snorted into her tea, ostentatiously choked and fluttered her fingers. "Your father or uncle or Wizard of Oz..whatever...is a Communist magician. How did he get to the head of the waiting list? Had he taken Khrushchev's place in line? My goodness, but doesn't he have the connections. First, a big apartment...well, bigger, and now a car." Vera caught a breath. "Now, we can get to the family dacha in secret, more or less."

"Nickolai is getting the car for me."

"And this bothers you?" The mischievous smile left Vera's face, a quick internal discussion moved her lips, then with a wave of the hand, she resolved the others' lifetime chaos. "What an advantage...two biological fathers. Now there's a miracle."

"I may have to turn down the car."

Vera paused, damping rising excitement. She had to reason with her beloved but idiotic friend. "Are you a moron?" she reasoned. "Why don't we leave the old people to work out their sins. Wait, we don't have 'sin' anymore, do we?"

Ekaterina licked a finger and opened her student notebook, searching. She reread a two-page passage quickly and satisfied, thrust it across the table.

Vera glanced down, a 'put upon' look on her face. "What?"

"Read!" Ekaterina stared into Vera's face as if she were expecting some glowing spirit to migrate from the paper to Vera's fingers and up the arm.

"Now?"

Ekaterina nodded, refilled each tea, sniffed the milk with mild surprise, and picked two sugar cubes from the bowl. "One sugar!" Vera warned without looking up.

"Sorry," she said. "Well?"

Vera looked back to the notebook turning it over as if thus it would make more sense. Ekaterina reached across the table, grasped Vera's hair to lift her face. "I have not the slightest idea what this means," Vera said.

"If you only paid more attention to the Marxism-Leninism lessons at Komsomol, my ignorant and best friend whom I love beyond all comprehension. Can't you see? The Imperialists have proposed to reserve twenty of the student exchange slots for students in the humanities, i.e., language students. Not all the slots are reserved for science and technology students!"

Vera removed Ekaterina's hand from her hair, but kissed the fingers. "You read that in there?"

"No, the director explained it. The Institute has two slots, which will be thee and me!"

"The capitalist devils, they are attempting to seduce us and I am ready. We could share a flat in Greenwich Village, talk with some beatniks and some Miles Davis to stop by to play Jazz."

"I would so love to study in America before we bury them," Ekaterina said, her tone wistful.

"Don't look so tragic. I am teasing you. Now, what's the matter? If you start crying, I am going to hit you." Vera brushed back a hair falling across Ekaterina's face and looked up. "Do you have a good-looking Russian guy in love with you, or is the KGB on your trail? Turn around," Vera commanded.

But as Ekaterina turned, a city bus had pulled up to the stop, and when it left, the admirer, or agent of state security, was gone.

CHAPTER EIGHTEEN

Father Frost retreated, then advanced. On Tuesday heavy snow fell rendering Moscow beautiful. Medieval Moscow had once been a small town. Tradespeople—butchers, merchants, weavers—lived in their sections. So it remained. Artists, military officers, Party officials, and workers lived in reserved blocks of flats near their work. Though successive defensive walls had been demolished and turned into ring roads as the city expanded, the old town remained. Though warm within his kitchen, the Muscovite's public face was grim. He didn't smile. Yet, the Russian kitchen bled onto the Russian street.

Normally, Danton walked to class. This morning Danton, wearing the Soviet Army Winter officer uniform, a greatcoat with a double row of buttons and Sam Browne belt, fur hat, and tall boots, rode the bus. Danton had nodding acquaintances along the route. Nodding was sufficient. In Suzdal, he was Danton Volkov, 'son of Volk," the NKVD officer named 'Wolf,' who trailed death in his wake. In Moscow, Danton was a simple engineering officer. Though not a veteran of the Great Patriotic War, he basked in the afterglow.

He walked the same route daily from his quarters at the Pushkin House on Staraya Basmannaya Street to the General Staff Headquarters on Znamenka Street near Old Arbat. The bus route passed the Chistiye Prudy metro station, down Myasnitskaya past the Chinese Tea House, then onto Kiev Station.

In the corner of his eye, an apparition reflected in the window of the teahouse, and he flung himself to the window, but the Number 17 bus black exhaust obscured the vision.

Distrust of the moment impressed upon the Russian soul. The Slav inhabited the plains between Europe's rich earth and the Central Siberian Plateau's sparse grasslands. The chariot- and horse-mounted herder learned from birth to defend his herd against predators with arrow, a youth's art suited to steppe warfare, the mounted raider lethal to a hundred yards. The Slav farmer's weapon was heavy hoe and ax, lethal to the length of arm and mattock. Drought periodically drove the steppe horseman to go where grazing land might be. With spring's greening, horsemen crossed the Ural passes to the banks of Oka and Kamemka Rivers. For millennia, the war between he who hunted and he who tilled the land was fought, as between Abel and Cain. In the emptiness of the vast plain, the Russian found salvation in the grand dream or the grand oblivion. This struggle would end with the Second Coming or world Communism. Until then...

She had disappeared like a fairy tale princess on a gray and rainy morning like Vasilisa, the Beautiful.

Danton dug into the pocket of his greatcoat for a cigarette. Fairy tales. He dismounted the bus at Kiev Station. Where did Colonel Professor Soroka fit in the mystery?

"We know that unobjective man guides himself using unexamined rules; Tartars are thieves and carry knives; Jews cheat good-hearted Russian, Ukrainians are stupid yet..."

Alexander Soroka paused as a teacher pauses to look hard at Artillery Captain Parchomenko. "...cunning." The students guffawed and Parchomenko grinned.

"In Swan Lake, Odette flies. In Ostrovsky's play, The Storm, The kettle drum is the storm. The producer and director knows his audience expectations and uses them."

Alexander Soroka smiled slightly. "Experience teaches truth and experience teaches false truths. The cat leaps upon the hot stove, screeches, and never again leaps upon a hot stovetop." A strategic pause. "And he never again leaps onto even a cold stovetop." Native Russian speakers nodded, slight smiles matching his own. Non-native Russian speakers slit their eyes, slower to translate the proverb. "We come to believe the most unscientific phenomenon in the face of all contrary evidence."

A passing cloud dimmed the auditorium, the graying light intruding a vision upon Soroka. 'There will be grain for all soon, grandma,' the young Soroka told the old woman. And she shrugged, 'We need less now.' She gazed distantly over new and crude white birch crosses dotting the snow-swept village cemetery. Soroka hardened his gaze as he had hardened his heart. He was a shock troop, a Komsomol, one of the 35-thousanders, the clunky Soviet word for the students sent into the countryside to collectivize agriculture. One believed in the future. The graves disappeared, his expression now a signal that the students would profit by attending to his words. They bent to their notebooks.

"Much is asked of you. As you learn how to deceive the enemy, you guard yourself against self-deception. As Lenin says, 'People always have been the foolish victims of deception and self-deception in politics, and they always will be until they have learned to seek out the interests of their class behind all moral, religious, political and social phrases, declarations and promises."

Which lesson might he derive from such nonsense, he, the activist, had orchestrated the Writer's Union attack upon the great poet, his verse, his novel, and his foreign prize, upon he who spoke Russian truths that scorched the heart.

Alexander and his brother had grasped Lenin to their hearts, 'Literature must become party literature. Down with nonpartisan litterateurs!'

And the poet replied, 'We've become like the Pharisees,' mouthing our empty slogans.

Soroka mentally shook himself. He had disembodied from his stage role of the great actor, great teacher, great believer. He lifted his voice.

"I finish with an anecdote from a foreign army officer. You GRU officers, pay special attention. He was, as far as I can tell, the first modern special forces officer, you soldiers who conduct reconnaissance deep behind enemy lines. Richard Rogers was a British special forces officer during the French and Indian Wars on the North American continent similar to Cossack irregulars in the Russian Imperial Army. This Richard Rogers organized a specialized reconnaissance force, which he called "Rangers," and after whom the American special troops have named themselves. He wrote Roger's Rules, guidance, which they were required to memorize. His first rule was thus: Tell the truth about what you see and what you do. There is an army depending on us for correct information. You can lie all you please when you tell other folks about the Rangers, but don't never lie to a Ranger or officer.

"Through deception, we survive. We will avail ourselves of this tool. We deceive the capitalist; we don't deceive ourselves. We examine carefully Lenin's guidance and how to apply it to our task to protect the motherland and advance the cause of Socialism throughout the world."

And deception is to the bonds of trust as hydrochloric acid is to the sinews of bones, he thought.

"Only by studying carefully the guidance of Vladimir Ilyich Lenin provides us in his collective works can we hope to have the clarity of vision required to bring about Communism in the lifetime of you young men yourself and the inevitable victory of the proletariat of all countries. Now, get out of here. See you next Monday."

Soroka looked over the officers repacking attache cases, lighting cigarettes, checking watches—who among these officers believed the horseshit he spewed—and noticed Larionov staring at him. The line of a play intruded upon Alexander Soroka's consciousness. 'Yon Cassius has a lean and hungry look.'

It had been a good role, this Cassius. Alexander enjoyed assassinating his brother, who played Caesar. Larionov. He thought to reassess the senior lieutenant's connections—his father was NKVD...rough customer. Soroka's warrant officer interrupted him with an urgent message. Nikita Sergeevich wanted to see him.

The First Secretary had been intrigued by the opportunity the new American president presented. Khrushchev, the peasant, visualized the boy president as a fop junior lieutenant or better, as the new landowner, son of the 'Barin', weak where the father was harsh and cunning. There was gold to be had at the manor house.

Soroka had his reputation in the Kremlin. He had snookered Roosevelt's vice-president. Thus, Soroka understood all Americans. Soroka thought differently; This President Kennedy seemed a dandy, the eternal lieutenant with a pretty wife, gangster father, and idiot mother and, as Napoleon said of Tallerand, *a piece of shit in a silk stocking*, but then, which was in charge post-Waterloo?

CHAPTER NINETEEN

"Katya, Katya, I've been looking all over for you." Vera stood in the vestibule before the concierge's window, the old woman eyeing her with official suspicion. "Ach, successful hunt, little peasant girl," she said, peeking under the cloth into Ekaterina's basket, before returning to her dispute. "You, Baba," Vera picked a mushroom from Vera's basket and waved it before the concierge's window. Mushroom hunting was a Moscow passion. Twenty citizens died annually eating poisonous fungi. "Taste?"

"Vera, enough. " Ekaterina tugged Vera's collar toward the staircase. "Must you be so nasty?"

"She..." The old and young exchanged venomous glances. "...has seen me a thousand times and still, she interrogates me. What does she think... that I'm an American spy?"

Ekaterina took Vera's hand. "Don't be agitated...I mean, more than your normal agitated self. What's up?"

"Hadn't you heard? Air Force Captain Yuri Gagarin has flown to the moon and back. There's a parade, then a big, big, big party tonight in the Kremlin. My father has an invitation, and I'll bet Alexander has one too. We absolutely must make new dresses today. I've stolen American magazines from school," she said, displaying two issues of McCall's from her bag. "Your mother can copy one of these Western dresses for us."

"These are beautiful, Katya." Irina stood at the kitchen counter sorting through the mushrooms. "But we'll have Alexander go through them too."

"Momma, I must must...must...must have this dress, this one right here!" Ekaterina pushed the magazine centerfold between her mother's eye and her motherly attempt to save the family from death. It had required only three flights of stairs for Vera to infect Ekaterina with the national hysteria. The Soviet Union had beaten the Americans into space. "Vera found two pairs of foreign...French!...shoes and Olga owes me two meters of cloth. Marina Fedotova owes you a bunch of favors. Couldn't the Bolshoi's costume shop help us?"

"Slow down, my angel, slow down." Irina rested her hand on her daughter's shoulder. "Girls, slow down. Vera, light me a cigarette. Katya, make tea. Let me think."

"Momma, we don't have time to think." Ekaterina twisting her hands, glanced out onto the balcony as if a beautiful brocade might have appeared from the cosmos. "Oh, why hadn't we been warned?"

"That Nikita Sergeevich is so impatient, can't contain himself, wanted a party right away. Doesn't he have any idea the time it takes time to get ready?" Vera said, an unlit cigarette in her lips fluttering like a squirrel's tail.

"Could you cut my hair like this?" Ekaterina asked, showing an American actress lounging at a California poolside.

Vera, leaning against the sink, tea and cigarette forgotten, raised a forefinger, the other hand snatching the magazine from Ekaterina's grasp. "The hairstyle does not suit you at all," she said. An argument was nigh.

"Ekaterina Nickolaeva, stop!" Ekaterina, vibrating in place, looked up. When a Russian mother addressed her child with name and patronymic, any child would pause. " Sit, both of you."

They sat. "Oh, please God help us," murmured Ekaterina looking to the ceiling. Communism was all well and good, but at the moment, God was more likely to provide the dress. They must, simply must, be beautiful. God forbid they attend the ball as frumps.

"Tea, Vera, make the tea," Irina said, crossing her arms. "You will trust me. I know how to create an effect. Ekaterina, you are not Kim Novak. You are Ekaterina, enchantingly beautiful..." She turned to Vera. "...as are you, Vera. You are both beauties. You will look like yourselves..." Irina paused for dramatic effect, "...only more so."

Vera, noticing the cigarette, lit it, taking a quick pull. Ekaterina shifted back and forth—was there no place to be comfortable—looking at Irina like an old believer gazing at an incense-wreathed Ikon of St. Gregory. Her mother had danced ballet under German shellfire. The Soviet Army newspaper, Red Star, had commended her organizational creativity. Might she even find nylon stockings? Ekaterina took the cigarette from Vera's lips.

"Ekaterina, call Alexander. Find out when the Kremlin ball begins."

"Momma, what are we going to do," Ekaterina whined. "It will take months to get everything together."

Irina put her hand to her child's chin to play her fingers across the young woman's lips. "People owe me."

And favors, some a decade old, were called. Precious products—nylon stockings, a pack of Marlboro cigarettes, twenty eggs—were given or promised. Moscow's intricate and unofficial networks fashioned to manage Communism's eternal shortages was set in motion.

Standing at rigid attention before a pillar in the St. George's Hall of the Great Kremlin Palace, Danton Larionov scanned the room without moving his head. His eyes came to rest upon Little Russia, a statue of a young woman, commemorative of the 1654 union of Ukraine with Russia. Pride overwhelmed Danton. A Soviet citizen had become the first man in space, which had dealt the main enemy a sharp blow. Danton, Soviet officer, the chosen one, of the next generation of Soviet soldiers, standing ready to serve Mother Russia after the heroes of the Great Fatherland War passed from the scene.

"Look, you useless dicks," snarled Senior Sergeant Georgii Konstantinovich Tsiklauri. The majordomo was a short and swarthy Georgian with a bushy mustache who spoke incomprehensible Russian save for his profanity which was oddly precise and articulate. He looked over what had been given him. He had requisitioned captains, our each from the five Soviet military services, all required to be over 6'4" tall, and unmarked. General Mikhail M. Vasilevskij, the commander of the Moscow Military District and the host of tonight's General Staff Victory in Europe celebratory reception, had a King Frederick Wilhelm I of Prussia complex. He wanted giants in his personal honor guard. The senior sergeant spit in disgust. "This..." he choked, "...shit I've been given to work with? You fuckers will serve as statues. The pimpled ones will work in the kitchen or in the dark. Those in front...I give a fuck if your ass is covered with pockmarks, and your dick hangs to your knees weighed with syphilis chancres...you're here to look pretty. Understand?"

None standing before the sputtering martinet met the requisition requirements save that they were all captains. The tallest, for God's sake, was barely 5'7", another was pock-marked, and a third wore glasses. Wartime losses and privation had depleted the population of large healthy men. He'd make do with what was available. Tsiklauri organized protocol for military receptions. Danton Larionov slid in under the criteria; his face was unpimpled. "You, little one, pay attention before I kick your nuts so hard you'll be chewing them!"

The majordomo's task was to manage the drinks early and the drunks late. When Soviet soldiers partied, they drank. The officers were war- and Stalin-hardened men, many of whom, when Nazi Germany attacked, had been awaiting execution, when they were given command of tens of thousands, whom they ordered forward to die by the millions. Twenty million dead? Forty million? Who counted?

The majordomo ranted on. "Pay attention, you assholes. I've been here forever, and any one of you fuck up, snitch vodka, munch a shashlik, I'll know, and I will personally shoot your ass. When it's over, you can all get shit-faced on the left-over slop, I don't give a shit." Tsklaura had served Stalin, it was said.

Air Force Captain Yuri Gagarin was the evening's honored guest. All Russia was enraptured. Fifteen years after the devastation of the Great Fatherland War, the USSR under the firm, but enlightened guidance of the Communist Party of the Soviet Union had recovered a ravaged landscape sufficient to send a man into space beating an America untouched by war. Danton daydreamed, his eyes wandered the Red Hall, for a moment, imagined himself a captain in the Tsar's Preobrezhensky Guard regiment, the elegant and slight Ekaterina of Suzdal on his arm.

"Don't spill anything!" The majordomo ranted on. "If you going to have wet trousers, you'd better be pissing yourselves. You paying attention, Captain?" Tsklauri pushed his mustachioed face into Danton's. "You're uglier than a goat's ass, but the best we got. You're on the snack and liquor table. When the plate is half-empty, get it refilled, and get it back. Same with the vodka trays...they need to be iced, and if they thaw half-way, get them out and into the freezer...and don't touch one, or I will personally stick my boot up your ass. Even a fucking Russian could manage that!" Thus, did the Major Domo continue his instruction to the crème of the Soviet Officer Corps of the Moscow Military District.

"Momma, my God, where could you have possibly found this silk? At the Maly? How is it possible that it hadn't already been stolen?"

"Katya, be still." Irina considered her child-woman. She had borne a child who had caused her years of gnawing anxiety, moments of gut-wrenching terror, and nightmares and, ah, the nightmares. It had been worth it. Irina had once thought herself incapable of loving. She, this child she bore, was beautiful. Irina loosened the tape measure a touch to not indent Ekaterina's breasts, calling over her shoulder. "90 centimeters...say 91 to be safe."

"Oh, Vera," Ekaterina pouted to her friend, also naked to the waist. "Mine are so small, and yours are so big. Lend me some of yours."

Vera, pencil and notebook in hand, jotted the measurement. "I could lose a kilo or two," she admitted. "Tomorrow, Katya, you can have some tomorrow, but alas, my weight comes off the boobs first, and I want all I've got for tonight."

Irina, pins held in her lips, stood, turning to a gaunt woman, hair in a tight bun at the nape of her neck, squinting through smoke from the cigarette hanging from the corner of her lip. "What do you say, Masha, can we make something of these two."

Maria Fedotova, the costume master of Moscow's Maly Theater, regarded two bolts of cloth, one white and the other blue, which lay on the divan, then picked up the latter pressing it to her nose. Tossing it aside, she fingered the white bolt, then looked from one girl to the other. "I don't know. Very, very difficult," she said. "Maybe, In three days...I am swamped, but I'll find some time for you, Irinochka."

Ekaterina closed her eyes. Vera's brought both hands to her cheeks. They were dead, Soviet ingenues walking. The ball was to begin in eight hours.

"Six hours, Masha. You have six hours," Irina pronounced.

"Impossible!'" She looked at Ekaterina, then Vera, then back again, her meaning clear: 'This is what you give me this to work with?' Thus Masha began the negotiations

"Perhaps six and one-half hours," Irina relented.

'No! the girls screamed in unison, silently.

Taking a drag on her cigarette, elbow cupped in hand, Maria Fedotova reexamined the mannequins, which were Vera and Ekaterina. "Those things…" With a wave of the hand, indicated the girl's Soviet undergarments—knee-length drawers, brown cotton stockings, parachute bras, "need to be burnt or buried. Show me the shoes."

Vera quickly crossed to the divan, unwrapped a package, and offered two pairs of shoes, one grayish, the other somewhat brown, for examination. "We'll dye them," Masha said.

Vera's eyes widened. She had borrowed the shoes. Natalie would cut her throat without a second thought were these shoes, which her father, a naval captain, had purchased during a port visit to Marseilles, were but a miniscule changed. However, this was now: her girlfriend Natalie was later. All die sooner or later.

"What color, Comrade Voskrensenskaya?" Vera, quick and independent Vera, cowed by no man, dared not cross the formidable Marina Fedotova. "Can you recommend who might dye them?"

Marina looked around as if searching for the source of the odd sound, laid a look like a cold iron bar upon Vera's soft shoulders as if to say, 'You need me, child. I don't need you.' "One pair blue, the other white," she answered. Vera blanched and grasped Ekaterina's hand. She was already dead, but perdition could wait till after the ball.

"Go," Marina Fedotova ordered. "Each of you beg, borrow, or steal a European bra." Each nodded, wide-eyed. And why not also a German Porshe sports car to take them to the ball? "And panties. I can't design over those god-forsaken bloomers." Holding back tears, the girls turned to the door.

"Girls, put on some clothes first," Irina said. Marina Fedotova looked to God to witness her trials. Ekaterina and Vera clutching bras, shirts, panties, and one another's hand, made their way to the bathroom.

Marina Fedotova waited until the girls were gone, then said, "I Can't make these dresses in less than two days."

"You have six hours."

"Impossible."

"What can make the word 'possible' appear on your lips? You've done it before."

Maria Fedotova brushed the silk across her face. "A shame to waste such cloth for a single," she said, expression covetous. "Which of your husbands obtained this for you?"

Irina waved her hand in the air as if harrying a mosquito. "Ekaterina will be as beautiful as it is possible to be. This, I want."

"Anymore where this came from?" Masha smoothed the bolt. "If you can get two more bolts…I'm indifferent to which color…then, perhaps."

"How much for the answer to be 'certainly.'"

"Hadn't Seryozha…that Diaghilev boy, given you that?" Marina touched the jeweled bracelet on Irina's wrist.

Irina considered for a moment the bargains she had negotiated throughout her life. She removed the bejeweled band and set it on the table. "You work here. I'll bring the sewing machine into this room."

"You look like hell, Irina. What's the matter?"

"The Bolshoi is in more than normal chaos. We're organizing an overseas tour, doing loyalty assessments. It's a hard business."

"You should see a doctor...go to the hospital for an x-ray."

"Doctor, Masha? Are you plotting the death of me?"

"Just saying. I'll need silk thread, Irinochka."

Irina spread her hands. "And you'll find it, Masha."

Captains Danton Larionov and Roman Baranov stood under the portico smoking. Light and cold rain fell on the Boyar Courtyard. They had draped cloths over their shoes against rain splotches, their white gloves wrapped in towels set between the balustrades. Everything was at ready; the tables set, hors d'oeuvres laid out, iced vodka on red trays, Slivowitz in black lacquerware bottles. The Yugoslav General Staff, by chance in Moscow, became guests of honor at tonight's reception. They liked their plum brandy.

"Lucky bastard," Roman blew smoke into the mist. "Yuri Gagarin is now world-famous, plus he had received a spot promotion to major."

"Why not?" Danton replied. "He studied hard...good pilot too, so they say. Gagarin's a good-looking guy, a former foundryman, a pilot, now a cosmonaut."

"All they did was strap a rocket to his ass, and shoot him once around the world. Now he's got it dicked."

"Right place... right time." Danton mouthed aphorisms, the Russian way of appearing involved without commitment.

"He's charmed, indeed," Roman replied, aware that Danton was not giving full attention, but not bothered. "My old man knows the range controller at the Tyuratam range. The first guy who was to be the big hero got his nuts fried off. The rocket blew up on the pad, fell over and took a hundred specialists with him, or at least 100 aluminum coffins were delivered to the range. The second guy is a world grand champion globe trotter, still circling the earth, deader than a doornail, still screaming 'Help me! Help me!' as far as I know, but they shut off the radio."

Roman was silent for a moment, then continued, thoughtful. 'We're a gregarious lot, we Russian. It's the odd Russian who goes off into the emptiness alone. There were the Cossacks, of course. Ukraine. It meant 'at the end' of the known world. You, Danton, you seem okay being alone. You hold your cards close, Danton. You may not go far, but your tongue won't trip you up." Baronov field stripped his cigarette and returned the filter to the pack. "But you need allies to get where you want to go. Think any of the Ukrainian Mafia, the guys Nikita Sergeevich brought with him, would have survived without covering one another's asses?"

"We have time for one more smoke?" Danton said. Roman lifted an eyebrow, saying nothing, merely shaking out a cigarette. The first principle of deception is truth, at least, some truth. Was Gagarin the first man into space? Maybe, maybe not. In any case, the first one to go, and return, alive. Had he circled the earth? Maybe, maybe not. Did it matter? The USSR launched rockets. Gagarin may have been on one. The world believed Gagarin was the first man in space. And he was Russian. American rockets exploded on television. Soviet rockets did not explode on television.

Who knew the real truth, but true enough was good enough for the moment. Serf women had once gathered wood in

Woman's Wood. Danton's cousins had practiced marksmanship at the NKVD rifle range in Woman's Wood. The dreaded NKVD Black Crows entered Woman's Wood. Shots echoed in Woman's Wood. Connect the dots. The story makes sense. Believe what you wished. Danton crushed his cigarette. Who dared call the storyteller a liar?

"Dearies, I just didn't have the time to do a proper job of it." Marina Fedotova folded her hands, her nails long and red, as if they did double-duty as knitting needles.

"Marina, I will give you my first-born son," Vera exclaimed. "They are beautiful."

"Do not promise your children yet, Verochka," said Irina, eyeing her with a tilted head. "Your bosom and butt are unbalanced."

Marina waved her hand in agreement. The seamstress unpinned Vera's back, grasped the strapless bra's elastic, and tightened it. Vera gasped. A few needle thrusts and Vera's bosoms rose towards the chin.

Irina smiled. "No breathing tonight, darling, understand?"

Marina Fedotova, chin held in hand, looked from one girl to the other, then to Irina. "Take off your bloomers," she said.

"Mother!" gasped Ekaterina.

"You go without undergarments, " said Marina. "Those Soviet underthings make you look fat." Nothing more need be said. They did as told.

Danton Larionov stood at parade rest in the heavy Soviet Army winter dress uniform, sweating. He faced south in the direction of Tula where lightning from the first spring storm flashed. He with Captain Baranov guarded the doors to the Tsarina's boudoir, his position giving him a view of the crowds swirling beneath the statue of Little Russia. The creme of Soviet society had gathered in St. George's Hall of the Great Kremlin Palace. Astronaut Yuri Gagarin was guest of honor.

The Soviet Marshalls were steaming. Marshall of the Soviet Union Malinovskij was enraged. The space flight had taken place in secret, it's success astounding the world. It also somewhat surprised the Soviet high command. Gagarin survived. Khrushchev had insisted Lieutenant Gagarin be promoted to major on the spot.

The celebration, thrown together in Russian fashion, was chaos. There was no vodka—Georgian wine, but no vodka The Kremlin larder had been pilfered. Danton and Roman had been ordered to requisition 400 liters of Stolichnaya vodka from the foreign exchange shops and make up any deficit with 'samogon,' moonshine, from the black market. Baranov negotiated like a peasant, purchased sufficient quantity of varied quality so that the big wheels—Three stars and above and civilian equivalent, could drink Stolichnaya, one and two stars drank moonshine, the remainder of the guests getting Georgian wine. A bead of sweat appeared beneath his hat band. Which liquor was Gagarin, the hero of the world, privileged to drink?

The crowd hushed. Danton slid his eyes to the left. A stocky civilian in civilian suit, dark hair and bushy eyebrows and looking like an Odessa gangster wearing a chestful of medals and surrounded by guards, appeared at the head of the Red Staircase. Another bead of sweat trickled down Danton's earlobe. Was the gangster allowed Stolichnaya or moonshine? A signal passed like a gamma ray through the crowd. A Long Range Aviation two-star general stepped from the gangster's path. Functionaries and officers vacated the space before the liquor table. Ah, Stolichnaya.

But, Colonel Soroka, also in mufti, and General Anton Gastilovich, General Staff Academy, hove into view. A second civilian; grey hair, face, and demeanor, accompanied the Odessa gangster, who nodded to Colonel Soroka.

The gangster looked Danton over. "Mine," Soroka said. "Trust me; trust him."

Danton flinched. Colonel Soroka had acknowledged him? What could it mean? Were the words an endorsement, or boars pissing on the ground marking territory? Was a spot promotion to Major in the pipeline with a follow-on assignment to the General Staff, or...?

"Von Manstein believed your bullshit, and he lost 2 million men." The gangster had decided to make nice. Danton assessed the gangster's campaign ribbons—Defense of Moscow, Malaya Zemlya, the Liberation of Kiev and of Berlin. General Gastilovich and Colonel Soroka had many of the same, meaning they had fought the same battles, suffered the same privations and distrusted one another. The gangster was no other than Leonid B. Brezhnev, Chairman of Presidium of the Supreme Soviet of the USSR. Danton stared straight ahead. The nail that stands out gets hammered down. The grey man was KGB chairman, Alexander Shelepin. Danton's Director of Curriculum, Colonel Soroka, spoke to the gods.

" Zhukov distrusted maskirovka, and we sacrificed millions." Professor Colonel Soroka replied unsmiling.

" Zhukov shot Beria," Brezhnev said, justifying Zhukov's direct action over duplicity.

"Give him that," Soroka said. "...Splattered that Ossetian's brains off the Lubyanka walls." KGB Chairman Alexander Shelepin's stare was cold.

Danton felt chill in the sweltering room. When the bulls fight, the grass gets trampled.

"That was a mess, I agree," Brezhnev said, and ever the politician, turned to the KGB Chairman. "Beria had his good points."

"When we have a moment, Comrade Brezhnev, we'll list them," said Soroka, ignoring Shelepin.

So this is how the Gods disputed; They pissed on one another's boots. Danton sensed the ballroom dimming.

Brezhnev lifted a frozen vodka from the table, with his fingers differentiating the Stolichnaya from the samogon. "It is a proud day to be Russian." He ricocheted the shot down his gullet.

"Larionov, flex your knees before you pass out," Soroka snapped.

"Larionov?" KGB Chairman Shelepin turned to examine the Larionov, then turned away, for there was a commotion at the Red stairway.

The commanding heights of the Soviet state crowded into the St. Georges Hall of the Kremlin, the hall packed, the air thick, men and women smoking like a Kulak's chimney, the noise echoing within Danton's skull. The reception line had formed, influence marked by their proximity to Lieutenant or Major Yuri Gagarin, who occupied the place of honor on Khrushchev's right, or mostly on the right for Nikita

Sergeevich was bouncing all over the place. Alexander Soroka moved about in the background, his function being protocol of some sort, sending runners to inquire the names of those he did not know, passing names to Brezhnev, who introduced the luminaries to Khrushchev, who presented them to Gagarin. Khrushchev—did the little peasant never tire?—was ebullient, hugging, slapping backs, exchanging great peasant kisses.

Brezhnev's attention had been caught by something or someone far down the greeting line. Likewise, the officers of the Yugoslav general staff, honored tonight with proximity to Soviet luminaries and well-liquored, had noticed what Brezhnev noticed, elbowing one another. Gagarin maintained his diffident smile as drunken Soviet Army marshalls planted boozy kisses on both his cheeks, lifting him aloft in bear hugs while their gushing wives pinched those cheeks. Lieutenant Gagarin—or Major Gagarin depending on how the pissing contest between the General Staff and Communist Party played out—would probably have preferred an engine flameout to one more hour in the Kremlin Great Hall. Danton flexed his knees. If he fainted, he would breathe fresh cold air the remaining days of his life at the Long Range Aviation base, Anadyr, on the shores of the Arctic Ocean. Would the night never end?

Brezhnev now fixed on the object out of Danton's line of sight. Had Lenin left his tomb to stand in line and share in this the greatest achievement of Communism? A woman, Danton guessed. Brezhnev was a ladies man, strutting for the beauties while ignoring the babas.

The receiving line moved glacially. The First Secretary of the Communist Party of the Soviet Union would not be hurried.

The object of the President's attention had now moved within Danton's line of sight but remained hidden behind the crowd.   He flexed knees, inhaled, gouged nails into his palms, imaging being elsewhere, fighting unconsciousness. For a moment, his line of sight cleared, giving him a quick glimpse of red hair, curvaceous breasts, and narrow waist. At the young woman's side was another, a wisp of a young woman, blond, to whom Colonel Professor Alexander Soroka was speaking. A shock coursed Danton's body snapping him fully awake.

The Soviet big wheels—Nikita Sergeevich Khrushchev, First Secretary of the CPSU, Leonid I. Brezhnev, Chairman of Presidium of the Supreme Soviet of the USSR, Soviet Army General, Anton Gastilovich, Chief of the Planning Staff, and KGB Chairman Alexander Shelepin—stood with Alexander Soroka in the Tsaritsa Chamber off the Red Room.

"Sasha, get us a bottle," Khrushchev, exuberant and tipsy, ordered Soroka, and elbowed Brezhnev. "Leonid, you cunt hound, I wouldn't trust you with little Miss Russia..." He waved toward the Red Room..." much less Tatyana." He laughed uproariously, this 'Tatyana' some secret between them. "Sasha," Khrushchev shouted, "you piece of shit in a silk stocking, where the bottle?"

Soroka looked to Danton. The strategic vodka reserve was hidden in Tsaritsa Chamber, beyond the conferees. 'Get it,' Soroka ordered with a curt nod.

Danton paled. His aching legs, immobile for hours, did not obey his brain, which buzzed from heat, stale air, noise, and inchoate emotion. On an April evening in Moscow, Vasilisa, the Beautiful, who one fine day had disappeared without a trace, had reappeared, as if from outer space. Ekaterina, the goose girl of Suzdal, was the ward of the wizard Soroka, advisor to the most powerful man in the cosmos, a crude drunken peasant. Surely, this was a skazka.

'Get the vodka,' the wizard's eyes ordered. Khrushchev slapped Danton on the shoulder. "Hey, kid, get a move on. I'm thirsty as hell."

The private stash had been hidden in the toilet tank. He brought the dripping bottle and placed them on some elegant writing desk. With a jerk of the head, Soroka ordered Larionov out of the Tsaritsa's Boudoir.

The Red Room was empty save for the boisterous Yugoslav contingent, some of whom were accosting Roman about where the booze and babes might be in the early morning Moscow. What had happened? Ekaterina of Suzdal, the Goose Girl, had been a princess in disguise. This evening, she had appeared dressed in delicate silks of ancient Bukhara, shod in silver slippers with a russet-haired full-breasted lady in waiting at her side. All paused before her beauty. But before the professor, she had bowed her head, and he touched her cheek.

'Irina?' he had asked.

'A migraine,' the beauty replied, eyes lowered.

What could that have meant? Alexander Soroka, the Sorcerer, who spoke truth to the Gods, was her protector. When she turned her face to Gagarin, the hero-captain gaped, mouth open, Gagarin's wife regarding the princess with a raised eyebrow.

The lights had been turned off, a few dim bulbs burning at one end and over the Red Staircase. He squinted. Danton, Son of Wolf of Suzdal, whose father had once been master of ten-thousand serfs.

"Hey, country boy, bite my dick if you don't need a drink." Roman had sent the Yugoslavs onto the streets of Moscow. "Did the big wheels leave any of the booze we hid for our hero Senior Sergeant?"

"The First Secretary and Colonel Soroka are guarding what's left."

"No shit?" Roman said. "Hear any secrets?"

Danton shook his head. "Strange night."

"Night's not over. We need to find a bar open at this time of night. I got a buddy who needs a drink."

"Where'd you send the Yugoslavs?" said Danton, then "Ah, fuck it, Roman. I'm exhausted."

"Gotta do it. C'mon."

"I will listen," Khrushchev said. There was a collective pause. Listen? Khrushchev? Unlikely. "Sasha, you start."

Khrushchev may well have been born an ignorant peasant but didn't survive Stalin and Beria by remaining an ignorant peasant. Soroka would have preferred silence, but the First Secretary was looking directly at him   "Nikita, I am uncertain what you have in mind, but deception starts with truth; it may be a sliver of truth, but the truth it must be. It is fundamental to success. The devil, however, is in the details...the implementation. One spy...or one fool can undo hundreds of hours of work." This is what Communism taught; obfuscation.

"Only idiots speak truth to capitalists," Shelepin said, quoting Lenin. Platitudes also served when one was playing for time.

"You support that, Leonid?" Soroka said. Brezhnev had served under General Gastilovich as the 40th Army's political officer. The 40th Army had as its primary mission front-level deception operations; the political officer was responsible for the unit deception plan; Brezhnev was by war's end was a past master of the craft. Brezhnev was wary of Shelepin; and vice versa.

"Truth, true, but partial truth," Gastilovich replied. "It is like the pea beneath the thimbles, which in truth is up the sleeve, that confounds the all-too-clever peasant who wants to win a little something at the cattle fair; it's there, but where?" Brezhnev too was not one to commit himself, but General Gastilovich stepped to the front, adding his two kopeks. "Deception is as are armored and infantry divisions, artillery, aerial support, bombs, and bullets is an integral part of the offensive." Gastilovich stopped there. He was an exceptional general, but no fool. All understood. Khrushchev had striven to move investment from military to civilian infrastructure; to reassure the Soviet generals, he said that the Soviet Union has thousands of missiles "that could hit a fly's eye at 1000 miles." No one believed him except, unfortunately, the Americans, who deployed in 1000 days 1000 ICBM Minuteman missiles across the American steppe. All present knew, but if Khrushchev shit his pants, and all would swear they smelt roses.

Nikita lifted his glass. "Comrades, to the inevitable victory of the working classes over Capitalist oppression." All raised their glasses. "We can do something with this Kennedy. He was only a lieutenant, for the love of Christ." Khrushchev, peasant-born and -raised, peppered his speech, with peasant aphorism and profanity.

"There is no hurry, Nikita," Soroka cautioned. Khrushchev's ideas were either brilliant or hare-brained. But Soroka's star was hitched to he who was once his student; another error or two and Brezhnev or Shelepin or some other up-and-comer would have fodder to clip his wings. "American presidents come and go, but there is only one Central Intelligence Agency, and there is only one CIA Soviet Division. Deceive them, and you deceive the whole imperialist edifice."

"No, Alexander Nikolaevich," Shelepin rejoined. "There is FBI counterintelligence, Army Intelligence..."

Soroka interrupted. "Their Minister of Defense is creating another military intelligence agency, like our GRU, because he suspects he can not trust the CIA. For now, the CIA tells the American president what is true and what is false. We can control the CIA Soviet Division."

"With nuclear weapons, we can not afford another surprise attack," Shelepin interjected. His face was pale and placid, his neck turning red.

Soroka shrugged, "Hitler controlled Stalin's mind." This, Khrushchev understood.

Soroka continued. "We've all read in detail the KGB and GRU analysis of the NATO war plan. They agree. Upon attack, the NATO forces retreat to the Rhine. Unless you,

Comrade Shelepin, have new information concerning NATO military options."

Shelepin slit his eyes. "The enemy surrounds the motherland--Japan, Turkey, Germany--with bombers, missiles, and cruise missiles. They built 1000 Minutemen missiles ..."

Soroka shrugged. He had spoken his truth and needn't repeat himself. He was in Khrushchev's tribe. Shelepin was not a current threat. However, if Nikita weakened...

"Oh, mother, it was wonderful." Vera snickered, looked at Ekaterina and both burst into laughter.

"Ekaterina and Vera, you are both drunk." Irina raised her eyes to the ceiling, ran her palms over Ekaterina's gown, and fingered the stitching on Vera's. "Well, you two seem to have held together well."

"Momma, I hadn't dared to cough, or the dress would have been a pile of cloth around my ankles. Alexander ordered a limousine to drive us home."

Vera broke in, "I just can't imagine how our dresses would've survived the Metro...the Air Force pilot—goodness was he good-looking... the wife was a harridan, though—looked straight down my bosom. Wonder if he saw I wasn't wearing knickers."

"Verochka, you home wrecker, he's married." Ekaterina, a severe expression struggling to erase the mischievous smile, pulled the tie at Vera's neck, and the gown top fell to the girl's waist. Ekaterina giggled. "Don't bend over else everything will fall out."

Vera, unabashed, shook her chest, and the delicate East German lace bra losing its struggle to contain ample Russian bosoms. She wiggled and gown falling to the floor, and she stepped out if it. "I want this dress for my next date," Naked, Vera struck an innocent pose. "Convenient, don't you think?"

"Both you little sluts," Irina's said, "Put nightgowns on now!"

"Momma, we had such a good time."

"Katyusha, darling," Vera said, "How did it feel to dance naked?"

"You tell me, lovely," Ekaterina replied.

"I swear one of the statue-captains was the one following you at Chistiye Prudi...no, at the Teahouse...you know, the one the bus took away."

Ekaterina pouted, "Why hadn't you pointed him out?"

"His post was across from Roman's." Ekaterina raised an eyebrow. "Baranov. Ah, you've never met him. He's a snake but had been stationed in West Germany...still has connections there. His family—his father is General Baranov––has a flat on the same floor as we at Timorevskoye. I should introduce you."

"I am trying to visualize the statue Vera's talking about, Momma. There was just so much going on."

"They are probably Alexander's students. I'll ask," Irina said. But tell me everything you remember."

"Think Alexander will introduce us to his cute officers?"

"He doesn't mix work with home, but we'll see."

"Momma, I am so tired," Ekaterina said and walked into her mother's arm. "Thank you so much, and I am so sorry you didn't come."

"Another time," Irina said.

"There'll never be another time."

"Come, girls, hang up your gowns and get some clothes else you'll catch pneumonia. Do you want water or tea? If you don't drink something, you'll suffer a three-day hangover."

Irina regarded her daughter's beauty and regretted that she couldn't take her to shop in Paris. The French had so many smart ways to hide or hint at or accentuate a young woman's beauty. There was a young officer smitten with her daughter? She'd inquire.

"Wait for us up there. We'll walk to it..." Larionov said. "and be out sooner or later." The driver, a war veteran, smiled wryly and pointed up Greater Lubyanka Street to indicate that he would park in front of the Ministry of Foreign Affairs. Three Russian officers stumbled out onto floodlit Lubyanka Square, the historical late night pose of drunken Russian junior officers since Russian officers existed, Baranov and Larionov propping Air Force still-Captain Gagarin between them.

"Eh, not bad," Roman Baranov said, gesturing to the departing limousine. "I could get used to that. All you Zoomies issued personal cars?" Baranov shuddered in the night chill.

"Nope, not all pilots, but all cosmonauts," Order of Lenin recipient Yuri Gagarin said.

"You shitting me?"

"I am shitting you. But, hey, there is only one of me. Would it cost the state that much?" Gagarin scanned the brooding mass of the Lubyanka Prison, the lights in a few offices seeming to form a skeptical and rheumy-eyed face that looking out onto the trio. Chance had lifted Gagarin from a foundry floor in provincial Smolensk to outer space, for the moment the most famous Russian in the world, more famous than even the American singer, Elvis Presley. Crowds had lined the route from Domodedovo Airport to the Kremlin. The cream of Soviet society feted him. Nina Petrovna Khrushchev pinched both his cheeks. It could have been different. He should have been swept up in the 1941 German labor requisition that sent his brother and sister as slave laborers to Germany. The steel beam that dropped from the hoist should have killed him instead of Dmitri Vassarionov. At the corner where Kuznetski Bridge Street intersected Greater Lubyanka Gagarin turned, lifted one hand in emulation of the pose of the Dzherzhinski statue. The Soviet cosmonaut spoke to the now-absent silent crowds. "I am a Soviet worker of modest desires. All I need is a beautiful car, a MIG fighter, and a bottle of vodka." He turned to his new colleagues. "Comrades, we are behind in plan fulfillment. Typical. The peasant screws the worker with a shortage of potatoes, thus vodka."

Floodlights cast long and formless shadows under the Lubyanka's yellow eyes. The three junior officers shivered and pressed against one another in drunken warmth. In the hour before the Moscow dawn, Lubyanka Square was as lonely as outer space.

"Danton Volkov Larionov," ordered Gagarin. "Find us someplace comfortable to the Great Russian soldier, and not an empty alleyway." It had been a sleepless seventy-two hours. Three days earlier he had climbed into a capsule strapped atop a Vostok 3KA-3 rocket. The capsule door would not lock, and the technician hammered it close with a heavy rubber mallet. He was already dead, would die alone, cold and forgotten. He had murmured prayers. If he survived, he promised, he would make his way to light a candle at the Church of the Holy Redeemer in Moscow.

He had survived. He had made his way to Moscow. The Church of the Holy Redeemer Stalin had long ago blown to smithereens.

"I know a place," Danton said. As of the moment, he was senior by date of rank, Gagarin as yet uninformed of the resolution of the dispute over promotion between Marshall Malinovsky and First Secretary Khrushchev.

Danton looked over Lybyanka Square. In 1953 Soviet Army trucks had spilled soldiers into the Square to storm the Lybyanka. NKVD officers who paused raising their hands were shot dead at their desks.

It was in reprisal, so to speak. In 1938, NKVD agents had arrived on General Staff Headquarters on Arbat Square, the Old Arbat of Pushkin and Bulgakov and Blok and Russia's poets, and imprisoned the Red Army high command, executing over time most, only Hitler's invasion saving the lives of the remainder. The three captains staggered past the Ministry of Foreign Affairs, where, in 1939, German Foreign Minister Ribbentrop and the Russian Molotov toasted the signing of a non-aggression pact that in days loosed Asiatic war upon Europe. Between the massacre on the Arbat and the massacre in the Lubyanka, the German Army scorched the lessons of Clausewitz into the Russian soul. German rationality combating Russian cunning killed thirty to fifty million soldiers and civilians, Germans, and Russians, men and women, children and grandparents, on the steppes, swamps and forests between Moscow to Berlin.

A racing Zhiguli sedan entered Lybyanka Square from Teatralnyi Proyezd', the rumble of rubber over cobblestone echoing in the enclosed space and disappeared into a closed passage, which invisible hands had opened.

"Here," said Danton. In the early morning light it was as quiet as death, the city abandoned. Larionov sensed a spirit pass through the locked gates of the distant metro station as the last NKVD executioner took the secret train north or west or east to a Russian forest, spinning the cylinder of his heavy service revolver, one bullet remaining. "...we drink."

"Money-wise, Sasha, things going all right with you?"

"Fine, Nikita Sergeevich, we are satisfied."

The First Secretary released Soroka's arm and spread his arms wide, taking in the room. "Ain't this a pisser, eh, Sasha? From a Donetsk mine to the Tsaritsa's bedroom, a real back-door man, eh? Like the suit? Made in England. Politburo took a vote...said we had to stop dressing like hicks. What's the world coming to?"

"I knew you were a good student, Nikita Sergeevich, but you have surpassed even my expectations. I'll pour you one..." Alexander poured two glasses] full, passing one to Khrushchev. "if you'll tell me where you buy your lottery tickets."

"Lottery ticket?" Khrushchev searched Alexander's face, then burst into laughter, cuffing Soroka on the shoulder. Soroka took the expected blow with arm extended in order not to spill the vodka. "Stalin's wife took a shine to me. Don't know why?" Khrushchev surveyed the boudoir, his mood pensive. "How did we survive, Sasha? Every night I'd leave Nina Petrovna, go out to Stalin's dacha not knowing if I'd see her again. Almost makes one believe in God." And as quickly, he bacame furious. "This is where that corrupt bastard deflowered our good Russian girls. We did that right...blasted the Tsar's perfumed ass to hell and back. To friendship...bottoms up..."

They clinked glasses. "No one deflowered here, Nikita. This is the Tsaritsa's 'boudoir,' or bedroom. The Tsar's whores were put up in the Terem Palace."

"Always the teacher, eh, Sasha?" They looked one another in the eye.

"Nikita, what in the hell are you doing?" Khrushchev had covered his privates with one hand.

"At the institute, you threatened to snatch our balls if we fell asleep."

"You all worked a full day while getting only half-rations, then came to night school to learn Marx and Engels. I was impressed with the worker's dedication, but you'd all get sleepy."

"A Jew teaching the ABCs of Communism? What did you expect us to believe?" Khrushchev said, grinning.

Alexander refilled the glasses. "Your jewels are safe with me, but on second thought, maybe I could get a good price for'em?"

And how's Irina Nikoleeva? Was she your wife or his?" Soroka was always surprised what Khrushchev stored in that brain. "I can't remember. I was no big fan of ballet. Still not. But damn if I wouldn't watch Irina spin around the stage for an hour or so. I'd watch her peel a potato for an hour or two, she was the looker, by God. Is she still? I go to the Bolshoi now and then because Nina Petrovna likes it. Prefer the Gopak myself."

Alexander smiled. The Gopak was a leaping and crouching Ukrainian dance. "She's fine."

"Glad to hear.   So was the ballerina your or your brother's wife,   though neither of you ugly pieces of sheepshit deserved her."

"Nor do I still," Alexander Soroka admitted.

"Wasn't Nikolai a left deviationist?"

"No, he had been allied with Bukharin."

"Ah, I had forgotten...right deviationist." Khrushchev paused, thoughtful. "I swear if all I had to do is clean up after Stalin, I would have enough to do for three lifetimes. But, they say in America, 50,000 people a year die in automobile accidents." Khrushchev continued as if to preclude his former teacher explaining the difference.   "Enough with the reminiscence. I have a reason to talk to you." Alexander nodded. So he had suspected. "I need you to snatch Kennedy's balls."

Alexander Soroka regarded at the Chairman of the Central Committee of the Communist Party of The Union of Soviet Socialist Republic. The Russian peasant as a class remained a mystery to the Jew of the Pale. Soroka offered the bottle, but Khrushchev passed. "I'm meeting the little twerp next month."

"I don't understand."

"The American President Kennedy. You snookered that other American, Roosevelt's vice-president. I want you to do the same with Kennedy."

"It's not the same thing, Nikita. Wallace was either a blithering idiot or holy fool. I still haven't decided.   In any case, he yearned to believe that Stalin's Communism had the answers. Kennedy is another kettle of kasha. Kennedy's old man was an Irish gangster; the boy should know a thing or two."

"He was a Navy second lieutenant, for Christ's sake. What could be more stupid? The Japanese ship commander just ran his ass over...wouldn't even waste a bullet on 'em. You'll come with me to Vienna and assess him." Khrushchev fingered his glass, looking off. "Isn't that something? We sent a Russian boy into space. We've progressed from walking behind a wooden plow smelling oxen farts and to flying into space. There is nothing Communism can't accomplish."

"Where's this bar you talked about?" Gagarin asked.

"Hey," Roman said and tripped over the curb. "Zoomies don't hold their liquor worth a damn."

"I can hold my liquor enough to kick your ass across the square and back."

"We want booze, not bloodshed. Turn around," Danton commanded.

They turned to face an alleyway. "This is where we piss?" Gagarin said.

"Yuri, how you got into space and back," Danton said. "GRU Captain Baranov, Air Force Captain... or Major, if the Party prevails...Gagarin doubts the professionalism of Soviet reconnaissance."

Gagarin and Baranov turned. "I sense a sliver of light," Roman said.

Gagarin said, "I sense distilled potatoes. My range finder indicates target at ten meters."

A passage appeared in what had seemed a blank wall. Deep within the alley, a red neon sign glowed no brighter than banked coals, as if it were the entrance to the underworld, the words Shchit I Mech, Sword and Shield, beckoning.

Gagarin straightened his shoulders. "Advance, finest sons of the motherland, to engage the enemy."

Danton pounded on the door to the Sword and Shield, the KGB's private tavern. "Kto?" growled a graveled voice from a speaker above their head.

"Larionov, Danton Volkov." There was a pause, then the sliding of a bolt. It was 3 AM. The business of the Lubyanka was all-hours.

The bar was long, the room narrow. The tables stood under hanging lamps. Large framed posters of past and present KGB directors hung behind the bar, save Lavrenti Beria, the space between Nickolai Yezhov and Ivan Serov empty. A mélange of photos of KGB heroes hung in the spaces between curtained windows. Heroic posters celebrating KGB construction projects—The White Sea Canal, New City Magadan in the Far East, Norilsk Nickel Mines—hung along the stairways ascending on either side of the bar. Three men, squat, short and broad-shouldered, with a fourth, who resembled a school teacher, sat at one table and regarded the newcomers. One leaned forward, speaking something with unmoving lips.

Danton sensed Yurii Gagarin tensing. Rocketed into space atop a Soviet-built rocket into outer space required one type of bravery; in the belly of the beast, another.

"Danton Volkov," said the school teacher. "You little prick, can it be you?"

"Arkadii Stepanovitch," Danton acknowledged. "I have a friend who has returned from a long trip. He needs a drink."

"Mother...." This Stepanovich looked to the bartender, thrust a finger to the sky; bring a bottle, circled the finger: Lay out a Russian spread; pickled herring and vegetables, black, brown and white bread with relishes, and iced vodka, then turned to his slowly comprehending comrades. "Off your asses. Where's your KGB sense of hospitality." Another gesture to the bar. Call KGB First Directorate, Internal Security. "It's Gagarin! "

Within minutes, the Sword and Shield had filled with Russians, boozing, eating, smoking, toasting, touching, and talking to Gagarin. Their duties; torture, confession, and executions, would be put off onto the day shift. Gagarin was thumped, embraced, and kissed, his vodka refilled after each sip. Danton stepped away from his host responsibilities. The Russian Gagarin knew Russian drinking protocol; he'd monitored his own state of inebriation; the hosts would refill his glass as he emptied it. No more nor no less.

Danton had moved to the doorway for air. The tall and thin teacher—Arkadii--joined him. "I was with your father in Kaliningrad. A man of steel."

"My father kept his counsel," Danton said. "I had not known he served there. When was that?"

"After the Pact uniting the Baltic States with the motherland in 39 and 40, we were sent to clean out a pack of counter-revolutionaries. Blokhin was our commander. Now there was a Communist to admire. Hard. No mercy...dispatched over 7000 counter-revolutionaries personally. He was not one to ask you to do what he wouldn't. We don't have hard men like General Blokhin and your father anymore."

"He was kind to my mother...to me."

"There you go. A hard but fair Communist. Don't make 'em like that anymore," he repeated.

"Blokhin committed suicide."

"So they say," said he who resembled a Polish school teacher. "Your father died of cancer?"

"So they say."

Arkadii pulled out a pack of papirosy and offered one to Danton. "He indeed smoked like a chimney."

"They make me dizzy," Danton said and declined.

"Let me know if there is any way I can help you," Arkadii said. He tilted his head toward Lyubyanka Square. "They'll know where to find me."

Arkadii saluted with his glass and moved off.

The cold air of the Moscow spring morning wafted across Danton's neck, and he stepped back into the noise. Loneliness as black and infinite as cosmos blurred his vision. In the classless Soviet Union, Alexander Soroka was of the Soviet *Dvoryanstvo*, the aristocracy. He spoke with the Gods. Ekaterina the Beautiful had seen Danton, and recoiled, as she had long ago on Suzdal's Illian Meadow. She was beyond reach under the protection of a powerful lord. Danton, the executioner's son, was born of the damned.

CHAPTER TWENTY

Rain mixed with snow fell over Moscow. Winter lingered over a despairing population. Danton Volkov Larionov stared through grimy windows into a grey and cold Moscow morning at the ice floes drifting in the Moscow River. Cigarette tar coated his mouth and nostrils; vodka fumes wreathed his brain. Danton looked into the grim future. He had glimpsed the seventh kingdom. A Suzdal prince, he had walked its ancient streets until the day soldiers came and the day the princess disappeared. Then one day, as if by incantation, she reappeared, as if from outer space, like Yuri Gagarin.

He looked down at his class notes. A paper, Fundamental Principals of Maskirovka, lay before him. 'A successful deception, like a successful theatrical production, has a clear objective--is the audience to laugh, weep or fall into deep thought. Does the deception convince the enemy commander to retreat, advance to his disadvantage, deploy his forces inappropriately? The scenario is prepared, rehearsed, presented, and assessed. Deception gives you secret powers,' sayeth the wizard, who incarnated the princess.

The briefcase landed on the table. Roman Baranov set his tea on the table and lit a cigarette. "You look like you've been run over by a vodka truck." Roman was smoking a Russian brand. "The blond last night... she's a looker. Nice ass."

"She is Colonel Soroka's daughter or niece or something."

"Doubtful," Roman said. "She's tall, blond and gorgeous. Soroka is short, swarthy, and ugly. Though her tits are a little small for me. Someone must have screwed his ballerina-wife while he was off saving socialism." Danton stiffened, but Baranov continued blithely on. "She was probably adopted. War orphan, probably. I found out some things."

"Her name is Ekaterina," said Danton.

"You know her?"

"Long time ago."

"Did know Ekaterina II did it with horses?"

"Roman, is there anyone on the face of this earth more foul that you?"

"Eh, touched a sore nerve, did I? I watched your mug all night, as if I had a choice, considering my posting opposite you. We, the best sons of the motherland, served as statues. I tried to pull strings, but Tsiklarus had a patron higher on the food chain than I, alas. When this Ekaterina, the Contemporary, appeared, I thought you were going to pass out."

"She had been a refugee in Suzdal for a short time in the summer of 1953. She was probably fourteen or fifteen years old, a kid."

"Ugly duckling into a swan, eh? Think she'll go down for nylon stockings?" Danton stared at Roman, who, unfazed, struck his chest. "Hey, you're my comrade, and I am a GRU officer. What good am I if I can't provide a fellow officer adequate reconnaissance to accomplish his mission? I know the redhead, her friend, Vera." Roman exhaled a thick roiling smoke ring across the table surface to dissipate against Danton's tea glass. "Soroka's political loyalties are divided between the Soviet Army and the Communist Party. The wife is a ballerina. This Ekaterina is a linguist who wants to travel."

"I'd drink her bathwater," said Larionov. "I'd drink your bathwater if you'd introduce me."

"What's a buddy for, eh? You'll do one for me someday." This was the way it worked in the 1960's USSR. Trading favors was the currency of choice.

"Where is she?"

The Chechen raised his hand, palms forward. "She had a tail. Couldn't approach."

Nikolai Soroka stared through one blood-shot eye. "What kind of tail, Hussayn?" The thug was confused. Nikolai Soroka repeated the question with a hard edge. "What kind of tail? Cop? KGB?"

Hussayn grimaced. "One or the other, but he was a dumb fuck."

"You tailed the tail? What did he look like?"

"A Russian, Blond, young, Maybe 25, maybe 30 years old."

"Where did he end up when you lost him."

"The Army Engineering Institute...Baumanskaya District."

Nicholas Soroka tapped out a papirosy. Was the Russian that had followed Ekaterina an undercover flick in training? Or had Alexander assigned one of his soldier-boy students to follow his daughter? Even genius could trip on his own foreskin. That took an aptitude, Nickolai supposed. His brother...Sasha, he could fuck up a wet dream. "No killing anyone, anything...not even a fucking cockroach..until I tell you. You fucking understand, Hussein, or I'll personally razor your nuts off."

Hussein nodded. He understood.

Nicholas stared into the cigarette coal. He was coughing blood and pissing ten times a night. He had dodged a million bullets, but this one...probably not. How much time had he remaining to get Ekaterina out of hell?

l

CHAPTER TWENTY-ONE

All autumn, the chafe and jar
Of nuclear war;
We have talked our extinction to death.
I swim like a minnow
Behind my studio window.

Robert Lowell, Fall 1961

The pride the Gagarin space flight had inspired transformed Moscow's grim public face into a grudging and fleeting smile that spring, 1961. Spring with the merest hint of green succeeding the harsh winter had restored the Russian sense that the worst was over. This Russian endured winter as he endured Russia's revolutions, civil war, famines, mass imprisonment, and purges. 'Life is getting better, sweeter,' or so at least affirmed the propaganda poster. 3-10 million had perished in that previous winter's famine. That the slogan appeared in the following spring. The calamitous Great Fatherland War still to come. Winter, war, siege, famine. Can not spring's redemption be far behind?

In 1961 as summer became fall and fall became winter, crises, one after another, agitated the nerves. The Headlines– –The Failure of the Vienna Summit, Bay of Pigs, the flight of Rudolf Nureyev to the West, the Berlin Wall, Soviet and American tanks confronting one another at Checkpoint Charlie. Would the next war be nuclear?

Ekaterina stood in a fog-shrouded forest clearing amidst whimsical wood carvings of human and animal figures, a scene so Moscow, so Russia, so Russian that she clasped her hands together. Long ago Baba Yaga in a fit of irritation had frozen a spring solstice celebration into woodcarvings. The young woman caressed the head of the poet elf. What had he done to raise the witch's ire? Might a young woman's touch return him to life? The Oak Grove in Ostankino District, once part of Prince Sheremetev's vast private forest preserve, was now being eaten away by advancing Moscow. What had it been like before the revolution? Had Muscovites been as kind and generous out-of-doors then as they were now at the kitchen table? Or did the old Russians walk onto the street with faces set into the same hard and harsh masks in defenses against a cold human sea? What was it about masks?

She looked up to another tall figure carved from a tree, a woman whose long hair flowed onto and merged with he robe. Had she been the Tsarina who had not pronounced the incantation to stay the evil flowing over the land? She, the statue tsarina, towered above the others, her cheeks weathered, as if tears had run the mascara down her cheeks that the lady in waiting had applied so carefully. Was she Mother Russia? Who had been the artist? Who allowed him to visit his whimsy upon this forest? Had he been a friend of woodcutters or perhaps himself a peasant, or maybe a member of the Academy? Had it been industrial soot or exposure to Russia that gave each face its tragic mien? Hadn't the English Druids also worshipped in the oak groves?

She had left a note for her mother: "Botanical Gardens – Mushrooms." Ekaterina waved farewell to the wooden people, and walked to the thoroughfare, peering up Akademika Koroleva Street. Some Communist Party big wheel racing from his dacha to a Kremlin meeting might run her over. But no, in the early hour and thick fog, the world was silent and constrained.

She crossed onto the grounds of the abandoned Ostankino Monastery, skirted the still ice-covered pond, passed by the silent carousel and boathouse and onto the meadow that bordered the Moscow Botanical Gardens. Snow patches remained in the lea of trees. The mushrooms she sought grew on oak and birch trees.

"A cup of tea would be just what the doctor ordered, Comrade Colonel-General Gribkov." Alexander Soroka, removing his fur hat and overcoat, addressed his host with elaborate Communist formality, and they shook hands, two Soviet tribesmen, the Army, and the Party, allies, for the moment.

"You didn't have to take the metro, Alexander Isaakovich. I would have sent a car." The office was austere. The requisite three photos—Marx, Engels, and Lenin—hung behind his desk, the Soviet flag to the right, the banner of the newly organized Strategic Rocket Forces to the left. Beyond the dest was an eight-place conference table. On the far wall were similar sized photos of Marshall of the Soviet Union

Rodion Malinovsky, Chief of the Soviet General Staff and of Marshall Sergei Beriyozov, Commander of the Strategic Rocket Forces. Gribok did not make three stars by being politically maladroit. Alexander looked for the one missing photo. Ah, ha. A signed photo of Khrushchev stood on the general's desk, indicative of either great respect or the chance to stick the damn thing in a desk drawer when the visiting high muckety-mucks passed through. Large windows lined the west wall which looked out upon Old Arbat street.

In the flood of post-Twentieth Party Congress rehabilitations and corrections of documents, ambitious Communists on the make embellished combat records. Gribkov was, however, a real war hero, his battle ribbons— the defense of Moscow, Defense of Leningrad, Three Orders of the Defense of the Fatherland, first and second degree and two Orders of the Red Banner with three Orders of the Red Star—earned in combat. In December 1942, in the Zhukov military debacle that was Operation "Mars" in which entire Soviet divisions had been decimated. Neither the Nazis nor the Soviets took prisoners. Zhukov, enraged that General Vassilevskij's Steppe Front had broken through to envelope Von Paulus's 6th Army at Stalingrad, poured Russian divisions into Von Manstein's waiting Panzers, and as General Vasilevskiy surrounded the Von Paulus' German 6th Army, Von Manstein devastated Zhukov on the Central Front.

Gribkov was one of the few who shone. Three German armored divisions had surrounded Captain Gribkov's corps until only three T-34 tanks out of 300 remained, losses so severe the three tanks did not have crew members. Gribkov drove the first tank to divert enemy fire upon himself, and when Gribkov's tank was hit, Gribkov got the survivors out.

Soroka waved off the generosity. "I like to ride the Moscow metro, that miracle of Socialist construction. I transferred at Revolutionary Square Metro station, petted the dog's nose for luck, and got off at Borovitskaya, so here I am. Takes more than a few flurries to divert us old soldiers, eh, General?"

General Gribkov was no fool. Soroka had been sent from the very highest level. Soroka and Gribkov neither friends nor enemies, shared a grudging respect. The then-Captain Gribkov, though a line officer, was also a General Staff officer.

General Gribkov made a sign to the attendant colonel to pour tea. "Wasn't the first time we met... in December 1942, Kalinin Front? You were on General Zhukov's staff during an inspection trip."

"I believe so, yes," Soroka responded, soldier small talk until the tea was poured. "You were already a major?"

"In 42, I was still a captain. In early 1943, I was promoted to Major after the second battle of Rzhev. Superstitious, Comrade Soroka? You touched the door frame when you entered a room."

"Did I? Perhaps when I'm distracted." They both had grown up in religious families, Gribkov's family Orthodox, Soroka's Jewish. Marxism rested lightly upon their souls. To Gribkov, Communism's convoluted flexibility was as opaque as an Old Church Slavonic of murmuring priests and smoke-filled censors. "Communism is a hard and logical science, but a little bit of luck now and then can't hurt."

They stood in momentary silence, the only sound the clink of spoons on glass, looking out at the intersections of the New Arbat with the Old Arbat Street. A heavy snow shower now obscured the Prague Restaurant some few hundred meters distant.

"We learned," Gribkov said. "We beat them eventually."

"That we did," Soroka said and lifted by the filigreed cup holder to his lips. "That we did." Soroka straightened. "But I've come to review Operation ANADYR? How many know about the operation?"

General Gribkov splayed his hand. Four. "Of whom Colonel Velikovsky is one," the general said, indicating he who had poured the tea. "You will be number five."

"How much transport?"

"170 to 180."

"Why all the hush-hush for such a small operation?"

Gribkov made a swimming motion with his hands. 180 ships. "The secure vault is there. Colonel Velikovsky handwrote the plan. He will sit with you and answer any questions. Write your comments, then leave."

"Cuba?" Soroka said.

Colonel Velikovsky nodded. They exchanged blank looks, then Soroka looked down. He shifted the pages to get the slant of the handwriting.

Alexander had once studied an American vice-president, read his file, shook his hand, looked into his eyes. Henry Wallace, professor and plant biologist, competent apparently, unlike Stalin's favorite, Lysenko, whose firm handshake and steady gaze, said he prized honesty and forthrightness. He was a man sorely disappointed with his own, and whom Alexander Soroka utterly duped.

Somewhere, this Wallace had thought, there existed a gruff and honest man to whom the common man gave honest and unreserved respect. Soroka provided the man he sought in the Soviet Far East, in Magadan, the New Soviet Man — Sergei Goglidze, an NKVD executioner and thug. Wallace yearned to be gulled; Alexander accommodated. It had been as a theater performance for children.

The current American president was not this Wallace. Nikita Sergeevich judged Kennedy a piece of shit in a silk stocking. Well, that he may well be—the father was a gangster with a good tailor. The boy inherited the tailor; had he inherited the cunning? If the boy were a gangster—pretty wife and tailored suit, notwithstanding—he would require the gun pointed square between his eyes before he'd negotiate in good faith.

Khrushchev was between a rock and a hard place. Three gangs—Army, Party, and KGB—each wanted more money. The First Secretary had foresworn execution as a management strategy. Alexander Soroka did not know what the Soviet-American correlation of forces was, but he suspected the American Secretary of Defense was telling a truth and that Khrushchev was lying; The Strategic Rocket Forces could not hit a fly in the eye at 5000 kilometers nor find its ass with both hands. Long ago, Alexander had employed sleight of hand to entertain his peasant worker-students so that they would master dull-as-dirt Communist doctrine. Too successfully, Alexander thought. Nikita Sergeevich figured he could work magic.

He wrote two and one-half pages in elegant Russian describing the plan's shortfall; The concept of operations was a piece of shit.

The day's rain had cleared the Moscow sky, cleaned the air, and washed the trees, so each oak leaf seemed to carry an electrical charge illuminating it from within. The evening sun skittered along the crowns glistened the raindrops, dusk settling among the trunks. The grime upon the faces of her carved wooden figures had streaked them about and below the eyes, making Greek masks, painted with pain as if almost freed of the long-ago incantation, but not. Who had carved them? None seemed to know. A Baba Jaga had arrested them, taken them from their loved ones, and cast their spirits to wander the endless taiga.

Ekaterina spied the Bashkir in black leather jacket leaning against an oak. In the direction where the cafe, she sensed a presence.

The voice came from behind, harsh, the words enunciated with care, "Good evening, Katyusha."

She gasped at his ugliness, her hand to her mouth, then caught herself, apologizing "I'm sorry. You had come to the apartment." He waved a hand. 'It's nothing.' Nichevo. He motioned for permission to sit. "Please, sit beside me," she said.

He who had returned from 'beyond the seventh sea' looked upon her, then the surroundings—the monastery and its reflection in the still waters of Ostankinskij Pond, a grove of trees with new leaves, the carved figures. The silence endured.

"Papa," she said, then repeated the unfamiliar word, "Father?"

He turned his single eye upon her, and it made her uncomfortable, afraid. He had become one with the carved figures, despairing, worn, features dissolved. But his single eyes was of the living, frightening, seeking vengeance. Upon whom? From whom to exact retribution?

He was the brother of a kind and gentle Alexander. He was her father, Nickolai, who had once been handsome, had played Macbeth on the stage, a Bolshevik, his eyes once blazing with lust for the bright and shining future, where pogroms were no more, and all were as...Jesus?

His gaze returned to her, the eye of the vengeance-filled Old Testament prophet cooled, the shadow of a smile rose to the lizard face, its texture like a hillside of cooling lava. He withdrew a cigarette from the packet, searched the inside pocket of his stained suit to find a small box of matches. He exhaled smoke into the still air, and a smile rose to her features as if her father were a human-inhuman character from an American comic book, and she suppressed it.

"I survived to see you dance, Ekaterina ...Katya...Katyusha. "He articulated each diminutive carefully on deformed lips as if seeking a lost time. "When you were born, my beautiful, I heard...one got news somehow in prison...Boris Andreevich... the director of Poltava Theater, had just been arrested and told me. I was filled with joy, and I knew you would dance, "Giselle."

"I grew, papa. I'm sorry. I am too big. The boys can lift me, but they can't carry me very far. I am nothing special."

"You are beyond beautiful, like your mother."

"Thank you, father. But bigger."

"The dream sustained me, my child." He closed and opened his lizard eye. Dream, nightmare, dream. Such as he had made the revolution, created the dream, which became a nightmare. "The dream sustained me," He repeated. "You are a Komsomol, eh, Katyusha?"

"It is how we get into the university, Nickolai Nikolaevich." Oh, God, what should she call him, he who might be her father? Comrade Soroka? Nicholai Nikolaevich? Father or Papa? Kolya?

"I was once a big shot in the Komsomol," said the specter. "Commissar for Agitation in Poltava Oblast." I knew how to arrange a spectacle." An expression appeared on his ravaged face—proud, chest-beating, Russian, not Hebrew. "That was something then, district commissar. Today, they are time-servers, Pharisees." He looked back into the branches of the budding oaks, a distant gaze cooling his smoldering eye. "In 1931, we were sent into the countryside to speed collectivization...to requisition grain. The Kulaks were hiding food... starving the revolution. My adjutant was a peasant. We found the wheat, rye, and oats. He could smell it buried ten feet underground, hidden in the forest, cached in the river. How could us city slickers know the difference between seed grain and hoarded grain? We took everything. When winter came... no, even sooner. We knew we had succeeded when they began to die—rich, middle, and poor peasants—by the thousands." He waved the vision away.

"Papa, the past is past. That was the Cult of Personality. We are approaching Communism now. The Report of the 22nd Party Congress says Communism is nigh." Slogans spilled from her lips as if she might build from them a wall of words against the Bolshevik flying squads, the Tsarist Oprichnina, the Mongol's steppe calvaries, the irruptions of the foul spirits.

The father returned his gaze to the daughter, then to his cigarette, a curl of smoke hanging in the still air.

"Had you ever seen a picture of me...before...when I was young?"

She bent her head, the trees diffusing behind tears. "No, Nickolai Nikolaevich, there are no pictures."

"No family portraits perhaps? Irina loved her camera...passionate photographer. I had bought her a German camera, a Leica, I think. Does she still have the camera?"

Ekaterina nodded. There had been an album of the dance troupe on tour, pictures here and there removed, in a few group photos, a face scratched out. The cancers had to be cut from the body. They metastasized. Stalin, the Ossetian seminarian, destroyed root and branch the enemies of the people, like Xerxes, King of Persia, and his Jewish consort, Esther, destroyed root and branch the family of her enemy, Haman. Death arrived in a black car, a crisply uniformed NKVD soldier with Tatar's eyes driving. She wiped the tear from her cheek. Besides her sat he whom they named 'vermin,' cursed in school rhyme and child song, gazing at the wooden statue of a father, a thoughtful daughter against his knee looking up in adoration. Long gray lines of prisoners, heads lowered, eyes to the ground, slid across her vision.

Silence had grown between them. "Would you like tea?" she interrupted. "There is a tea house there, through the woods."

He lit another cigarette, his gaze fixed on the carving. "The Germans saved my life. I was imprisoned on the outskirts of Kiev. A decision was sent down. Instead of executing the prisoners, we were given a choice—volunteer for the suicide battalion or be shot, a choice to die under the open sky or in a dank execution cell." He spit on the ground. "It was the least they could do for loyal and dedicated

Bolshevik, don't you think?" A shaft of sunlight penetrated the oak canopy. Ekaterina nodded dazedly. It was the least they could do. "We were given rifles, one for every five, our rags for uniforms." He snorted. "Some even had shoes." He lifted his face to the sun, breathed deeply, bitterness gone. He had become the Russian soldier, no longer an enemy of the people, but the finest son of the motherland marching resolutely forward into battle with the enemy. He lowered his head and continued speaking, now to the ground. "I became a political officer of a suicide battalion. Political officer!" He crushed the cigarette pack in his hand. "I was their rabbi, the priest!" After another pause, he continued. "The Hermes knew what they were doing that day. They passed us through their defensive line; when the main attack was launched...well, the Nazis had them zeroed in and wiped 'em out...probably 8000 men. I pushed through to the Pripyat marshes, joined up with the partisans and fought there until the Red Army passed through."

"But why the Gulag?"

"Who knows? Because I was the commissar of a penalty battalion and didn't die? We partisans were loaded together with Soviet prisoners of war. We were divided at the Railroad junction in Vladimir, the Russian POWs were sent north to Norilsk, we politicos for some reason were interned in the Suzdal."

"Suzdal," she murmured.

His body alert, sniffing the air like a rat. The Asiatic had signaled. "A white carnation. You'll receive a white carnation. Go to the Metro station written on rice paper the Saturday following the week you are given the message, then eat the rice paper." And her 'father' was gone.

"So the name of the operation, Marshall Biryozhev." Alexander Soroka said.

"Anadyr."

"And you are the operational planner, Colonel Vasilevsky?" Alexander asked. "Why is that?"

"My handwriting is good."

"This is a joke?" Colonel Vasilevsky did not respond. The operations plan was in three handwritten copies. This was how it was done during the Great Fatherland War. Responsible officers read the plan and memorized their actions; no notes were to be taken. Alexander thrummed the table, stood, and went to the samovar to add hot water to his tea. "Cuba?"

The Marshall nodded.

"Impossible," Soroka said. "Can we fiddle with the timelines?"

"I doubt it."

"The Americans know a great deal about our missiles," Soroka murmured. The American war secretary had publicly laid out the Soviet missile order of battle some months earlier for domestic political consumption. They had campaigned on the missile gap; there had been none. The American war secretary had pacified his political opponents and agitated the Soviet General Staff. Nikita's erstwhile 'allies' now knew the Soviet Union's weak position. The First Secretary's enemies had tried once to remove him, but the Army had sided with Khrushchev. If Khrushchev did not placate the Army, next time they would oppose him. Nikita's fate was Alexander's fate. There would be no expanded apartment; no foreign service assignment for Ekaterina.

"Where are these things being emplaced? How many Cubans live around there?"

"There can be no flaws," Biryozov pronounced. There was a balance in deception planning—time versus attention to detail versus security. There were always mistakes. The enemy must eventually detect the inevitable flaws.

"An increased tempo of activity tips the enemy to increase his reconnaissance. A simple soldier smokes a cigarette at the wrong time or the wrong place and the enemy to question the deception story. The Cubans are no problem. We'll plant the truth among them." There are spies or security lapses or compromised codes, or a stupid-ass soldier falls in love with the wrong pussy. Moving a division twenty miles undetected through a forest had failed often enough. Two-hundred ships sailing 8000 miles over the ocean..." Alexander gasped at the thought, "The ships pass through the Straits of Bosporus? Why not ship the missiles from Vladivostok through the Panama Canal?"

Marshall Biryozov waved impatiently. "It's been decided. Make it work." He spilled a drop of tea on a document. Colonel Vasilievsky hurried forward with his handkerchief to dry the paper.

A light summer wind gusted into Ekaterina's hair, swirled her skirt as she exited the Kitai-Gorod metro station. The Bashkir stood opposite at the entrance of one narrow and ancient passages to the merchant's section of the medieval city. He moved off amidst the disgorged passengers. She trailed behind several tens of meters following him into a passage, then another until it dead-ended at a small courtyard. Was this all necessary? He had disappeared, but a door to the left was open. She entered, descended a set of stairs where another passage lay to the right. Dim bulbs spaced at 20-meter intervals faded away, faint pinpricks, continuing perhaps only in her imagination. The air was damp and close, the walls closing upon her, and she struggled against wisps of claustrophobia pressing her throat. She sensed distant footsteps and followed.

"Here, child," the voice said. She jumped. The gloved hand found her elbow. "This way."

They passed into what she sensed as a vestibule, and then through the second heavy iron door. She gasped. After some moments, "I have no words..." she said, but the Bashkir had disappeared. The room was large, well-lit, though two doorless dark passages led off to the left. Within, Brocade hung on the walls; Indian carpets covered the floor. Floor and table lamps lit the room and carpet to advantage, but the ceiling was high and dark. The far wall was bookshelves before which a ladder on wheels leaned, its top-end unseen in the dimness. She looked around. A cloud of smoke rose from a high-backed chair in the French provincial style, and she felt her features twist in fear, for there sat Koschei the Deathless, he who might be her father.

"Tea?" he said. He indicated an ornate Indian divan. "Sit," he said as if tasting on his tongue words he had never spoken, "my child." He leaned forward, the light illuminating a face absent features save a single glistening eye.

"How...?" she said.

He waved off the question. "There are dachas in the Moscow forest which make this look like an izba." He obtained these treasures as one gained treasure. A massive

Russian man appeared our of one dark passage, a large silver samovar service in his hands and set it on a table before Nikolai, nodded, and left. He who had delivered the tea had been the Moscow policeman who had approached her that long ago cold morning at an Ostankino trolley stop.

"The was how the aristocracy lived before the revolution," she murmured.

"Life returned to normal as it had once so senselessly sundered."

"Pasternak," she whispered. "How...?" She who could chatter for hours in three languages could at this moment find but a single word. "Momma's ill, Nikolai Nikolaevich," she finally said. Nikolai Nicklaevich gazed into her face as if he were at the Tretyakov Gallerie puzzling over a Chagall or a Rembrandt self-portrait. Of course, Ekaterina understood that men thought her beautiful, suffered the gaze and approaches of foolish boys, yet the single glistening eye unnerved. "Momma's very ill," she repeated.

But he had begun to speak, first in single words, then the fragments joining, difficult at first to puzzle out, spoken through lips rigid with scar tissue.

"We are slaves in the land of the damned," he said. "The Tsar organized a pogrom here and there, killed some Jews, then the Cossacks would arrive and kill some Russians. It all worked out. The Bolsheviks believed in equality; they killed everyone." The single eye glistened. "As did I. The NKVD sergeant had emptied his Markarov...it had a nine-shot clip... into a column of us prisoners. He walked away, cursing himself. He had only killed eight. I then had vowed to kill Sergeant Larionov." He snorted, startling her. "What should happen, but an Army detachment arrived and shot the bastard." The eye squinted upwards as if peering through a keyhole into the past. "Bunch of the others too. It gave me some pleasure, but not as much as I would have hoped. A slice of black bread would have pleased me more."

A barely sensed humming had become loud, the room grown hot, her brow sweat-covered. She remembered the long lines of prisoners marching through knee-high snow, their eyes fixed on the foot rags of the prisoner before them. Socialism could not possibly allow such cruelty. Yes, yes, mistakes could be made. Trotskyite saboteurs would slip iron filings into the machine's grease cups, even becoming guards, right? Her heart pounded so that she felt her ribs could not contain her pain. She had not seen them. She squinted, as if into the past.

"Ekaterina, my darling, you haven't touched your tea."

She lifted the tea glass from the table to finger its filigreed silver. The wealth within Ali Baba's cave disappeared into whiteness as if a blizzard has swept into the room. Out of the whiteness appeared long lines of ragged gray men marching towards and over her. The glass fell from her fingers.

Danton waited in a alcove passage in the Revolutionary Square Metro Station, where Roman Baranov joined him. Roman set his issue Soviet Army officer brief case aside Danton's, who nodded to the matching briefcases. "I've reworked your paper...incorporated the criticisms. Looks good to me."

"Good, good," Ramon Baranov smiled. "I should read it before I turn it in."

"We get assignments in August," Danton said. "When are you going to get me together with Ekaterina?"

Roman grimaced running his hand over his face. "Dunno. Soroka seems to have some sort of hard-on against you. If he finds out I've got you together with his little precious, he might fuck over my assignment to Berlin." The old woman jostled him hard. "What the fuck, grandma?" The crone had shoved Roman against the marble pedestal, and rubbed the nose of the statue of the bronze dog.

"For luck, sonny," she cackled and raised her broom to his nose. "Don't looks as if need any, rich boy," she said, picking up her trash bag and moving on.

The Revolutionary Square Metro Station was populated with human-sized heroic statues. The young men had chosen to stand next to the border guard and his dog, which was said to provide luck if its nose was touched.

Danton smiled. "It's typed. You had better read it a thousand times. They are going to question you out the ass."

"Yea, yea, I'll read it. What's it about?"

"Technical camouflage in a desert."

"What the fuck...We don't have deserts in the Soviet Union."

"Read a geography book. Kazakhstan?"

"Can't get a piece of ass any place else?" Roman moved the conversation back to renegotiating the terms of the original agreement—introduction to the Ekaterina of Suzdal.

"She's not that kind."

"They're all that kind," Roman replied. "And I'm warning you, country boy. You'd better get on her, then get away. She's bad news. She has some Chinks tailing her. She's some kind of hard-currency whore."

Danton suppressed his urge to fling Roman into the path of the on-coming train. Drunks pitched onto the tracks every other day. Oddly enough, that Roman held the twenty-page tactical deception plan Danton had written in his brief case saved his life. Though Roman the Kulak deserved to die, Danton would have to answer questions.

Chairman of the Presidium of the Supreme Soviet of the USSR, Leonid I. Brezhnev wrapped General Professor Anton Gastilovich in a massive bear hug while pulling close Soviet Army Colonel (Reserve) and consultant to the International Department of the Communist Party of the Soviet Union, Alexander Soroka. The three, veterans of the 17th and 40th Armies, had the war in common. "My dear comrades, we'd knock a few back, but we have business, then I have a meeting with Kunayev...he's Party Chairman of the Kazakh Communist Party now..." Kunayev was Brezhnev's man. "We need more cotton, much more cotton...."

"You're a busy man, Leonid," Soroka said. Brezhnev was ambitious, moving his people into key positions.

"Way too busy." Brezhnev indicated his desk with three dozen telephones, each a direct line to some influential Soviet leader. Ostentatious consumption was discouraged in the puritanical Soviet Union, but the more telephones on your desk, the more critical your role to the Socialist undertaking. "There's hardly time to fart. So, down to business. Prognosis, Sasha?"

"I am worried," Alexander Soroka said.

"This is different than normal, Sasha?" Brezhnev laughed.

Gastilovich raised a finger. "The Americans are building 1000 silo-bases Minutemen missiles across the American plains. If we don't counter them, the Capitalists will be in an advantageous position for a surprise attack."

Soroka spread his hands. "Which shows how deception improperly conceived bites you in the ass. Surprise attack and correlation of forces were phrases freighted with meaning, terror even, to the war generation. Untold Soviet millions had perished when Hitler's surprise attack set the Soviet Army on its heels unable to stabilize the front until winter froze the German tanks. Each of the three has seen frozen fields so thick with the dead that it seemed one could walk a kilometer without touching the earth. Stalin had executed the statisticians who had conducted the immediate post-war census. "Nikita bragged that we were deploying ICBMs like piroshki; No one ..." The actor Alexander paused for effect. "but the Americans believed him and voila, they have deployed one-thousand Minuteman missiles."

"What was that American unit like our 40th Army, Sasha?" Brezhnev diverted the conversation. The conversation was running askew.

"The US Army 23rd Headquarters Special Troops. It functioned much like our 40th. The British had a similar unit... I've forgotten the designation. I have their unit histories if you're interested."

"When I retire, Sasha, when I retire," Brezhnev waved. General Gastilovich looked up. He had not known this fact.

Another phone rang on the desk; Brezhnev glanced, noted its position, his patience nearing its end. "But I repeat, Sasha. What's your assessment of Vasilevsky's plan?"

"It's a piece of shit."

"That's short, but not sweet, Sasha." Leonid rotated his hand. "More detail. What do you mean?"

"The Americans will uncover the ship movements. They will think we're up to no good. I propose that we tell the truth that we're moving missiles to Cuba. We have nothing to hide. The American hands are dirty. They invaded once. We are defended the poor and mistreated."

General Gastilovich raised an eyebrow, non-commital. He'd seen truth work deception miracles, but he straddled the fence. His position was only a temporary discomfort. "It is already decided," Brezhnev said. "Make it work."

"Hey, Verochka, wait a moment," Roman Baranov called down the dim hallway. Vera pressed the elevator button several times as if her impatience might bring it up faster.

"What?" she said as he came up to her.

"My dear friend, you treat me so suspiciously. What have I done to you?"

"You are a serial liar and a dishonest son of a bitch. You lie because you savor the taste of shit on your tongue. But I always know."

"Am I lying now?" He straightened his shoulders, froze his face, and set his eyes on the framed poster of Lenin.

"Your lips are still moving, jerk."

"Hey, woman's intuition is powerful stuff." He relaxed his face into a smile. "I have a favor to ask."

"When hell freezes over with proof provided by two honest Russian men."

"You make it hard." Vera pressed the elevator button several more times, causing the ceiling light to flicker. "I still have Salem cigarettes."

"I don't smoke."

"I have a friend who is hopelessly in love with your friend, Ekaterina. He wants to meet her."

"No."

"What do I have to do? I admit it, I'm a jerk, but he's a fool. A good woman can manage him."

"What do you owe him, Roman? You don't do squat without payback."

"Until the arrival of Communism...next year or the year after... we remain socialist. We don't trade in money, we trade in favors. I owe him one."

"Get fucked."

"You volunteering? I still have one lot of West German prophylactics."

"Screw yourself."

"Ai, you have a dirty mouth. C' mon, Verochka. The son of a bitch is in love. Your Katya can end or save his life, as she wishes. It that such a big thing?"

"Tell you what..." Vera searched through her rich collection of epithets but realized there was no insulting Roman. "Bring him to the summer garden on Saturday. I'll look him over."

"Let's take the stairs," Roman said. "We, the nomenklatura, the vanguard of the proletariat, have defective elevators. There is something wrong with that."

"You are a spoiled brat is what you are." She slapped the back of his head as he pushed open the stairway door.

CHAPTER TWENTY-TWO

"Out, out of here, you beggar." The bum shied as the heavy-set woman gripped the collar of his tattered army greatcoat and bounced him off the door jam.

"Captain...Major...' the hideous toad croaked. "...Colonel Soroka!" The interloper was drunk. His back to the commotion, Alexander turned from his conversation with the French photo-journalist, his wife and daughter at a window table in Moscow's Prague Restaurant on Old Arbat.

"Stop, Sofia," He rose, murmuring to his table companions. *"Un de mes garçons...de la Guerre...gravement blessé."*

"C'est dur, n'est-ce pas..." The woman touched Alexander's wrist, then motioned him to his duty, repeating, *"C'est dur."*

"There's work for such as these..." Sofia loosed but did not release her grip, watching her catch suspiciously, ready to bang him once more against the wall. "...in the new lands. If he drove a tank, he can drive a tractor." Sofia Petrovna, the day manager of the ritzy restaurant and night club, brooked no nonsense from veterans. She had been a Moscow fire warden the winter of 41, had stomped out two incendiary bombs herself, had done her part for victory over Fascism. Veteran reunions, emotional and turbulent Russian affairs, were taking place with increasing frequency, indeed, but there were leeches about wearing discarded uniforms, and she'd have none of it. During the war, there was discipline. A summary execution now and then puts an end to a great deal of shirking.

"Come, sit, Sergeant, there's a park bench." Alexander put his arm across the bum's shoulder and guided him to a street bench in]view of the clients. The French couple had watched a Soviet war film or two, the emotional scene where the hero-captain did not separate himself from the post-war lives and welfare of his men. Alexander pressed his face close to the bum's face. "Kolya, what the fuck are you doing?"

Nickolai's single eye bored into Alexander. "Wolf Larionov's kid is sniffing around Katya."

"You sniffing your cocaine?"

"The Larionov that's your student."

"Larionov, the engineer? You're full of crap. How many Larionov's are there in the Soviet Union? A Million?"

"Volk. NKVD...Suzdal," Nickolai rasped. "I vowed to kill him, but the Army got the SOB first."

"That was then. Now is now. Young Larionov has killed no one."

"Get rid of him or I will."

Alexander grasped his brother at the shoulder to look in into that single eye. "We are so innocent, eh, Kolya?"

"Get rid of him," the brother repeated. Nikolai Isaakovich wretched himself from Alexander Isaakovich's arm and stumbled away. The Moscow policeman eyed the bum, tapping his club against his palm. An Asiatic youth in leather jacket flipped a match into the street and moved off after Nickolai Soroka.

The sky, visible through an opening in the crowns of the oak and linden, was clear save for a few towering cumulonimbi. A movement of air rustled the leaves and skittered across the pond waters to disturb the V-wake of a swan and two cygnets. A summer cafe had been fashioned in the shore clearing, tables around a dance floor, a five-piece combo playing waltzes, polkas and now and then a surreptitious forbidden foxtrot. Dancers, mostly elderly, circled the floor. At the water's edge, shaded beneath a Russian elm, a table of young men and women, among them a few older men; bearded, thus artists, flung arms and pointed fingers, shoulder-to-shoulder in the warmth and intimacy of the Russian kitchen, arguing, the remains of dishes strewn like a battlefield diorama. Here and there, vodka bottles stood upright, dazed, and depleted survivors. Over the din of music and voices, Danton sensed his name being called.

"Danton," Roman Baranov shouted and waved across the clearing, "Over here!"

Danton paused, the memory in black and white, another full table, the soft hands of women touching his face, the heavy laborer hand tousling his hair, loving noise, and smells caressing his soul. He inhaled to fill the emptiness within his chest, making his way through the moving couples.

"Pickled onions and potato salad remaining...vodka or beer?" Roman slapped his shoulder, his voice loud above the din, turning to address the table while their attention remained on the newcomer. "My friend and comrade, Danton Volkov Larionov. I will bring him around in due course." Friendly faces nodded in his direction, hands waved in greeting, before returning the issue of the moment. Danton scanned the table, looked at a young blond woman at the water's edge, subtracting a decade from her age. It wasn't the storyteller. "Well, Danton, at least I am happy to see you."

The red-headed woman in a long skirt and tight short-sleeved white sweater, her nipples suggested—like American sluts at a Rock and Roll concert—watched him. Russian women wore 'Khrushchyovki,' the heavy corset and bra so named because the contraption formed them into the image and shape of Nikita Sergeevich. He drove the thought from mind; he was not a complete idiot; she had been Ekaterina's companion at the April ball. As in a fairy tale, he would answer the riddle or his picked bones would decorate the witch's gatepost.

This Vera's expression changed from suspicious to amused. "Sit here," she commanded. "I've seen you around Moscow."

"I'm not sure," Danton said.

"One more lie, Danton' son of Wolf' Larionov, and your future is bleak indeed," Her smile was not a smile. Roman smirked, shifted his chair between Vera and Danton, searched for a bottle opener, then with his teeth removed the bottle cap. "Go talk with Neizvestny," she commanded. Roman shrugged, handed the beer to Danton, saluted. Danton felt the center of the crosshairs on his throat and descend to his heart. Of such women as these, the Soviet Army made snipers.

"I saw you with Ekaterina at Gagarin's affair, then once at the Teahouse on Myasnitskaya," Danton said.

"How do you know Ekaterina?"

"She stayed with the Ukrainian Women's Cooperative in Suzdal a few months in 1953."

"She told me. You are in love with her?"

"She told stories."

"Answer me directly, Danton' Son of Wolf," she said, stressing the patronymic, "Misdirection irritates me mightily, and I am beginning to take a dislike to you." Danton felt the blow; the interrogator backhanded the suspect. She seemed to share the thought for though she did not smile, her visage softened, not with kindness, but a sort of amusement. "You peasant boys...as did your mother and your grandmother and great-grandmother...tell stories. Can you read and write, peasant boy? Suzdal was a gulag. Your father was either a prisoner or a guard. Which?"

"Guard."

"NKVD officer or enlisted?"

"He started as an enlisted, a major when he died."

"How?"

"Suicide."

"When?"

"53."

Vera nodded. Recent Russian history was oral, unwritten. Her family was military; In 1953 the General Staff visited upon the NKVD the purge the NKVD visited upon the General Staff in 1938. Some few may indeed have committed suicide. "How many innocents did he murder?"

"The mark of Cain disfigures us all, doesn't it?"

"Well, listen to you, Danton, Son of Wolf," she said, enunciating his patronymic, "raised Orthodox, are we?"

"During the war, Grandmother attended...and attended...and attended mass; thus, did I. To answer your question, I've murdered no one." Danton's obfuscation seemed to bemuse Vera. Spoken or not, those come of age after Stalin was either birthed in a sea of blood or born innocent, as they chose to believe.

"Verochka, dear..." The bearded man stood at her chair, "Masha and I must leave. You'll come to the exhibition at the Manezh?"

"Ernst, I wouldn't miss it."

"Life's getting better."

"Yes, ...sweeter." There was irony in the back and forth, variations on words printed on posters hung on every Vladimir-Suzdal factory, school, and collective farm social center. It was a phrase from a 1935 Stalin speech; the 1932-33 famine, six to twelve-million dead. "Best of luck with the exhibition."

Vera watched Ernst and Masha chatting and greeting as they cross the dance floor, then returned to Danton, her face hard. "What are you thinking?" It was the interrogator's backhand. Danton flinched. "Look, Danton, you mean less than nothing to me, but I owe Roman a favor...but it's small this favor. I'll consider whether I introduce you with the Storyteller."

He nodded. Vera was a Russian woman; if he crossed her, she'd gut him. Vulnerable and helpless would be his facade.

Ekaterina stepped out of her shoes to lay next to her sleeping mother, closing her eyes to avoid speaking with her fathers. Fathers. What would it have been like to have had either intense, opinionate, and righteous man around during her childhood?

She would not have had Bukhara. The sun always shone, the skies deep blue, the hills voluptuous, the desert horizon changing color minute to minute. And when you brought your eyes to its street, a chaos of hues the width of color spectrum pleased your eyes.

She smelled her mother, the vanilla scent she favored, like the markets of Bukhara. The Communists allowed peasant markets during the war, smells of such intensity as to challenge the colors of the desert and the mountains for the impression they made upon the child's senses.

And when Irina, the Ballerina, her mother appeared during breaks in her tours of the front. It was as if a tiny fairy in white like a tuft of thistle, cool on hot. The Bashkir women would show the queen her mother Ekaterina's teeth and nose and legs. "Healthy. She grows like a weed." Then, the women displayed Ekaterina's feet, for the child's foot foretold how tall the child would grow. There was much shaking of the heads." I fear the poor men won't be able to lift her." Twittering.

Russian women, wives of powerful men, passed the war far from the front or managed the cotton gins and weaving plants, who gossiped how the prima-ballerina allowed uncivilized slant-eyes who'd collaborate with the Fascists if given a chance to raise her child. But the women did no more than chatter as if a wizard who lived in the distant foothills might suddenly arrive, for the ballerina had friends too.

So Amenya had raised her, and Ekaterina was grateful. To protect her, three—Irina, the Ballerina, Alexander, the Magician, and Amenya, the cunning peasant, had conspired against the gods, faced unrelenting danger, endured scalding fury. They lied and plotted and deceived that she might survive and thrive. She fell asleep to the sound of her fathers' murmuring.

Kolya sniffed the soft breeze that wafted into the room to sway the embroidered Ukrainian curtain and lift a hair fallen across Irina's forehead. Mother and daughter slept. Irina had not joined the Party; she couldn't be bothered; she would dance to advance Communism. Her parents were Uniat, townspeople who traveled abroad. Irina had studied in Warsaw, performed in Paris and Berlin, and returned to Poltava. There, two tall, gawky and intense Jewish boys from the Pale dedicated to the practical and consuming task of building Communism and inculcating Socialist culture in the crude peasantry, uninterested in frilly and refined women. They were rude and abrupt; with a sad and elegant glance, she laid him low.

He escorted her across the Great Square of Kiev, and he blurted out his proposal. In the noonday light lightening struck. Irina accepted. In those heady days, crisis was constant. The Communist Party ordered him here and there, food and fuel always in short supply. She asked for little; little by little, his faith in Communism weakened; his faith in Irina firmed.

Those who purged were purged. The Terror with its random violence—arrests, disappearances, mass murder-- paused. It paused as the Plague paused, flaring anew, killing those whom it had previously spared. Bukharin was executed in 1938. None were secure; all waited. All save Stalin expected the German invasion; people hoarded salt and flour and sugar and tea. Refugees told tales of what they did to Polish Communists and Jews. It was unclear what the Germans did to the children of Communists but not what they did to the children of Jews. Nikolai and Alexander arranged a summer and fall Poltava Ballet Company tour of the far east. Nikolai was arrested in April.

He was now old. He could do a few things.   Alexander had nodded off. Behind his mask, Nicolai returned Ekaterina's smile.   Nickolai and Alexander, two Jewish gangsters, one in the Party and the other not in the Party. Next year in Israel, eh? Was it a Russian thing or Jewish thing this imminence of Armageddon? One could rarely go wrong in Russia foreseeing the end of the world.

Irina Soroka woke, watched through half-closed eyes those whom she loved, who loved her, and awaited the next wave of excruciating pain rising from beneath her ribs. Was it cancer, or was it heartache? Long ago, Diaghilev had offered her a room and a place in the corps de ballet in the Ballets Russes. She had refused. Makarov had hinted at prima ballerina at the Kiev, and she had returned with the Soviet State Ballet from Paris. She shifted in bed, and sensed her men start and half-rise, but felt her daughter asleep at her side.

She made a decision.   She had made decisions. Arrangements had been made. Irina wondered at the deceptive flexibility of the Russian verb. With the simple addition of the 'sya' suffix, one changed from actor to audience, acting or acted upon. She danced, and they watched; she watched, and they danced. It had been as if she had stepped into the little boat on that slip of a stream in Ekaterina's Botanical Gardens–– the Yauza River, was it? And rowed, but the current speeded up, tossed the boat tossed hither and yon— to the Moscow River, and the Volga and to the Caspian Ocean. Her beloveds were thrown from the ship, disappearing and reappearing, now a hand, now a terror-stricken face in the boiling waters. Balanchine vowed he would leave his wife, Geva, for her but she understood that he was a snake, and she would be cast aside when another Russian beauty appeared. So it was. He did leave Geva, but for someone else, whom he also cheated on.

A wave of pain rendered her face rigid and eyes open. She shook her head, no, and they sat back, alert. The pain subsided. She looked around. Alexander had obtained the second apartment; Nickolai had furnished it. Irina smiled at her husbands, and they were relieved. Ah, she thought, a Russian woman should have two husbands to have a life appropriate to her station. You are the lucky one, aren't you? When Irina met the Soroka brothers, everything was possible, the future limited by one's imagination. If they could imagine it, so it would be.

They had imagined the dream but not foreseen the nightmare. What was it about the Russian Intelligentsia that inured them to evidence? Here Nickolai and Alexander, the commissar and the impresario, sitting in tatters before the dying ballerina, who stayed true to beauty as she understood it. For some reason, the Communists, crude peasants who wouldn't have understood a pas de deux from a pair of deuces, honored ballet. Ballet was safe. Fairy tales were suspect. Who decided these things, she wondered.

The air fluttered the curtain and moved a wisp of her daughter's hair. She is more beautiful than I, she thought, and the ballerina gently reordered her child's lock and fell into a fitful sleep.

Irina opened her eyes, looked at her sleeping woman-child and waited until a wave of pain and nausea subsided. Medical care was free in the Soviet Union, and worth every kopek one paid. Ach, sardonic Jewish humor, she smiled inwardly; it'll be the death of me.

 She had cancer for the love of God. She had ducked and wove and charmed and ignored and danced herself crazy to survive and thrive, so like a Russian woman. She picked strategies to protect her child, deceptive, sometimes even truthful, always truthful in the deceptive world of dance. You thought the Bolsheviks were murderous back-stabbing thugs? Try dancing at the Bolshoi.

She had loved both these men, and one of them was Ekaterina's father, and she had married Nickolai, and Ekaterina came from God knows where, tall like her fathers, graceful and Ukrainian like her mother, a storyteller like no one on earth.

She signaled to her men, lifted a finger to her lip, gestured to approach. Each sprung from his chair. Ekaterina snuffled, shifted, brushed her hair away from her face and, still asleep, snuggled closer to her mother.

"Find a priest," Irina said. "I will make my confession." Alexander inhaled. "What is the Communist Party going to do, Sasha? Take away my party card?"

"It is difficult," said Alexander. He had moved heaven and earth to double their living space from 110 square meters. It was said that Marshall Zhukov wanted an Orthodox funeral; The Party denied his last request.

"It will happen," said Nikolai. "Which church?" Nikolai glanced at his brother. In 1957, the Communist Party had launched an anti-religious campaign which was now coming to a crescendo. Another bullet in the ammunition belt of his enemies. There was freedom to be had when one was labeled an enemy of the people; when one lived by white slavery, protection rackets, and corruption.

"A Father Tikhon lives in the shed behind the Cathedral of the Holy Trinity." She waved in the direction of the Ostankino Pond. "Go," Irina said and smiled the gentle smile of a Russian woman who sent fierce warriors to fetch her lunettes.

They stood in the hallway between Alexander's two apartments. "She needs to be in the hospital," Alexander said.

"They're hellholes," replied Nikolai.

"They're getting better," Alexander said.

"Life's gotten better... every day in every way."

"Some other day your sarcasm, Kolya."

"Stalin inspired us, don't you think?"

"She needs morphine," Alexander said, ignoring the jibe.

"It will kill her."

"She needs to be in the hospital to get it," said Alexander.

"She wants to stay here," Nikolai said. "I'll get it."

Alexander looked down at his hands, helplessness sagging his body. After some pause, Alexander spoke. "And a priest at the graveside."

Nikolai raised his hands, like a Jew of the Pale, in exasperation.

Nickolai gazed upon his ikon, the image which held his faith in the face of unspeakable suffering. She was dying. Irena, the slight, windborne like the dandelion; Irena, the strong, a steel beam against the whirlwind.

He had been the skilled dialectician, matching the brainiacs of the Bolshevik Party. Such was the intellectual that could fashion fact from the air, build edifice from mists the color of concrete, assured in the rightness of Communism as workers and peasants died by the tens of thousands.

Stalin, the Clumbsy, understood the dialectic: death ends it. The con men and murderers mouthed the slogans, memorized the incantations, disputed the intellectuals with such tools as they commanded—terror and hope. The pistol trumped the dialectic.

Nickolai smiled, the mask of scars unmoving. In the Gulag, he had become a gangster. To survive, this is what one did. He knew something about being a gangster. He had been a Bolshevik. He had loved to read Isaac Babel's Odessa Stories. He had first visualized Benjamin Krik, the Jewish Odessa gangster, through the Communist lens; Krik, the capitalist, to be destroyed. He came to emulate him. Kolya, the Bolshevik, turned gangster, a distinction without a difference.

Irina of the gods had descended to earth, chose Nickolai, the organizer, then, Irina, the survivor, took Alexander, the dreamer. She winced in her sleep, her breathing uneven. "She needs morphine," said Nikolai.

Alexander paused before the concierge window. The latter poured tea in her own sweet time, sipped, slowly pulled her log-book forward, and picked up the pencil. "And who is this?"

"Write one fucking stroke on that page, I'll cut your tits off," Nikolai rasped. She started, her enormous bosom rising to advance, looked into to the single enraged eye, and pulled back, her gaze widening to a scarred moonscape of a face, taking in the crude tattoos on his neck, the army greatcoat on a warm and sunny summer day. The pencil dropped.

"Sofiya...Hero of the Soviet Union...head wound," Alexander murmured. They exited the building into the courtyard.

A short man in workman's cap and overalls fell in behind. "Get morphine," Nikolai ordered in Yiddish. Two brothers moved off, one in good standing in the Party, the other in the underworld, each an adept in a world without laws, each in his own way a Jewish gangster, like Benya Krik in Isaac Babel's Odessa Tales.

"Momma," Ekaterina murmured. Irina felt the soft evening air waft across the bed, watched it move a strand of hair on her daughter's brow, flutter the girl's eyelash, open her eye. The young woman looked around. "How long have I slept? Where've your husbands?" she said and smiled.

"I've sent them on an errand. Let me look at you once more," Irina said. "Stand," she commanded. Ekaterina slid carefully off the bed and took the ballet third position. "Now, turn once." She pirouetted slowly, the tear sliding down her cheek. "Is there anything you want to ask me, my darling?"

"Oh, momma." Ekaterina dropped her pose and slid back next to her mother, the child now twice the size of the mother.

Irina, the Russian mother, made short work of the distracted child. "Ekaterina, I will be dead soon, and you will regret not learning secrets. Now, be practical. Your fathers and I, we Russians, have lived chaotic lives, haven't we? You wonder which, Sasha or Kolya, is your father? I don't know. Does it matter? I have loved both."

She exhaled. Ironic that the disease should strike her in the breast, which she, the ballerina, never had. That was not what men noticed. Her face, her eyes, her presence, this was what beguiled. She regarded her daughter once more. From whence came this beauty at her side, full-bodied and - breasted, tall and blond? The Ukrainian mother is always surprised at that which issues from the bony gate, the legacy of armies that had crisscrossed the vast steppe.

"You were an honorable woman, momma. I believe that."

"Nonsense. I was as honorable as I could be and still live, Ekaterina. Nikolai had been taken...arrested. Alexander had his suitcase packed, still free." Irina grimaced against the wave of pain as Ekaterina fluttered her hands, helpless. "Free? What a word? The Germans freed them all, didn't they? Only a Russian would understand. Instead of Russians murdering one another, the Germans took upon themselves the task, so we Russians could make our cause common. Ach, I can make no sense of it."

Murmur "Momma," was all Ekaterina could manage.

"Ekaterina, you are a storyteller, you can find more words than 'Oh, momma!' Now talk to me." Ekaterina smiled, the room swimming beyond her tears, and by a force of will, suppressed the question haunting her, but her mother read the words in the girl's eyes. "Does it matter? They both love you."

"And you know, Ekaterina, how much I loved you, don't you? I couldn't always be with you, but I did what I thought was best."

"I've lived a protected life. I am grateful."

"It will not always be so; I won't be there to protect you, to warn you, to unleash those..." Here, the ballerina smiled, "...those fierce Jewish warriors." In the twilight, they smiled.

"Darling, you are a storyteller. That's what you must do."

"Momma, that is my dream to study in England or France or Germany."

"Not in America?"

"Impossible," Ekaterina said.

"Well, then my dearest child, I will make your two fathers work on that. Aren't you glad I've organized so well your future?" She raised an eyebrow, and Ekaterina could see what made young men, Russian or Jewish, stupid in her presence. "You are beautiful, Ekaterina, but innocent. Have you yet made love to a man?"

"Momma, will you stop!"

"Do you think I am chilled, darling child, you blush so and heat the room?" she teased, then spoke firmly. "I was born to speak truth, but such truth as could be expressed in the curve of a wrist, the tilt of an arm..." She made some unseen motion in the darkness. "If the world survives this nonsense, I want you to move to the United States. I want you to find happiness. Leave this god-forsaken land. I wish I had followed Balanchine, but I would not have had you. I wish Nureyev god-speed. I will talk to your fathers, fierce men who will change the rotation of the earth for you. Now, I must sleep, my darling, but stay with me."

CHAPTER TWENTY-THREE

BOOK III

All autumn, the chafe and jar
Of nuclear war;
We have talked our extinction to death.
I swim like a minnow
Behind my studio window.

Robert Lowell, Fall 1961

The atomization of society within the hurricane of
Stalinism from which gangs, clans, tribes, mafias organized
themselves, associations based upon shared experience,
ethnicity, marriage, interests, formed themselves into bands
like serfs escaping into the wilds of the steppe, Cossacks
bands without law or tradition creating new traditions of
eternal verity. Some tribes throve while other were destroyed
root and branch, the few members as might have survived
sold into slavery in the markets markets on the Black Sea or

into the Gulag. It was a steppe tradition and in this the Bolsheviks revived their Mongol heritage.

Hebrew? Survive? Perhaps. Thrive. Never. A Communist? Survive? Perhaps. The Leningrad Party Organization were as consumed in Stalin's flames as those who opposed Moses in Sinai, consigned to wave burning censors in a volcanic landscape exuding methane gases. ;

All autumn, the chafe and jar
Of nuclear war;
We have talked our extinction to death.
I swim like a minnow
Behind my studio window.

Robert Lowell, Fall 1961

Ekaterina sat at a corner table of the Moscow Writer's Club. She had left instructions with the concierge to bring to her table he who, according to Vera, adored her. A tall, grey-haired gentleman approached her table, motioned her not to stand, and touched her cheek with the back of his fingers. "I convey my regrets, Ekaterina Alexandrova. Your mother was a treasure upon this earth."

"Thank you, Comrade Tvardovksky." She inhaled deeply as if providing room for her heart. "We had so little time."

"As do we all. I met your mother first in 1942 when she danced for the troops before Kharkov." Alexander Tvardovsky, editor of the literary journal, Novy Mir, and author of the soldier's epic in verse, Vasily Tyorkin, moved his craggy features into the semblance of a smile, seeming to look into the past. It had been the eve of the second battle of Kharkov. Marshall Timoshenko would launch his attack the following morning, break through the enemy lines, and retake Kharkov from the German 6th Army. "She danced on a stage set on oil drums with two accordions playing Tchaikovsky. The ten thousand in the audience and I fell in love with her." The Germans allow the attack to advance, counterattacked, enveloped the offensive, and three-hundred thousand Soviet soldiers perished. "And why is our young beauty sitting alone?"

"I am meeting a boy I had known in Suzdal."

"Suzdal? I had not known. Irina also lived there?"

"No, just me...a short time...in the summer of 1953. Grandmother had returned to Poltava but didn't know what she would find. I was left with women's goose and sheep cooperative, a Ukrainian collective that had been stranded in Suzdal...from Poltava Oblast."

"Ah," He said. The oddest things happened in that caldron, unfathomable loss and, on some odd and rare occasion, a thing of sweetness. "And you were happy there?"

Ekaterina paused a moment, thinking, then said, "Yes, on the whole, yes..."

He smiled at her pause. It was how the Russian confronted a happy memory. It was stolen, undeserved, to be punished for being cherished. Tvardovsky's father, a landless soldier, came to own four cows. He perished, a kulak. "Katya, darling, Send me one of your short tales, 5-600 words...in the old language, but on a contemporary theme. I'll find a place for it." He raised his hand, stopping her protestation. "Enough. Just send it. I'll tell you whether it's good enough. So, tell me about the young man."

"I'll introduce you." She shivered, straightening her sweater over her shoulders, brought her tea to her lips before setting it back. She half stood, then sat, raised her hand to wave, struggling with memories both warm and anxiety-filled. "There he is."

Danton Volkov Larionov stood to the side of the entrance door in a mismatched and ill-fitting suit that blended with the dismal Soviet curtains so that for a moment he appeared to be a blond head wearing a tie and white shirt but without a torso. The concierge stood at his elbow, prepared to escort him out, were no one to claim him.

Ekaterina signaled that Danton was her guest. He looked much the same, save that he was no longer a teen. She had been afraid of him in Suzdal. On the meadow beneath the medieval town's towers and turrets, cupolas, bells, and walls, this hard-faced youth with a fishing pole scared off some a dozen young thugs, but as if he were taking her for his own. She diverted him with a fairy tale. All through the summer, she fussed the Ukrainian women for tales, so that when Danton, the Brutal appeared, she had a new story, like Scheherazade. She learned little of him. He had lost an uncle and his mother in the war, his father often absent. Always afraid, She had over time cajoled his story of loss, surmised his loneliness and came to sympathize, but still fear him, as if giving wolf meat that he not devour her.

"I leave you with your friend, Katya," Aleksandr said. "Remember, send me a story."

"Sit, Danton," she said. He stood at attention before her. "Please sit down." He thrust the bouquet forward, then leaned back, anxious, watching her face for a response. It was ludicrous. "I bought them from a Georgian vendor. It's all I could find. I'm sorry. You don't like white carnations?"

"No, no, Danton Volkov," Ekaterina started speaking, took a breath, brought her hands to her cheeks to form a smile. "No, no, Danton Volkov, I am so pleased. I don't often receive flowers. Thank you so much, I am so pleased...surprised...really pleased," She chattered on. "I'll find a glass of water to put them in... to preserve them."

"No, you needn't. The Georgian said they will last several days. They were picked yesterday in Tbilisi, or so he said."

Each interrupted the other until Ekaterina in a grand gesture indicated he should speak. He looked left and grinned widely, exposing his teeth. Ekaterina did not understand. "Look," he said. "No incisors. The wolf can change his teeth." Ekaterina, fingers to cheeks, shook her head slowly, not understanding. "I have had an incisor tooth removed. Well, it was knocked out in a tumble. I am in the Army...I have nothing to do with the KGB."

Ekaterina leaned slightly back. Was he drunk or crazed? She smelled no alcohol. The collar of his shirt was clean. Was he really in love? What might she do with this she did not know. "Danton, I beg of you to sit, please. I have classes at 2PM. That gives us at least an hour. Tell me what you've done since Suzdal."

"You don't remember," he said. "The first story you told me that summer in Suzdal was the magpie and the wolf and that the wolf could not change his teeth." His smile was that of an innocent boy displaying his first fish. "I've changed my teeth."

For a moment, Ekaterina was perplexed. It had been a Bulgarian tale, the magpie advising the wolf that yearned to change his savage ways. It was impossible. The child's tale was dark in meaning. The wolf can't change his teeth. Man can't change his essence. The Russian word for magpie is 'Soroka.' Danton's patronymic was Volkov, 'son of Wolf.' The young woman nodded in dawning awareness. How is it that she just now realized this?

The late August high-pressure system lingered. The days were warm and still, and a haze hung pleasantly in the air. Cool fresh air descended flowing through the worker resorts along the Volga, Pioneer camps sprinkled upon lake shores, the dachas in villages on spokes of commuter lines that radiated out from the city. The nights brought the Muscovites into the streets and parks to smoke, eat ice cream, and just sit in the cafes. Vacations would end soon; on 1 September the children would return to school, the factory workers to their lathes to overfulfill the Seven-Year-Plan already collapsing under the weight of corruption, incompetence, and cynicism.

Alexander entered Alexeev Cemetery at the gate before the Church of Our Lady of Tikhvin, turned right to pass through the second gate to walk along narrow passages between crowded tombstones. Eyes—the photos well off Soviet citizens had engraved on their headstones— watched him pass. In the southwest corner stood the sage-green marble monument. He dropped to his knees, clumsily made the expansive Orthodox sign of the cross, and snorted. He was a Jew, for the love of God. The vast cemetery diminished, retreated, disappeared until only her eyes, dark, wide-set and calm, remained. The photo had been taken in 1931, the year the brothers Soroka had been called—the 'flying brigade'—to fix the theatrical disaster. Some Communist big-wig was expected to attend opening night. The phrase' heads will roll' was not a figure of speech in the 1930s Soviet Union. The stage manager, associated with a Trotskyite cell in 1925, had been arrested and shot.   As Alexander raged at the cast, she had stepped from the wings, and as he spun to berate some other group, she gazed upon him, and he stilled.

He had not failed her. By hook or crook, he had arranged for Irina to be deep into the rear as the Germans swept over Ukraine. The infant Ekaterina had been raised far from carnage and want in the sun where food was plentiful, and disease abated.

"Irinochka, where in God's name can I hide the child now?"

Khrushchev was committed to moving nuclear weapons to Cuba. He was poking the bear in the cave. The American President Kenney was young. Could he resist his general staff? If war came, there would be sun-drenched mountain slopes far from the front. In Alexeev Cemetery, August 1962, Alexander gazed upon Irina as he had gazed upon her in August 1932; stupidly. Were he to have been executed at that spot at that time before the whole Poltava company, it would have been a life well-lived.   He laid the bouquet of white carnations atop her grave.

The room was damp, humid; the water stain traced the wallpaper seam to the floor, the paper separating at the ceiling.   Danton snuffed his cigarette in the overflowing ashtray as the radio intoned the music station's half-hour time signal 'Moscow Nights.' The announcer began the newscast— the corn in Kazakhstan thriving, or some such. The common room radio buzzed, sizzled, went silent, stinking smoke curling upwards in the still air. He looked without seeing, took his last cigarette, and lit it.

A fever burned in his skull. He had emptied the little remaining in the vodka bottle, which stood empty on the table, the desolation in the room matched that in his soul. What had happened? He had been first in his class. He deserved at least the post in Zossen-Wunsdorf, Headquarters of the Group of Soviet Forces Germany. Baranov? Possibly, but what would it have advantaged Roman? The black marketeer had gotten his assignment to backwater Dresden, where the soldier-capitalist could revitalize his export-import business without the mission interfering.

It would have been Alexander Soroka, the Director of Studies, who alone decided the postings. Soroka was the saboteur, no doubt about it.

Russian anti-Semitism which hung like cigarette smoke over the Russian kitchen table, so pervasive and unnoticed, flared in Danton's mind. The Yid? The Yid had stabbed a loyal and trusting Russian soldier in the back. Danton was a smart Russian, a threat, first in his class and the Jew exiled him to Anadyr, the heavy bomber base on the Chukchi Peninsula. Anadyr? They had thought it a joke, a metaphor for the end of the world. He had been assigned to the end of the world. The Jews. They exploited the good-hearted and trusting Russian dry.

Stalin had died too soon. In 1953, the Suzdal gulag had been preparing a reception area, a transit camp, facilities to cleanse the Soviet Union of

He hurled the vodka bottle where he did not know, barely noticed the shattering window, the slow movement of air into the great hall of Alexander Pushkin's city house. Vera had informed on him.   A sob escaped his throat. Ekaterina was a Jew.

Ekaterina clenched her fist so as not to rake her nails across Vera's face. Vera, orange-red hair flared like a lion's mane, was not to be cowed. "Katya, you're having your period? I swear I'll drown you, you don't stop being such a bitch!" Ekaterina deflated, her fury gone, and burst into tears. Vera turned apologetic. "Oh, Ekaterina, I thought a few days at the dacha would do you good. Oh, my God, we must be the best of friends, even ovulating together on the eve of the full moon."

"I am such a horrible person. How do you stay so calm?"

"Compared to you, I'm calm. Everyone knows when to avoid me, and if you don't get out of my sight very very soon, I will indeed drown you. Go for a swim, now!"

"I didn't bring a swimming suit." She was now giggling or hiccuping. "I am so sorry. I don't know what I was thinking?"

"Stop apologizing...I swear."

"I know. Or you'll drown me."

"You'll borrow one of mine."

"I can't. Your boobs are too big."

Vera inhaled deeply.

"Verochka, I am so sorry a thousand times. Your breasts are beautiful," Ekaterina wept. "But I can only wear a one-piece."

"You will wear what I give you," Vera said, a pause after each word. "Here, a pair of shorts." She sorted through the laundry basket. "And here's a shirt. You can be like Sophia Loren climbing out the water...denim shirt...for all the world to see and admire like in the movie 'Boy on a Shark.'"

"Boy on a Dolphin," Ekaterina corrected through quivering lips.

Vera softened, placed her arms around Ekaterina's shoulder. "I know, Katya, how much you miss your mother. Cold water. It always works. Swim to the rocks." She waved towards the stone escarpment that formed the lake's northern shore. "You'll feel better."

"Okay," Ekaterina whimpered in English.

The mid-afternoon sun beat down, the air still and thick. Barefooted, Ekaterina picked her way carefully across the scree to the few feet of sand along the lakeshore. How could the water be so painfully cold? She scanned the beach, self-conscious. On the veranda, mothers cleared dishes off the lunch table. The three generals--Baranov, Vera's father, Gregor Vishensky, and an artillery general, whose name she had forgotten—were seated beneath a maple tree, smoking, deep in conversation. Older guests napped. The young people had gone to the Vishensky dacha. Ekaterina was alone at last.

She stepped into the water, squeaked at the cold, and looked around if anyone heard. Russian mothers could surround, query, and scold and correct like a flock of crows if somehow you caught their attention. The cold water drained the heat and, oh, blessed waters, the nervous energy from her skin. She plunged and swam in an easy crawl to the middle of the lake. There, she paused to look around. A cheer rose from the Vishenky dacha celebrating Roman's assignment. She swam in the opposite direction. The aspen wood shaded the shoreline, and she shivered stepping from the water, made her way to a sun-drenched and private rock outcropping. She looked about. She was completely alone. She took off the shirt and shorts, spread them to dry on the rocks, and lay down to warm herself in the beautiful sunlight, and fell asleep.

She woke chilled, the rock ledge now in the shade, and started. "Danton, you startled me."

He looked down at her. "I apologize deeply, your royal highness." He was standing on her bathing suit.

She crossed her arms over her breasts. "They said you weren't coming."

"I changed my mind."

"Danton, please turn around. I don't like the way you're acting."

"Ekaterina Soroka, the Princess of Suzdal," he said.

"Danton, you frighten me. You're drunk."

"I'm not," he said, his eyebrows raised. He looked out over the lake, scanning the dachas lining the eastern shore. "Aristocrats... the aristocracy." He spat a thick gob which landed beyond Ekaterina.

"That's foolish," she said. "We're all equal in the Soviet Union." She said it as if it were a catechism.

"My father was a hero...fought corruption...shot the blood-sucking lice." He drained the bottle and threw it, and it shattered on rocks where she must pass barefooted. "You look like a whore."

"I'm leaving." He blocked her path. She pushed past, and he grabbed her wrist. "You're hurting me." He touched her breast, gently, as if feeling a finely wrought sculpture. "I'll scream."

His grip tightened, eyes cold, as on that gray day or was it a nightmare, when the blow brought her to her knees, his expression freezing her in place, his grip forcing her back to the rock.

Soviet troops in heavy winter gear stood sweating on the Moscow Vnukovo airport's oven-hot asphalt tarmac. In army-fashion, they had been hustled to the TU-134 airliner, the doors to which remained closed. Parkas and packs lay scattered about as glistening men, naked to the waist sought shade beneath the wings. Two civilians in short-sleeved shirts and cropped hair and carrying briefcase sauntered to the plane.

"Viktor Ivanovich, long time no see." The regular army colonel knew the new arrivals. "What the fuck..."

"I am an agricultural expert," the ersatz civilian replied smirking, '...corn."

"Khrushchev miracle corn that grows in icebergs?" The regular army colonel wiped his hands before extending for the handshake. "Don't you know where you're going?"

"Don't you..." responded the ersatz agricultural expert, "know where you're going?"

"Up to the Arctic circle, Viktor Ivanovich, and you're going to freeze your nuts off." The regular army colonel was waving his arm in a generally northern direction. "Where's your pack? Already on the plane?"

Viktor Ivanovich turned to his companion and said, "I suppose we can tell then now." He waved in the opposite direction. The regular army colonel was perplexed. "Think, Andrei Andropovich, think!"

Andrei slapped his side, uttered a series of 'mother' curses, and enlightenment suffused this face. "Cuba!"

The aircraft doors swung open, the ground crew began moving stairs to the plane as troops began searching for their equipment.

Danton, also enlightened, muttered his own mother curses. He had been deceived.

CHAPTER TWENTY-FOUR

BOOK IV

"Oh, lucky Vera!" Ekaterina murmured.   Ekaterina Soroka perched on the edge of the chair in the lobby of the Hotel Ukraine. Vera had already departed with her tour— politically advanced English professors with their wives, church activists and Quakers exuding goodwill towards the Soviet Union.

She searched her purse for a pencil, finding it, but forgetting what she had wanted to note down. The nervous mouse scurried up and down her throat, its furry back wisping along her esophagus. She reached into the open satchel at her feet, withdrawing typed class notes from the In-Tourist guide training course.

'They're students, sympathetic to us,' Ivan Markov had said. 'Why are you worrying?' Was he simply an idiot? How did such fools attain positions of responsibility? Markov hated her. Ekaterina wasn't from Moscow, and everyone knew how xenophobic Muscovites were. 'By the way,' he added. 'The KGB is investigating a report of a Trotskyite agent among your tour group.' She inhaled, expanding her chest to crowd out this thing skittering in her throat. The responsibilities of an In-Tourist guide-translator were enormous. She was the human face of Communism to the world. It was the likes of her, a Komsomol, who would manage the transition to Socialism so that when capitalism collapsed—this year or the next—it would not end in war.

She fingered the cushion, found the stitching had begun to unravel. She stood, turned the cushion over, but the unfaded fabric contrasted. The Hotel Ukraine had opened four years ago, and already it looked worn. She returned the cushion to its original position. The CIA assigned Russian-speaking agents, children of the counterrevolutionaries, to plot their return to power, stealing the factories away from the workers, forcing the peasants back into serfdom. Tourists had to be watched. There were dozens of secret military and scientific institutes in Moscow. Every day on the #11 streetcar she passed the Space Institute in Ostankino. Would the CIA chief, John McCone, allow poor people to come to the USSR to be overwhelmed with the glories of the Soviet workers' paradise? Of course, he inserted anti-Soviets among innocent foreign sympathetics. She visualized his sharp teeth, and leering grin, his hands folded around a dagger held behind his back in the youth magazine, Krokodil.

She paged through her notes, picking questions with replies randomly.

Question: If the USSR is a peace-loving nation, why did you develop and explode the hydrogen bomb?

Answer: The Soviet Union tested its first hydrogen bomb on August 12, 1953, seven months after the United States tested its hydrogen bomb on November 1, 1952. The peace-loving citizens of the USSR know the horrors of war all too well, attacked by the Nazis without warning. Hundreds of thousands of Soviet citizens died. It is still hard to imagine the suffering we have collectively endured.

The mouse in her throat moved to her stomach, where it turned into a hedgehog. Vasilisa the Beautiful could not have been more nervous approaching Baba Yaga's house set on chicken legs to snatch the knight's thighbone. The tour schedule was cast in concrete: first; the Moscow Art Museum. Second; the Kremlin, Red Square, and Lenin's Tomb. Third; shop in the GUM, and lastly, return them to the hotel no later than 7 PM. She would write her report and be on the metro with plenty of time before the underground closed at 11 PM.

Oh, Where were they? Why was she so nervous? Could it be that difficult?" Her group was already 15, no, 20, minutes late. Ekaterina glanced at the bank of elevators where two lifts had remained stuck at the 23rd floor for the last several minutes. Should she get them? Had the Trotskyite saboteurs jammed the elevators? Would the Americans understand her English? What if they asked for another guide? Ekaterina willed the elevators to move when a waterfall of freezing waters seemed to cascade from the ceiling, causing her to flush from the roots of her hair to her shin bones. Maxim had not yet arrived! Ekaterina jumped up, then sat. Should she call In-Tourist? Would they laugh? 'ach, Katusha, you think this is WWII. They're Americans!' Or worse. 'Ekaterina Soroka, you are a Komsomol. You are expected to solve such little problems.'

A tiny voice whispered in her soul that the Trotskyites had destroyed Socialist property and the Americans and Maxim and Ludmilla, the wicked witch In-Tourist guide would never come, and the tourists were now a matter of State Security, and Ekaterina could ride the metro to the Botanical Gardens where she would write a one-word report...*Nichevo.*

She again reviewed her notes. Why is the Soviet Government encouraging war in Africa and Asia? We support freedom-loving people everywhere to choose their Socialist destinies. We know what war is and want nothing to do with it. We have suffered war more than any people on earth. All peace-loving peoples on the earth must join to stop America from arming Germany with nuclear weapons.

The CIA sent émigrés to pose hostile questions to confuse inexperienced Communists, to sway loyalty, to cast doubt. Competent In-Tourist agents and Komsomol activists quickly assessed group composition and determined which were the enemies of Socialism to organize allies against the enemies to win over the neutrals. Simple, isn't it?

"Why do women dress so badly in the Soviet Union?" Ekaterina closed her eyes. The hedgehog flexed his spines. The question was not in her notes.

Oh, where are they? Can nothing be on time in Russia? She stood. Across the lobby sat a young woman reading a manuscript. She wasn't Russian, but unaccompanied Americans were not allowed in the Hotel Ukraine. Ekaterina looked again. She was not movie-star beautiful, but she was lovely. And petite. Brown hair, skin lightly tanned, teeth white and straight. Beneath an embroidered denim vest, she wore a black t-shirt with a tangerine scarf around her neck. Ekaterina looked again. A light shade of lipstick. Mascara so delicately applied that only a woman would notice. But she wore men's baggy trousers. Ekaterina wanted to finger the seams to see how she had tailored the pants to complement her boyish form.

Spanish, Ekaterina decided. But where was her chaperone? Someone— mother, brother or uncle—always accompanied Spanish girls. The young Spaniard checked her watch, exhaled, and sunk into the chair, legs sprawled and crossed, the manuscript above her head, foot keeping a...waltz tempo. The manuscript was a musical score. She was a foreign student attending the Moscow Conservatory.

Ekaterina gasped. Oh, God, her shoes! They were ankle-length brushed leather half-boots with three-inch heels of three...no, four shades—brown, green, maroon and some other color—that blended, yet contrasted, showing off the young woman's beautiful foot. Of course, even were the young beauty club-footed, those boots would complement her outfit.

Italian. She could only be Italian. But In-Tourist didn't place Italian Communists at the Hotel Ukraine. She smiled to herself. She felt like Bezdomnyi in Master and Margarita questioning the Devil. The girl was Margarita. The Italian girl was as Ekaterina imagined Margarita. She had heard that the manuscript, which she had read on a winter's night beneath Uncle Sasha's bed at 11 years old, had been published in Italy.

Ekaterina looked down at her own shoes, which looked as if carved from blocks of wood. Her feet looked enormous in Soviet shoes. When the USSR attained Communism, might we Russian women have beautiful shoes? Why not now? Turin, Italy had a Communist government, and Italian women had beautiful shoes. If she could only visit Italy for a day, she could buy pairs of gorgeous shoes, at least two, and she would take good care of them. Well, one couldn't wear them during the Moscow winter; the slush was so corrosive.

The young Italian woman's music score had fallen to the floor, her eyes regarding the ceiling murals. Ekaterina sensed sadness in the young woman's carriage. Was that a fashion accouterment, like her boots? How could she be sad when she wore such beautiful boots? Men adored beauties who wore clothes subtly, wore sadness subtly, and whom they could protect.

The wail of sirens rose from the street. A black Zhiguli with militia escort flashed by, some Communist big shot hurrying to some crisis or another. Oh, where was Maxim and the awful Ludmilla?

The Italian girl sprawled in her chair, her music score above her eyes, her handbag visible, large, elegant, leather. Would there be such beautiful purses after the transition to Communism?

An elevator arrow began to descend, then the other. The first door slid open, then the second, and Oh God, disgorged twelve. Where would they find the room on the bus? Markov had told her eight!

Ekaterina considered the lobby door. Should she run away? A stocky unsmiling Russian wearing clean worker coveralls entered the lobby, flipped open his passport to the guard, who, expressionless, stepped back respectfully. Maxim had arrived. At his side and one step back, a squat woman in a shapeless print dress, gray hair in a severe bun and rimless glasses, wearing shoes like Ekaterina's. Maxim, a bus driver and KGB sergeant, had arrived with Ludmilla, the guide, who drilled Ekaterina with a sour look. 'Hooligans, these young people! For this, we sacrificed?' Ekaterina turned back to her charges. Thus did the Soviet soldier go into battle against an entrenched enemy to the fore; NKVD execution squads to the rear. The soldier had a choice. Probable death before, certain death behind.

The tall and gaunt woman with an expectant smile was searching the lobby, spotted the Italian girl first, and her smile turned cold. It was only later that Ekaterina recalled the look for as she was trying to decide how to manage with two extra American tourists, the second elevator door opened spilling nine additional tourists, a short and stocky female at their lead, who spotted Ekaterina, smiled broadly, extended her arm like a broadsword and charged. The hedgehog in Ekaterina's throat grew into a wolf. Was this how Prince Vladimir felt in 1382 as he watched the Mongol Horde darken the plain before Kiev, the smiling Batu Kahn at their lead.

"Catherine, Oh, aren't you the young thing, May I call you Kathy? Do you spell it with a K or a C?" The woman shook her hand vigorously. "I am Helene, Helene Moore. Nearly finished with my dissertation…about Mayakovskij. He's a Soviet Poet. Do you know him? I so do hope we visit his commune today. I know his American friend, you know…his girlfriend. That's why he committed suicide. Because Stalin refused him permission to leave Russian. Let me introduce you to Miss Stein. She is an associate professor at Bronx Community College."

Ekaterina looked at Miss Moore, mouth open, for she understood not one word Helene spoke, but detected insult in the cascade of words directed at Miss Stein.

Miss Stein, all sharp corners—elbows, knees, nose, and cheeks—pushed forward to take charge. "Ah, Kathy…" She spoke slowly, enunciating each consonant, rounding each vowel. "Miss Moore's English takes some getting used to. She's from Brooklyn. The Midwest, where we speak with the best American accent, hasn't had a great effect upon her dialect, has it?"

Ekaterina blinked. This insult a Russian could understand.

With a smug glance, Miss Moore speared Miss Stein, who reacted with heat. "Julia, at least I was organizing the workers. You wear the sweetest little beret, don't you? But, dearie, not French workers in Greenwich Village, are there?" Helene's eyes teared over. "While we, my comrades and I were confronting the beast in his lair." She turned to Ekaterina, thrusting her finger into her sternum. "Wisconsin! Joseph McCarthy!"

Helene Moore looked over her glasses with a smile that did not go deep. "I am sure, Julia, you were useful out...there." Ekaterina sensed there was a muzhik somewhere among this group whom these two babas were fighting over, as among the Ukrainian women at the Suzdal' Goose Cooperative. Her In-Tourist notes did not address cat fights.

As Miss Moore and Miss Stein stabbed one another with ice pick smiles, students began to wander off. All was not amity in the leadership collective.

Maxim lit a cigarette as Ludmilla's wheezing breath spread hot and damp over her neck as the mouse, hedgehog, and wolf in chaotic unison bounced against Ekaterina's breast. The object of the women's jealousy came into focus. Alyosha, the Lazy, light-boned, dark-haired, blue-eyed and a jerk—had lit a cigarette, leaned against a wall, and gazed across the lobby at...the Italian girl?

It was as if Ekaterina were back in Suzdahl herding geese, and Miss Stein, the lead goose, was pecking Miss Moore, who was squawking. Someone was going to be bleeding before this day ended. And Alyosha, the Lazy, was across the lobby flirting with the Italian girl.

Ekaterina ordered her internal beasts to calm themselves, turned to the bus driver, and ordered. "Maxim, Viktor just arrived. Commandeer his bus. We have too many for yours." Maxim inclined his head, stubbed his cigarette out on the marble floor, and went out. Maxim, the KGB sergeant, outranked Victor, the KGB corporal, and this would teach the young Victor the stupidity of arriving on time, much less early. "Ludmilla, go with him. Ensure the bus is clean." Ludmilla slit her eyes. 'You will die for this want of respect, you young whore!' but like a soldier assigned to the suicide battalion, Ekaterina was already dead.

Miss Moore turned to Ekaterina, a sheen of moisture on her brow. "Kathy, you can't know how much I suffered organizing against the Vietnam War in Wisconsin. I mean, who knows where it even is? Yes, yes, I am sure the Russians suffered terribly in their war."

"Miss Moore, Miss Stein, could you get the group ready," Ekaterina said. Miss Moore looked at Miss Stein, the command being passed wordlessly. 'Get them moving, you fat strumpet.' Miss Stein moved slowly, resistant. The students had scattered...like geese. The Italian girl stood, her eyes meeting Ekaterina's, and she smiled.

CHAPTER TWENTY-FIVE

The nut struck the debris before SP-4 Richard Belisle's face, waking him. Without stirring, eyes closed, he searched the surrounding jungle for errant sound; heavy breathing, careful footstep, the slide of rifle bolt, a harsh command to stand, the shot. The noise, however, was cacophonous and comforting, summer monsoon rains in the Annamese Cordillera falling in cold and dismal torrents on the trees, on his poncho, in his face. He opened his eyes. Twenty feet distant, Ntaaj, their Montagnard tracker, gestured and disappeared behind his blind.

In the half-light, Richard checked the dull luminescence on his watch face. Ntaaj had let him sleep four hours. He had ordered two-hour shifts, no more. But were Richard to critique him, the latter would grin; white men, white time, who could make sense of such nonsense?

SSGT Dieter Leibrock, PFC Richard Belisle, and the Meo tribesman, Ntaaj, lay ten miles deep into Laos, depending from which point on the tortured tri-border region their position was measured. The mission was road-watch. Higher-higher wanted North Vietnamese troop movement into the

Central Highlands tracked. It was 1964. War was in the air. Officers anticipated medals, warrior words and three-star endorsements on their officer effectiveness reports, and accelerated promotion. Enlisted goals were less exalted; Do the job and get the hell out of Dodge. He had a woman at home. Come hell or high water, he'd survive the NVA, the regiment's head paper-pusher, and even this ex-Wehrmacht.

Sergeant Leibrock moaned. He was sick, wracked with malaria and dysentery, and threatening Rick's survival in so many ways; a fevered cry within bad guys earshot, one less rifle when the shit hit the fan, debilitating bulk to carry to the rendezvous point.

Richard pulled down the mosquito netting over his Boonie cap, slithered from sleeping bag to the fallen log, and raised to his knees behind a bulbous growth, then slowly shifted to gain a clear field of view. A white face was the full moon rising. A twig snapping was a building collapsing. He was back home, bow-hunting whitetail deer. The cross-border patrols needed more and younger men, arty coverage, better radios, or airborne radio relay. A few more Montagnards in trail and front wouldn't hurt either. Richard considered his NCO, but would decide tomorrow what to do with him; If they were lucky, he'd die overnight.

He propped his elbow on the log and despite the early hour reflexively glanced up that no sun to reflect off the binocular lens. and glassed the river crossing, followed the jungle-hidden trail up the mountainside, pausing were the foliage thinned, then the jutting karsts and two gaps. It was as it had been for two weeks; rain and flood-swept. But the current surface had taken on a certain agitation where underwater boulders and karst left their image in the water's course. The waters were subsiding. Soon, the skies would clear, the roads dry, and troops, porters and bicycles appear.

That, however, the next patrol would observe. He sat back against the log, swigged water, retrieved a packet of Saltines from his backpack, and touched a young woman's plastic-encased photo sewn into the flap, the St. Adrian's medal and made a quick sign of the cross. He apportioned God and his girl thirty seconds each day. She was pregnant, as was, apparently, Kitty. The three—God, Marie-Jeanne, and Kitty— would manage. And the ten-grand survivor benefit split four ways would benefit no one. He closed his pack. He allowed himself one more whine. Ntaaj had three wives. How was that fair? Thirty second up.

But despair threatened survival. He tipped his canteen to the northwoods, the farm, the cows. Mosquitos ate their fill. With butane light and hot nail, he went even with leeches; sometimes, they got blood; mostly, he got them. But his gut bacteria fought amoebic dysentery to a standstill. Shit-covered tails slapping him across the mouth had inoculated him against the world's voracious bacteria. He returned to the log.

A shaft of sunlight broke through the clouds illuminating the waterfall at the valley's north end. Save now and then, the NVA road honcho on his motorbike checking the condition of the Ho Chi Mihn trail network, it had been blessed boredom.

The monsoons were ending. Come tomorrow dusk, they'd move to the rendezvous point, a two-day walk where, if they could make radio contact, a helicopter might arrive, assuming battalion had a helicopter to spare. Despite hell, high water, leeches, slopes and a batshit crazy chain of command, he'd survive. He had a kid to raise.

"Ntaaj," Rick murmured. He paused the binoculars at the crossing. "Sergeant Leibruck, We got company coming...two hundred meters up from the river."

"Was? Slopes?" SSGT Dieter Leibrock, awoken from his nightmare, grunted in thickly accented English, a chill shaking his torso. He elbow-crawled to Richard trailing a stench of urine, sweat and diarrhea. "Was? "Ach, ja. Slopes."

Rick hand-signaled Ntaaj. *'Les vilains."* The two men shared a limited fifty-word French-Montagnard-English lexicon and the hunters' vast hand signal vocabulary. Richard turned back to SSgt Leibruck. "See that gap where limestone...that white stone...karst outcropping, where the trail dog legs back down to the river." Rick moved Dieter's binoculars. "There are two boogies on that outcropping, Sarge. Lookie there, one's a round-eye." Rick passed the binoculars to Leibrock, with his finger adjusting the sergeant's angle.

"Frog? " Dieter squinted, shaking his head to clear his vision.

"Ach, ja. Da ist er." After a moment, he said, "Russkii."

"The white guy?" Rick said. "Nah. He'd be Polish, probably the International Control Commission inspecting for violations of the Geneva Accords against Laotian Neutrality."

"Russkii," Dieter reaffirmed, face dripping sweat, his eyes the fear-filled fourteen-year-old belt-feeding an MG-42 machine gun over a cold and rain-swept river crossing in Pommerania.

"Regard," Ntaaj said, *"La bas."*

"Crap," Rick murmured. He grabbed the binoculars back. Two NVA soldiers towing a heavy rope had stepped into the river, the cable to permit heavily-laden soldiers to cross without the current sweeping them away. Rick made out a Vietnamese with holster on hip, gesturing commands. "Not smart,' Rick thought. Marine officers wore shoulder-holstered .45s and stood out like albino-bucks against a spruce tree line.

"Schießen Sie den Russen," Sergeant Leibrock said.

"He's probably a Polack. He's got a transit and theodolite. He's an engineer or surveyor or something with the United Nations or something like that." Rick returned his attention to the outcropping, about the same height from the water as the American patrol, five-hundred meters according to the binocular's range-finder reticle.

"Schiessen Sie!" Dieter repeated the guttural command, tome brooking no opposition, the sergeant's fevered minds-eye seeing a Soviet Army patrol recce'ing a water crossing for follow-on T-34's.

"The sergeant is supervising the crossing. The OIC is on the karst. Those the two that need shooting," rules of grammar lost to rising tension.

"Hai," Ngaaz called out. At a gap in the foliage midway between the river and the outcropping, three soldiers were setting a mortar tube. *'Pas ben."*

'No shit, Sherlock,' Rick thought. Ngaaz shrugged. It was no good big-time. "Dieter, we'd better get out of Dodge."

Leibrock pointed. "Shoot him."

Rick recalculated. Plan A: Get out of Dodge. He had one in the oven, probably two, to raise. He had a girlfriend to marry.

Plan B formed quickly. Rick signed to Ngaaz with a touch to the hip, a finger to the crossing. You shoot the NVA sergeant. Fuck discipline. "Sergeant Leibrock, I'll take the longer shot... shoot the white man. You shoot the two in the water. "

"Schiessen Sie," Dieter repeated. Rick and Ngaaz looked at one another. Rick raised one finger, pointed to himself, then across the valley. The tribesman nodded, set his iron-sighted M-1, nearly as tall as the rifleman, over the log. They had apportioned the targets. Shoot the leaders.

Rick checked the elevation and range adjustment on his Weaver 2.5x 330C hunting telescope, that a neighbor, a WWII Marine range instructor, which his dad a bought for fifteen dollars, had the farm implement dealer forge M-1 mounts, and mailed to Ricky in a box labeled 'Christmas cookies.' He set the cross-hairs in the space between the NVA lieutenant and the white man, inhaled slowly, and murmured, "let the shot surprise. Let the shot surprise."

The crack, the kick, the empty casing ejected over his head, the M-1 settling back to position. The Vietnamese officer lifted from the ground and was gone. The white man—Russian or Pole or French—looked to his left as if someone had told a joke, which he didn't quite understand.

"Get the fuck down, stupid fuck," Rick coached. He moved the cross-hairs over the white man's chest, lifting the reticle just above the transit, letting the gunfire of its own accord. Ngaaz shot broke Rick's concentration. He moved the cross-hairs back to the white man futzing with his theodolite. "Doesn't deserve to procreate," Rick murmured.

The M-1 recoiled, and the white man disappeared as if the motion picture camera had been stop-motioned and the director moved the white man off-camera before restarting the camera.

Single shots now punctuated the air, like the incipient patter of rain on a barn roof. Rick moved his scope to the river. The spume of water arose before the lead soldier, who looked at it, as if curious, then disappeared underwater, like a crocodile had grabbed him from beneath. The second soldier, framed in the crosshairs of Rick's scope, looked perplexed into the swirling brown waters, understanding coming to his eyes, his head turning back to the shore. This spume rose at the soldier's rifle strap, and he too disappeared beneath muddy waters.

The fall of rain grew heavier as bullets now clipped in the trees, but far above their heads, a leaf here and there falling about them.

"We get out of here." SSGT Leibrock had returned from somewhere in Central Europe to somewhere in Laos. "You two...Back. I kill the mortar crew. I stay here until you are set."

Rick scanned the clearing. The white man, Russian, Polish or French, had been a handsome guy. Why'd he stand there so long...four or five seconds...after Rick had shot the Vietnamese?

He'd think about that later. Leibruck had come through, and Rick thought it was lucky he hadn't snuffed him. He crabbed his way back. The mortar crew was higher on the priority list.

CHAPTER TWENTY-SIX

Ekaterina sat in the dark midnight lobby of the Hotel Ukraine, the same chair as in the morning, buried her face in her hands, brain vibrating. She felt that if someone lit one of the myriad stray hairs hanging like fuses about her face, her head would explode, splattering English phrases about the lobby, but in proper grammatical order, for surely random chance and gunpowder could create the better English sentence. Why didn't the whole world speak Russian where case and declension made word order so unnecessary? It had been an awful day. Students smirked, looked to the sky, wandered off in mind and body as she translated Ludmilla's convoluted Communist-speak, which on the page glowed with hope in a shining future, but translated, was as pinched and shriveled as the mouth that spoke it. Who would believe such nonsense? She began the day as a translator and, as the day progressed became an editor.

Ach, the group leaders! Helene, like Trotsky, wouldn't shut up. Miss Stein, like Stalin, watched with a cold eye, as if she wanted to sink a pick ax into Stein's thick skull. Ekaterina had to manage the flock of geese, one randy drake strutting among them. No, not geese! Geese could be managed. They were goats, one randy ram among them. Alyosha, the Lazy—what was his name, Alexander the Snake?—slithered to her at Lenin's Tomb. "I am a Marxist," he said. He was as much a Communist as Nicholas II, though deserving of the same end. He was only flirting, but The KGB foreign agent recruitment form was sixteen pages long. When would she have time to fill it out? And besides, Ekaterina had obviously been the second choice, which a girl just loves. He had gone after the Italian beauty, who with the gentlest smile and Italian *Savoir-faire* sent him after the next possible conquest, which had been Ekaterina. Did these American's not understand that the Soviet Union's greatest shortage of all was privacy?

Ekaterina regarded her high heels, a Western plot introduced into the Soviet Union to render Soviet womanhood bitter, anxious and anti-man, thus causing a population crash. Did buses run this late on Prospekt Mira? Ten blocks. She'd just have to walk barefoot. Why hadn't she carried different shoes?

Beyond the room's fluorescent hum, an odd sound caught her attention. She lifted her head and listened, brow wrinkled. It made no sense. She rose and padded barefoot across the lobby to investigate.

"Allo?"

"I'm sorry," the voice whispered. "Is it forbidden to sit in the lobby so late? Ah, you're Ekaterina. That's your name, isn't it? Oh, my God, are you still working? You must be ready to collapse." Had the weariness addled Ekaterina's brain or was she sleepwalking and composing a wondrous tale? The Italian girl of the beautiful boots was nursing a child! She spoke in the quiet voice of a mother settling a disgruntled infant. "Come, sit next to me," she said. "I have only my mother to talk to, and if I move, Chrystelle will wake, and I'll be settling her the rest of the night." The Italian girl-become-mother looked at her oddly, then smiled, her likeness like the Botticelli's Madonna of the Tretyakov Gallery.

Ekaterina caught herself. "Your English is so good."

Marie Jeanne laughed, caught herself, and rocked the child, who snuffled, rose to wakefulness as both young women held their breath, then drifted off. "No, not Italian. I'm from Canada. My name is Marie Jeanne, 'M.J.', or so my friends name me. I shake your hand, Ekaterina, symbolically, lest we wake the little *dictatoresse* here. She's as bull-headed as her father."

"Ah, her father is where?" Ekaterina's weariness had disappeared. It was midnight in Moscow and reality was hours away. This girl-woman of impeccable taste with stories from beyond the sea might become a girlfriend. Marie Jeanne slumped slightly. There was no wedding ring on the Italian-Canadian girl's left index finger.

In 1945, the twentieth century wars paused. After thirty years of episodic slaughter, two nations remained standing, the US and USSR. Each arms itself with doomsday weapons. Stupored by unrelenting death, sobered under threat of nuclear conflagration, yet another generation groomed for *The Long War*.

For much of the latter half of the twentieth century the Soviet Union loomed as a brooding presence over American political discourse. To some observers, the Soviet Union was less threatening, to others more, but to all a threat nevertheless. It was a state so obsessed and so successful with secrecy that it was impossible to perceive to what extent the threat against which the U.S. prepared so assiduously existed in reality or only in its fears.

This was no accident, as the Communists were wont to say. The flip side of the coin of secrecy is deception. The Soviet Union may have had neither intention nor desire to initiate war with the United States; however their widespread use of deception undercut that assiduously cultivated perception.

On one fine day, the Soviet State imploded. Discussions of war between the Soviet Union and the United States, once chilling, disappear from memory.

The *Long War* series examine the Soviet and American post-WWII war of deception through the eyes of four protagonists, who were but children when in 1947 the Soviet Union designated the United States as 'the main enemy.'

Each side sought advantage indirectly where war was Armageddon. advantage indirectly, by proxy war or perceptions management; theater, deception, lies, bluff. Rarely—Korea, Vietnam, Afghanistan—were main force units committed.

Richard Belisle and his French-Canadian childhood friend, Marie Jeanne Charbonneau, cross paths and cross swords with Danton Larionov and Ekaterina Soroka. They trust and betray one another, give faith and deceive, become fast friends and bitter enemies, each striving to live within a moral code in an immoral world. The novel series addresses deception in war and peace in a 20th century world of contrived and real ambiguity.

Spirit Falls (Book I)

English Language ISBN-13: 978-1-7338827-0-5
Ebook ISBN 978-1-7338827-3-6
Russian Language ISBN-13: 978-0615840260
Dual-Language ISBN: 978-1515283959

Spirit Falls, Book One in *The Long War* series, is an affecting story of childhood friendship growing into profound love, a coming-of-age novel set in the empty and hardscrabble landscape of Michigan's Upper Peninsula.

The Korean War rages. A six-year-old girl in overalls appears in the one-room Spirit Falls Graded School on Michigan's isolated Upper Peninsula. Marie Jeanne Charbonneau, French-Canadian, and Ricky Belisle, Serbian and Scots-Irish, befriend one another, and wander the forests, lakes and swamps, their parents occupied with their own injuries. As they mature, strangers come to town bringing with them new influences and a longing for the wider world. A Lake Superior storm brings the two teenagers face to face with death and the knowledge of good and evil, driving them out of Eden into the world.

The Wounded (Book II)
ISBN-13: 978-1-7338827-1-2

Wounded find Ricky Belisle and Marie Jeanne Charbonneau have left their remote Lake Superior village, a world circumscribed by Life Magazine and the Saturday Evening Post, the radio, stories told around a kitchen table during winter storms, and such news as an occasional visitor might bring from the city.

Marie Jeanne, younger by months than Ricky, wiser by years, understood that two created such meaning as vague words—love, respect, sharing, kindness—conveyed through shared experience; a cup of coffee, a sunset, a birth. M.J. saw the world built in this order: man and wife, immediate and extended family, community, nation.

Richard, however, would be judged worthy by "them," the men in his clan, his tribe, his nation. Yet, truth be told, that wasn't the complete calculation, if calculation there were. In the eyes of most, Ricky had proven himself worthy. It wasn't enough. He would prove himself worthy of his childhood friend by clearing the debt his parents took on for his sin. And, had his priest been wiser or better read, he might have introduced the young man to the teachings of St. Augustine, "Lord, make me chaste, but not yet."

He makes his way across the American south seeking redemption and adventure. Soldiering, the family profession, is no longer an option; it is the nuclear age. He plays baseball, is jailed, injured, laid low. M.J. finds him on a Colorado mountain recovering from injuries to body and soul. Indifferent nature tests them yet again.

Executioner's Son (Book III)
ISBN-13: 978-1-7338827-2-9

It is 1953. Danton Larionov, son of NKVD major Wolf Larionov, lives in Suzdal, ancient Russia's capital and spiritual center. Its medieval fortresses, monasteries, and nunneries are now an NKVD Gulag. Screams punctuate the night. Woman's Wood, a tract of ancient forest, emanates deathly silence. The *rasputitsa,* Russia's spring thaw, ejects those buried in mass graves, brings the murdered to the surface, as if rejecting Stalin's victims buried with proper rite and ceremony.

An apparition, the fifteen-year-old goose herder, Ekaterina Soroka, appears on Illian Meadow. The all-powerful sixteen-year-old Danton drives off young hoodlums threatening her to claim, a Soviet *droit du seigneur*, the beautiful stranger for his own amusement, but she transfixed him with a *skazka*, a tale. All that spring and summer along the banks of the Kamenka River, he attends to her inexhaustible font of tales.

Stalin dies. The executioners are executed. The Soviet prince is laid low. On a autumn day Ekaterina disappears. Danton vows he will seek her if he must search *beyond the seventh sea and beyond the seventh kingdom*. He joins the Army, an engineer, travels to distant lands—Kiev, Cuba, Laos—in service to the Soviet State, seeking his teller of tales. Then, in a distant forest in a distant land, he discovers not whom he seeks, but the American executioner, US Army sniper, PFC Richard Belisle.

Broken Codes (Book IV)
(Release date: 2020)

Broken Codes is a political thriller set in 1973 on the ancient and bloodied trails of Thuringia, in the decadence of underground Berlin, and in Soviet Post-Vietnam push against a weakened American military. Captain Jon Einarsson, a young US Air Force officer, United States Military Liaison Mission officer attached to the Group of Soviet Forces Germany, seeks the glory that escaped him in Vietnam and also the good times that escaped him growing up in a small town in the Upper Peninsula of

Michigan. Post-war West Berlin provided this young bachelor officer good times aplenty.

At a party Jon encounters American newspaper stringer, Molly Nielssen, seeking entre into the journalistic elite. Young, hungry and focused, she manipulates Captain Einarsson using sex and beauty for access to Berlin's newsmakers, entertainment and good times. Much to her inconvenience, they fall in love.

In 1973 Berlin on the front lines of the Cold War, the young lovers become witness and weapons in a Soviet-American cold war drama writ close and personal. The hard, cold and disfigured Soviet security chief, Lieutenant Colonel Danton Volkov Larionov, has a personnel antipathy to US Army major Richard Belisle. Jon and Molly suffer a sense of their own provincialism before Marie-Jeanne Belisle, a concert pianist of startling beauty and grace. Equally enamored of the Major and his wife is the Soviet translator and press attache, Ekaterina Soroka.

The October 1973 the Combined Arab armies invade Israel, the Yom Kippur war which brings the Soviet Union and the United States to the brink of nuclear war. Major Belisle deploys the USMLM teams to East Germany to monitor Soviet preparations for war. Colonel Larionov will take the eve of nuclear war to wreak some private revenge upon Major Belisle. Through a *legerdemain* Major Belisle renders Jon Einarsson the target of Colonel Larionov's vengeance.

Resurrection (Book V)

Resurrection, the final book in the *Long War,* is a tale of struggle between two opposing captains of two opposing armies of two opposing states, sons of fathers and grandfathers who fought in their country's wars spanning the 20th century. The Soviet Union collapses. The colonels Belisle and Larionov must confront the damages wrought within themselves, their families and their peoples.

Richard Belisle, exhausted, once suppressed traumas resurfacing, sits dazed at the bedside of his dying unconscious father at the VA hospital, Iron Mountain, Michigan. On the opposite side of the world, Danton Larionov witnesses the collapse of the Soviet Union, the cause his family had served for three generations.

The Commander, Houghton-Hancock VFW post, invites Colonel Michael Richard Belisle to address the members, aging WWII and Korean war veterans. The post commander's son, Jon Einarsson, who had served under Belisle in Berlin, returns home. He struggles to make sense of his family's past, his worship of Army Colonel Richard Belisle, his love for the journalist.

Jon Einarsson and Richard Belisle have coffee. Jon proposes Richard take an end-of-career NATO assignment in the German Alpine village of Garmisch-Partenkirchen as the resident expert on Yugoslavia. The colonel, Mrs. Belisle and family arrive as Yugoslavia descends into genocidal civil war.

ABOUT THE AUTHOR

Townsend comes from a long line—father, grandfathers and great-grandfathers—of soldiers, American and pre-American. Slavic on his mother's, deep-south redneck on the father's side, his parents managed money poorly and told stories well. Spare, pithy, lasting the duration of a Pall Mall cigarette, the tales were to entertain while teaching. No one is completely useless, he was told. He can always serve as a bad example.

He learned this lesson—storytellers are treasured, liars are vexing and both are often one and the same. The craft is shared; the objectives differ.

His stories and novels arise from family history, fables and stories told around the kitchen table as well as his own experiences in America's late 20th century ambiguous wars, deceptions and counter-deceptions.

Fluent in Russian and German with a combat vocabulary in French, Townsend is a graduate of the University of Wisconsin (BA), studied at *Freies Universitat Berlin* (Certifikat), and awarded his MA (Russian Area Studies) from Georgetown University. Since leaving the intelligence business, he has turned his attention to writing stories and essays, an early passion waylaid by life and work.

The *Long War* is a novel series addressing deception, war and peace in a 20th century world of both contrived and actual moral ambiguity.

In 1947, the Soviet security services named the United States as 'the main enemy.' The Cold War was joined. Four teens, born half-worlds apart, children of their nations' greatest generation, come of age in the 1950s, each in their small-town Eden, cast out to encounter one another on the front lines in the war for control of the imagination.

The novel series follows four main characters: Two Russians; Danton Larionov and Ekaterina Soroka, one American; Richard Belisle, and a Canadian; Marie Jeanne Charbonneau. These four cross paths, destinies, and swords as they stalk, deceive and love across the world. They trust and double-cross one another, fast friends and bitter enemies, give faith and deceive while striving to live in accordance within their moral codes in an amoral world.

Townsend and his wife, Patrice Naparstek, live comfortably most anywhere—Rovinj, Croatia; Dresden, Germany; Dubai, UAE; Boulder, Colorado; Semur-en-Auxios, France, Madison, Wisconsin—but return periodically to the northern Wisconsin family farm to breathe deeply.

·